"When the land forgets its King, the magic forgets the land."
— The Verdant Chapel Scrolls

THE DRUID KING

BY

EMERSON FORESTER

PAPER SAINTS PRESS

ISBN: 9798999384119

First published by Paper Saints Press 2025
Phoenix, Arizona, United States

Edited by the author & Marlow Fen

Illustrated by author & Wynn Calder

Cover design by author & Wynn Calder

First Edition

The Storyteller's Scroll

Chapter 1: Portals Before Supper 9

Chapter 2: The Book 17

Chapter 3: Pip, Potions, and Potential Disasters 23

Chapter 4: One Door, One Path 33

Chapter 5: Reagan 41

Chapter 6: The Druid 47

Chapter 7: Welcome to Balderon 59

Chapter 8: The Enchanted Tea Room 69

Chapter 9: The Ball Room 81

Chapter 10: The Balcony 91

Chapter 11: The Cottage 101

Chapter 12: Inside Ysmerra's Manor 113

Chapter 13: The Ruins of Balderon. 125

Chapter 14: Zombie Bride 135

Chapter 15: Fate & Destiny 147

Chapter 16: Swamp Hag 153

Chapter 17: The Kapre 161

Chapter 18: The Shack 169

Chapter 19: Calla, Evra, Sorrel 175

Chapter 20: The Warning 183

Chapter 21: The Hollow 193

Chapter 22: The Lagoon 203

Chapter 23: The Garglegs 217

Chapter 24: The Bazaar Of Endless Paths 227

Chapter 25: The Purple Woods. 243

Chapter 26: Murlus. 251

Chapter 27: The Deal 261

Chapter 28: Owed Loyalty 271

Chapter 29: The Treetop Path 283

Chapter 30: The Day the Sun Descended 291

Chapter 31: Valla & Arithel 301

Chapter 32: The Time Prison 317

Chapter 33: The Prisoners Escape 327

Chapter 34: The Prisoners Escape Part 2 343

Chapter 35: The Return 355

CHAPTER 1

Portals Before Supper

A loud knocking echoed from inside the house. Ysmerra, the former shaman of the elf tribe, was startled. The sound rippling through her manor in Thistlemire Woods. Her foresight warning her of what would come to pass.

As she sat in her rocking chair, fingers curled over the armrests, it began to sway without her urging it. As if it was possessed. Her mind was wrenched from the present and dragged into the depths of a trance. A sharp gasp tore from her lips and blackness swallowed her eyes.

An image sharpened to two tribal elves, cloaked in black and worry, standing at her doorstep. Desperate.

The shadows of the vision swirled like storm winds, then unveiled a beautiful young elf and darling little boy. Their faces eerily illuminated in flickering candlelight, surrounded by sigils and arcane symbols. A book. An incantation.

The unintentional rocking of Ysmerra's chair was growing frantic and more erratic.

Time fractured. Shadows swarmed, then peeled back, revealing a figure wreathed in shifting darkness. His eyes gleamed with hunger. His voice slithered around them like chains and a leash. The children stepped past the veil, vanishing all traces of them from existence.

The vision fragmented again, forcing her deeper beyond time. And there, for the briefest moment, she glimpsed something worse... his intentions. The soul-fire being stripped from their bones.

Ysmerra's grip tightened around the armrests, the wood creaking beneath her. Her mind moved swiftly. Planning. Calculating.

The blackness that had washed over her eyes faded. She gave herself a brief moment for her heart to still, her breath to catch, and the rocking chair to stop. With a swift, fluid motion, Ysmerra rose from her chair, grasped the smoky quartz orb of her cane, and headed toward the library.

Something was watching. Waiting. The air pressed against her, thick and knowing, drowning out the usual scent of parchment and candle wax. Something unseen stretched across the cavernous library, weaving between the cobwebs, clinging to the beams of ancient, dark wood.

She ignored the lurking, uninvited guest, as it seemed to present no immediate danger, and pressed forward. There was no time to waste.

She ran her fingers across the spines of the centuries-old cracked leather books.

The books groaned, shifting restlessly within their towering shelves, as if waking from a long slumber. They began whispering, faint but growing, in a language only Ysmerra could understand.

Ysmerra stood before the library with arms wide open, eyes closed, connecting her thoughts with theirs. The books began to settle into silence.

She said aloud, her voice calm but commanding, as if calling upon an ancient rite.
"Show me what I wish to seek."

A book slipped free from the shelf, gliding toward her, fluttering its pages like a bird's wings as it opened to a page where the ink glowed to illuminate the passage meant for her. It hung expectantly mid-air before her eyes.

She read the glowing passage.

"Love Potions for the Desperate and Damned"

She deadpanned.

The book shuddered as if embarrassed, then hurled itself back onto the shelf. Another book took its place and glided over to her.

She skimmed the illuminated text.

"Go Back In Time"

The book responded eagerly, shifting up and down in gleeful approval.

She shook her head.
"No! Absolutely not. They never turn out well."

The book slammed shut and flung itself back into the wall. The library responded by letting a book fall off the shelf and hit the floor with a resounding thud.

Ysmerra rolled her eyes. "We'll have none of that today. Thank you."

They gently sent another book toward her. She grabbed it with both hands and brought it closer, reading the luminous ink.

"Portals"

A flicker of relief passed through her—barely visible. Her lips curled into a small smile, eyes glinting with quiet satisfaction. "Yes. You'll do quite nicely."

She set the book down on the clawfoot round table, cluttered with scrolls and open books. Then yelled sharply.
"Pip! Get in here!"

There was a gust of wind, and her assistant appeared in the doorway, arms crossed, grinning like a fox caught mid-heist.
Flipping his copper bangs off his face.
"What's the emergency?"

The woodland elf quickly recognized what was in the forefront of her mind. Her vision, the spell. The grin slid right off his face as his eyes narrowed slightly, and he uncrossed his arms, suddenly alert.

Ysmerra didn't waste time. She slid the book across the cluttered table, its leather cover scraping softly against the wood. Her tone brisk.
"We don't have much time. I need you to procure the items for this potion."

Pip planted one hand on his hip and tilted his head, eyebrows raised and he said dryly.
"Last time you said 'just a few ingredients,' and we ended up with two talking squirrels and a very distressed goose."

Still looking through books and scrolls, Ysmerra didn't even raise her head. She replied matter-of-factly.

"The squirrels were absolutely essential. And the goose? Completely under control."

She paused, tapping her chin as she rifled through a leather-bound book.

Pip grabbed the book, glancing at her with a skeptical squint.
"Let me guess. You want me to wrestle a minotaur or steal some of its urine?"

He muttered something sarcastic under his breath as he glanced at the ingredients.
"We've got most of these… but…"

He scoffed under his breath, scanning the ingredients list. He looked up. voice pitching into a confused whine.
"Tears of a mermaid?"

Ysmerra gave him no response. Not even a twitch.

He looked back down and continued reading the spell's instructions with a growing sense of betrayal. Blinking slowly, mouth pulling into a grimace.
"Urine of a minotaur? I knew it! Why is it always urine!…"

Pip continued aloud, his voice rising with every absurd item like he was personally offended by the spell itself.
"Wax from a goblin's ears? You've got to be kidding me!"

Ysmerra let out a sharp breath through her nose, her patience visibly thinning. She gave a slow, deliberate nod and an exhausted glare. Dragging her words like a stone.
"Yes. That's what it says."

Pip exhaled dramatically, snapping the book shut with a groan "This is going to take me all day."

Ysmerra tapped her fingers on the table. Her gaze sharpening as she locked onto him.
"We need the portal opened before supper."

Her voice dropped lower now. Serious. Heavy with something unspoken. "The longer they're there…"

She trailed off, lips pressing into a tight line, her brow furrowing like she'd just let herself consider what that actually meant. Then turned her attention back to another open scroll.

She waved a hand at him without looking. Done with the conversation. Gave him a tired shooing gesture, like swatting a fly. "Just get moving."

As he turned to go, she didn't even bother lifting her head—just raised a single finger in his direction, eyes still on the pages. "Don't forget the spit of a troll."

Pip rolled his eyes so hard it might've required a healing salve and tossed his head back with a groan. Then announced with great suffering
"Wouldn't dream of it."

And then, with a faint shimmer, a whoosh of air, and the softest puff of cinnamon and ozone, he vanished. Leaving only the faintest scent of mischief in his wake.

PIP
Right. I've got the lists. You want me to pick up anything else while I'm out?

YSMERRA
Yes. A snack. Something crunchy.

PIP
Crunchy like toasted bat wings... or crunchy like roasted sunflower beetles?

YSMERRA
Surprise me. But nothing with legs still attached this time.

PIP
Noted. Legs... optional.

YSMERRA
Like a fish trying to climb a tree.

PIP
...Right. Crunchy. No legs. Got it. See you later.

YSMERRA
And don't go to that one vendor in Mosscreek. Those eyeball pastries were dreadful.

CHAPTER 2
The Book

Dread coiled deep in Ysmerra's stomach. Sharp and relentless. No tome in her vast library held answers about the creature she'd seen or the fate of the young elves it had taken.

Her thoughts snapped to the book. The summoning text. The invocation spell that unleashed this nightmare.

Had she missed something? A warning? A clue buried in the margins?

Her nails dug into her palm as her fist clenched at her side. She had to find that book. Whatever it held, it might be the only thing standing between her and the truth or more tragedy.

She had to go to the room where it all began.

Ysmerra closed her eyes, drawing a deep breath to center herself. The world around her faded into the shadows of her mind. She reached for the vision that clung to the edges of her thoughts—the image of the young elves, their faces glowing in the candlelight. Her heart ached at the sight of them, but she forced herself to look past their faces, focusing on the room instead. The bed, the bookshelf, the sigil... the candles.

Her eyes fluttered closed and her mind sank deeper into the vision. She was searching for something... anything that might guide her forward. Trying to establish a connection, a bridge, a path she could follow.

Focusing on the details of the room, Ysmerra tapped her cane sharply on the wooden floor and whispered, the words flowing like a soft chant.

"Alari En'Vaya."

Wind, Carry Me.

A rush of energy spiraled around her, pulling her deeper into the vision. The wind hummed, charged with power. She repeated the words over and over, each syllable anchoring the vision. The current intensified, momentum building, spinning faster around her until the sensations began to fade and the energy settled.

After a moment of stillness, she opened her eyes and was standing in the very space she had envisioned.

The candles scattered around the room were still burning, their wax long melted into shallow pools. Tendrils of incense curled lazily in the air. The room was just as she had imagined it. Dim, quiet, suspended in time.

Except... everything was slowly fading into nothing. The furniture, the bookshelves. Everything was beginning to blur at the edges, being erased from existence piece by piece. The candle flames bent unnaturally, casting long shadows that devoured nearby furniture into an ever-growing abyss.

She could feel the space slipping, as if the room itself were holding its last breaths.

In the center of the room, a massive sigil had been drawn in thick, white chalk. It felt somehow disconnected from the lingering oppressive energy that permeated the rest of the room. The sigil pulsed faintly, as if alive and waiting. A low hum thrummed beneath the floorboards. Faint, but constant.

Ysmerra's eyes caught the book's cover, gleaming faintly in the dying candlelight. Her hands trembled slightly as she picked it up, the rough texture worn beneath her fingertips. She lingered, staring at the cover before tucking it under her arm.

The, she felt it. Unseen eyes grazing her every move.

The room felt heavier now, its instability growing with each passing second.

She took one last look around the room, trying to capture every detail before it vanished into nothingness. She turned away and a sigh escaped her lips as she spoke the words,

"Selorien Thar'Amin."

Pathways, Open Before Me.

Two of the candles' long, wavering shadows ripped off the walls and floated before her. One by one, the others followed, merging together to form a dark circle, their edges emitting an intense light. Through it, a passageway back home.

A wave of warmth enveloped her, pulling her into its gentle embrace. She stepped forward into the shadows, leaving the room to fade into the darkness behind her.

The energy surged, and in an instant, she was gone. The glow of the shadows dimmed and drifted back to their places along the walls.

In the blink of an eye, she was back in her library, but the room and what it meant, lingered heavily on her chest.

A haunting remembrance in the silence.

PIP

Okay, I've been insulting this troll for fifteen minutes straight and he just won't spit. I'm losing daylight here. Any ideas?

YSMERRA

Did you try comparing his hygiene to a barnacle's backside?

PIP

Yup. I opened with that one.

YSMERRA

Try: If I had a silver coin for every wart on your chin, I could bribe the gods to erase your reflection from every scrying pool.... Or: You're the reason potions come with warning labels.

PIP

... Nothing. He yawned. I feel like he's heard them all.

YSMERRA

Say his mother brews tea with her own toenails.

PIP

Eww. Okay...OH there it is. Yup. That one landed. Direct hit to the cheekbone. We have slime.

YSMERRA

That one's a classic.

CHAPTER 3
Pip, Potions, and Potential Disasters

The familiar surroundings of her library offered little comfort. Ysmerra eased into her reading chair, the old leather groaning beneath her. She stared at the book as if daring it to reveal its secrets.

She whispered, "Lor'nia Varthil." *Bring Forth Light*.

The candles flared, illuminating her reading nook. Her fingers traced the book's cover.

The Path of The Forsaken Hand

She opened it to the invocation spell first. It was covered in tiny, cramped warnings:

DO NOT ATTEMPT THIS SPELL WITHOUT A FULL MOON

She narrowed her eyes.

CAUTION: FLAMES MAY BECOME SENTIENT

She raised a brow.

PORTALS ARE PRONE TO MOOD SWINGS

She set the book down and rubbed her temples.

Who wrote this nonsense? A drunk gremlin? What kind of lunatic enchanted this thing?

The spell was either brilliant or completely nonsense. Possibly both. She didn't have the luxury of choosing a saner option. There was no turning back, not even from a moody portal.

Suddenly, there was a loud thud and a distant crash from the hallway.

Pip yelled. "It's fine!"

A second later, he burst into the room. Disheveled, grinning, hair sticking out at every angle like he'd just run through a bramble patch.

He announced, triumphantly holding a half-eaten apple.
"I'm back!...And before you say anything, the vase wasn't that important, was it?"

Ysmerra exhaled through her nose, long-suffering, and rubbed her temple even harder.
"Get started on the spells. Brew the potion. Set up the altar."

He took a dramatic bite of the apple. With his mouth full, he repeated "Got it. Spells. Potion. Altar."

Ysmerra gave him a withering stare as he chewed obnoxiously loud. "Don't add anything weird this time."

He paused mid-bite, tilting his head, eyes glinting with mischief. "Define weird."

She lifted a finger at him with a warning tone. Half amused, half threatening. The corners of her lips twitched, betraying her amusement.
"I mean it, Pip."

He held up his hand in mock surrender, a goofy grin spreading across his face as he saluted her.
"One perfectly normal, boring, no-fun-whatsoever locator spell coming right up!"

And with that, he vanished in a blur down the hall.

She returned to the book, reading it from the beginning.

Meanwhile, in the apothecary, Pip began working on the spell. It was a chaotic sanctuary. Every inch of shelf space crammed with jars and vials filled with ingredients preserved in varying states of decay. Each jar was labeled neatly in alphabetical order, from *Absinthe Root* to *Zirconium Dust*. Dried herbs and animal bones hung from the ceiling like chandeliers.

With the cauldron afire and the grimoire balanced precariously in one hand, Pip scanned the directions. With uncanny speed, he darted across the room, snatching something with one hand, and before the dust could settle, he'd already gathered half a dozen more ingredients.

On a high shelf, a jar caught his eye—

DO NOT OPEN UNDER ANY CIRCUMSTANCES.

He gave it a little shake. A muffled growl vibrated through the glass. He said, excited while stuffing it into his pocket. "Good to know."

With a dramatic flourish, Pip added ingredients to the cauldron with an exaggerated *splat*. The potion bubbled violently, dark emerald liquid splashing in angry bursts.

He danced around the room, skipping between shelves, grabbing things with reckless abandon, triumphantly throwing them in with no regard for precision.

The potion hissed loudly, sending up a wave of foul-smelling smoke. Pip stirred it with a long, crooked wooden spoon, humming a little tune.

He looked around at the mess. Half-empty jars, ingredients spilling over, bones scattered across the floor, and magic swirling through the air. He wiped his brow, smiling.

The cauldron burped, sending up one last puff of smoke that smelled oddly minty.

The potion, now a deep, fluorescent green, settled into calm. He transferred it into a glass bottle and jammed a cork into the top. *"Potion of the Unseen Path*. Done!... ish."

He peered into the grimoire.

The next part of the spell called for *Gareth Ash. A* fine powder made of crushed beaks, fangs, bones, horns, and other odds and ends. The recipe didn't explain how to convince any of these creatures to donate parts willingly.

He plopped a sack full of questionable ingredients on the table with a grimace. Something inside it snarled. Possibly in protest.

Grabbing the mortar and pestle with the enthusiasm of a chef about to make a disastrous soufflé.

He rolled up his sleeves with far more confidence than the situation warranted, and muttered.
"Time to get grinding."

Reading the first item on the list.
"Griffin beak? Of course it's a griffin beak."

He reached into the bag and pulled out a jagged yellow beak, curved and sharp, like a weapon forged for face-stabbing. Pip looked at it with a mixture of guilt and apology. He gave it a sheepish pat before dropping it in. Wincing at every crack.
"Sorry, buddy. Nothing personal... "

Read the next ingredient. Stopped. Blinked twice.
"Nope. Absolutely not."

He looked around the empty room as if someone, anyone might back him up. "I don't get paid enough for that... Oh wait, I don't get paid *at all*."

He paused. His eyes narrowed with dramatic realization. He waved a hand.
"Ya. Next."

He turned back to the grimoire and scanned the next item.
He leaned in, squinting at the next line like it might change if he stared long enough.
Dried goblin's eye.

He held the shriveled thing at arm's length before letting it plop into the mortar. He pressed the pestle down, but the eyeball shot out like a cannonball, bouncing off the counter, ricocheted off a bookcase, and vanished under the nearest shelf.

He dropped to all fours, scrambling across the floor like a gremlin in search of treasure. The bag tipped over behind him, releasing a slow tumble of mysterious odds and ends, some twitching, others moaning.

When he finally found it, the eye was dusty and dented. He scooped it up with the corner of his sleeve, muttering curses and set it in the mortar.

The pestle squeaked with every press, and Pip's hand cramped from the effort. He set the pestle down and thought for a moment as he rubbed the cramp in his hand.

He lit up with excitement and dashed to the enchanted weapons room, returning moments later with an oversized mallet covered in magical runes.

He declared gleefully.
"Meet the Pulverizer!"

He gripped the handle with one hand, tapping the mallet's heavy head into his opposite palm with theatrical menace. Grinning like a cat about to break something expensive.

He knocked the mortar aside like the sight of it disgusted him. Then slammed the mallet onto the rest of the ingredients with such an impact that it made half the jars on the shelf rattle.

He hammered away like a troll on a deadline. Dust clouds erupted like a volcano having a tantrum. Bone fragments flew like confetti at a haunted wedding. Remnants ricocheted off the wall. Gray powder clung to his hair, sleeves, and eyebrows like a tragic baking accident.

When the carnage was finally over, he scraped what was left into a seashell bowl with the flat of his hand.

He blinked once. Slowly.
"Perfect."

Meanwhile back in the library, Ysmerra was slumped in her chair, flipping through the ancient tome with a scowl. Page after page

offered nothing but stars aligning, poetic truths, personal prophecies, and half-finished thoughts.
"Useless! This whole thing is useless!"

She was ready to snap the book shut and hurl it across the room. But, then she saw it. Hidden in a paragraph of nonsense was a name.

Clear. Defiant. Eternal.

Slowly, she leaned closer, the frustration softening from her face like a veil being drawn back. Her eyes widened, focused and sharp, glinting with something fierce. Triumph. She whispered,
"I found you."

The name pulsed in her mind like a beacon: *Zarriq*.

That alone would be enough to pinpoint his location, wherever beyond the stars he was hiding. The hunt had truly begun.

The silence stretched for half a beat. Then pop.

Pip reappeared in the middle of the library with a proud little spin, and a flower tucked behind his ear like a prize. He declared,
"All set. Just waiting for you."

Ysmerra glanced up, pretending not to notice the flower. She simply reached for her cane with the dry composure of someone about to make a deeply questionable life choice.
"Let's hope this doesn't explode."

Pip gave a radiant grin, tapping the flower like a king adjusting his crown and replied cheerfully,
"Fifty-fifty odds."

And with that, they made their way to the ceremony room, while above, their uninvited guest clinging to the beams was still watching.

Still listening...

Waiting.

YSMERRA

There's a 50/50 chance this explodes.
What ingredient did you leave out?

PIP

...The toe jam. From a volcanic gnome.

YSMERRA

Oh honestly Pip. You had ONE job.

PIP

Last time, a gnome bit me and chased me up a tree,
then declared a blood feud. Now there's a hex on my
laundry.

YSMERRA

You're lucky I don't put a hex on you.

PIP

Fair. Well... maybe the jam's optional? Optional-
adjacent?

YSMERRA

Maybe. We'll just see what happens.
Worst case scenario, we re-create last
month's bog sprite incident.

PIP

I still can't open the pantry without a
bribe and a shield.

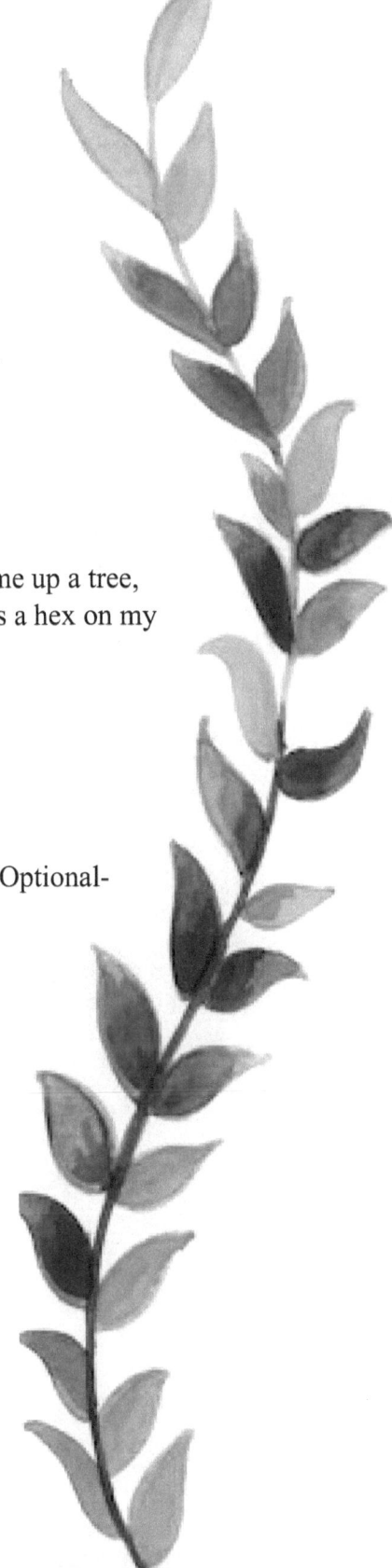

CHAPTER 4
One Door, One Path

The ceremony chamber awaited, dimly lit by a fireplace. Pip settled off to the side, cradling a small drum in his lap. He gave it a gentle tap, the sound light and steady, like a heartbeat.

Ysmerra set her cane aside with care, then removed her shoes. The soft fabric of her shawl slid from her shoulders, hanging loosely around her arms. She stepped into the center of the room, barefoot, letting the chill of the wood ground her in the magic she was about to summon.

She tilted her head back, gaze lifting to the moon visible through the glass ceiling above.
"The moon watches."

She let the tension drain from her shoulders, her breath slowing with the rhythm of Pip's drumming.
"Now, we begin."

Before her lay a simple wooden table. Weathered, knotted, and deeply scarred by countless rites long passed. Upon it were four objects: a carved stone, a feather, a crystal that seemed to pulse faintly, and a twisted iron key. Each item represented the elements that bound realms together: earth, air, fire, and spirit. At its center rested a clay bowl, filled with black soil from a burned forest.

Ysmerra knelt before the altar and placed the book *The Path of The Forsaken Hand* upon it, and opened it to the page of the invocation spell that had called forth Zarriq. She reached for the feather, collected from a griffon's fallen plume. Dipping it into cursed tar, laced with obsidian dust and snake venom, she wrote the name *Zarriq* onto aged parchment. Her voice weaving a chant into the letters as she sprinkled *Goreth Ash* upon the ink. The chant swelled softly, the energy in the room tightening like a drawn bowstring.
Pip's drumming had gotten louder... and more dramatic.

Ysmerra looked over her shoulder.
"Why do you insist on playing that drum every time we perform a ritual?"

He paused mid-beat, his expression going utterly blank as if she'd just asked why the sky was blue.
"I like it. I think it adds ambience to the ceremonies."

She stared at him a second longer, unblinking.
Then she sighed, turned back to the altar, and muttered,
"Fine. But keep it rhythmic."

Pip gave her a mock salute and resumed with exaggerated focus, as if he were summoning the dead through sheer vibes alone.

Ysmerra took an obsidian knife and drew a shallow line across her palm. Her blood dripped and pooled into the soil. The dark drops swallowed without a trace, thirsting for her offering. The magic surged, and without warning, strands of her silvery hair fell, drifting like feathers to the ground. It was a quiet reminder that blood magic always demanded a price. Subtle, but with each spell cast, the toll was paid in a piece of her youth, a fragment of her beauty, a part of her vitality, something small always slipped away.

She whispered, "Laerá Shi Vaerán, Laerá Shi Cindúlin."

Forth From Shadow, Forth From Time.

It began to deepen and echoed within the room, until it seemed layered as though joined by a chorus of countless unseen faces.

Ysmerra rose slowly with deliberate grace, her eyes ignited like molten gold. She grasped the parchment bearing Zarriq's name and tossed it to the floor. She stood before it holding the seashell bowl of *Goreth Ash* in one hand and the stone bowl of blood-drenched soil in the other. Slowly spilling their offerings over his name on the ground, the ash and soil intertwined and hissed of ancient power.

In the short silence that followed, dark vines erupted with a violent snap, curling and twisting, weaving and knotting themselves into a large archway.

"Vaerá Shi Lóte, Ará Shi Amarillë."

Let This Door Be Bound To Fate.

She reached deep into the pocket of her long skirt and drew out a single seed. Ysmerra placed it at the arch's center, pressing it firmly into the soil, then poured the green *Potion of The Unseen Path* over it. The seed cracked open. A soft, eerie glow spilled from its split husk, and the light spread outward. Roots spread rapidly, snaking their way up the vine-covered arch. A heartbeat later, white flowers bloomed along the vines.

She placed her hand on the nearest blossom, closing her eyes. She saw a cottage nestled in a quiet garden, with stained glass windows, its roof covered with moss. The portal would rest there. Veiled by bloom and stone. Protected by charm and illusion. It would wait for the girl.

The inside of the archway was a swirled mass of shadow and mist. Slowly, it began to stabilize until it resembled a still, dark pond. The twisted iron key lifted into the air and turned, creating the sound of unlocking a door that echoed through the manor. The crystal fractured, its shards flying directly into the front of the dark pond. From each shard, faint silver vines began to grow, winding like creeping ivy, until it resembled a door.

Ysmerra grabbed the floating key and placed it into the ivy door's keyhole and commanded,

"Ilvé Lóte, Ilvé Silén."

One Door. One Path.

The portal pulsed once, sealing its purpose. Then she opened it. The glow from her eyes faded and returned to their usual icy blue. Pip stopped drumming, his attention pulled toward the door and what mysteries lay beyond it. Ysmerra looked over her shoulder and flashed him a grin, then without hesitation, she walked through it. Pip jumped to his feet, startled. She left without a word or giving him any instructions to follow or even checking if it was safe.

Ysmerra came right back through the door. But Pip was nowhere in sight.

A little concerned, she shouted for him. "Pip?"

There was a rustle, followed by the unmistakable sound of hurried footsteps. Pip zipped in, a washcloth draped over his shoulder as though he'd been deep in the throes of some urgent task. His face was flushed, an exaggerated look of frustration masking his natural curiosity.

Pip huffed, clearly unimpressed by her sudden reappearance. His arms crossed tightly, though his lips twitched upward as if he was trying to suppress a grin.
"Where have you been? You were gone for hours!"

Ysmerra stood there for a moment, silent in thought, tilting her head slightly, calculating the time difference.

Her voice trailed off with a soft hum, the weight of the realization sinking in.
"Hmm… interesting. A mere step to me there, yet hours here. Oh, that changes things."

Pip's expression was a mix of annoyance and curiosity, but his tone remained sharp as ever.
"Changes what?"

Ysmerra's fingers traced the edge of the ivy-covered portal beside her as if the answers were written in the leaves.
"A lot can happen in a few hours. And not all of it is pleasant."

Pip threw his hands up in exasperation. His voice tinged with playful frustration, exaggerating every movement
"I got so bored, I reorganized the herbs alphabetically. Then I cleaned out the cauldron. Twice."

Then his eyes narrowed, and crossed his arms with a mock pout.
"You could've at least told me you'd be late. I only made dinner for one."

Ysmerra's eyes rolled, the corners of her mouth twitching with exasperation. "Oh for heaven's sake, I didn't know time would leap ahead of me."

Pip's uncrossed his arms, eyes wide with relief, couldn't hide the question bubbling on his tongue.
"How long will the portal stay open?"

Ysmerra, always savoring the present moment, closed her eyes, drawing in a deep, fragrant breath of the flowers surrounding the portal. After a pause, her lips curved into a knowing smile.
"Midnight, I'd say... enough time for a proper welcome, I should think."

She tilted her head, almost as though listening to something distant, her fingers idly tracing the edge of a flower petal. Then, she spoke with that familiar playful mystery.
"Now, we wait... for her steps to lead her here, as if the very wind whispers her name."

Pip blinked, leaning forward. "Who?"

Ysmerra paused, her gaze distant, as though listening for the name and trying to pluck it from the air itself.
"Reaganna... Reagan"

Ysmerra's voice lingered on the last syllable. It clung to the silence like a prophecy waiting to unfold.

PIP
So... snacks and cards while we wait?

YSMERRA
Absolutely. I earned something crunchy.

PIP
They were out of crispy root clusters. I got moss-cheese
twists, eel-puffed crisps, and something called
"ScorchPuffs" with a warning label I can't read.

YSMERRA
*M*oss-cheese? No. The last batch tasted like wet roof
shingles.

PIP
That's oddly specific... Wait a second... There's a patch
missing above the west turret.
Was that *you?* Did you... did you eat part of the roof?

YSMERRA
It was a gingerbread-house spell gone awry.
I won't fuss with you over the details.

PIP
You *ate* the house?!

YSMERRA
I was under a spell!

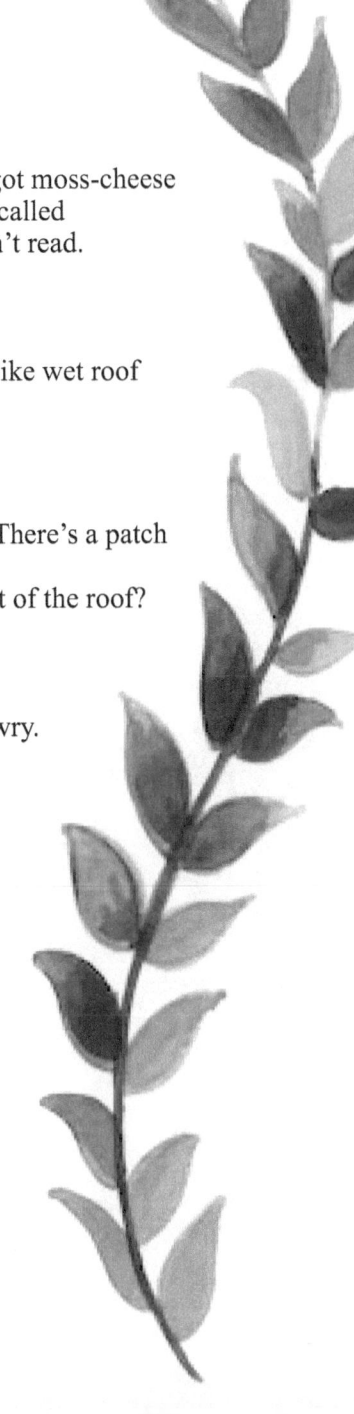

CHAPTER 5

Reagan

Reagan sat by her window, the moonlight casting a faint glow over the worn book in her hands: The Path of The Forsaken Hand. Her eyes kept glancing at one passage: *I would have never known the wonders hidden beyond the veil of despair if I hadn't invoked the druid. He didn't just shatter the chains that bound me, he showed me the path to power and freedom.*

Night had draped itself over the forest. Candles flickered from every nook and surface, filling her room with a twilight of golden mosaic light patterns. She sat motionless, her eyes on the worn pages but her mind elsewhere. Incense smoke twirled like silent wishes through the air giving an illusion of peace in a world that offered none.

Reading about the tales of a man whose life had been a treacherous labyrinth of choices and consequences, made her think about her own life. A tangled web of expectations and duty.

The door creaked open and her mother's voice sliced through the stillness like a distant bell.
"Reaganna. We're leaving. Watch your brother. Just some tribal matters. We'll be back soon. Keep Kayleth out of trouble."

Reagan didn't even flinch. Her eyes stayed fixed on the words.
She could hear her mother's footsteps fade and the front door close.
She was lost in thought. Dreading the day when the tribes ink would claim her, binding her to a life she'd never chosen.

She sat cross-legged on her bed, with the battered book resting on her lap. Now on the page with the sigil for invocation.

It began to rain outside. Little droplets of water hitting the glass. She stared out the window watching the rain hit the trees. The sound of the downpour filled the room, steady, rhythmic, but inside her, the storm grew louder. Then, a raw undeniable urge compelled her to do something, to act, to change her circumstances. To not feel helpless.

If the druid helped that man, then he could help her too. To change everything, or help her escape. The thought coiled around her mind like a serpent, squeezing out fear and replacing it with reckless need.

The need to draw it overwhelmed her. The book had laid out perfect instructions for how to invoke the druid.

She wondered. *Could I? Could I Escape?*

The rain outside intensified, as if urging her forward. Her heartbeat quickened to match its rhythm. The need to draw the sigil burned within her now.

She talked herself into it. There was no turning back.
Racing with excitement she practically jumped off her bed and over to her desk looking for a piece of chalk. Rummaging through drawers trying to find something to write the symbol with. She found it, a small piece of white chalk. She slowly picked it up. Her fingers trembled, not with fear, but with anticipation. Looking at it she knew it was meant to happen.

She grabbed the book off her bed and dropped to her knees scraping the chalk against the wood. The symbol taking shape with each careful stroke. The edges of the drawing seemed to shimmer for a moment before she completed it.She sat back admiring the preciseness compared to the book.

A soft thud broke her concentration. Kayleth, her little brother, appeared at the door. His tiny face was framed in the doorway, his eyes wide with curiosity.

The sight of his cute expression brought her back to reality. She felt unbelievably silly for believing the book could possibly be real. She was relieved.

Kayleth came into the room, running into her arms, hugging her. She didn't want him to see the anxiety that twisted inside her. He was so young, so innocent, and she didn't want to burden him with her fears. His touch reminded her he was there and that made everything feel a little less heavy for her.

He took a couple steps back and sat down in front her. He pointed to the book.

She smiled, trying to keep her voice light.
"I just got that one today. You want me to read it to you?"

She often read to him at night. He nodded his head enthusiastically with a smile. She picked up the book, settling into what she thought would be another usual quiet night.

She started reading to Kayleth, putting on her most theatrical voice, exaggerating the tone and rhythm of the words to make the story fun and entertaining.
"After the symbol has been drawn, get into a quiet meditative position and close your eyes."

Then closed her eyes obnoxiously slow, arms drifting upward in an over-the-top mystical prayer pose. She opened one eye dramatically to peek at Kayleth's reaction.
"Focus on your intent. Focus on the druid."

With extreme showmanship she sprang to her feet, reciting the next passage like a full-blown sorceress in a tavern play. Her hands flew into the air like she was summoning a thunderstorm, commanding it from the heavens. Her voice rising with each line.

"In the name of power long forgotten, I call to you. I seek the one who waits. Hear my cry! Awaken from the ashes of time. Let the one who answers my call come forth. Come forth and answer... Show yourself...Zarriq"

Kayleth erupted into a fit of giggles, clapping his hands with delight at her wild, grande gestures and the drama she poured into every word.

She glanced down at Kayleth. His laugh made her smile ear to ear.
"You like that huh? I can do more like that. I—"

And just then, the windows burst open with a deafening crash, the panes slamming against the walls.

PIP
How long does it *take* to walk through a portal? I
feel like we've been playing cards for hours... I
raise you my last soul-binding charm, and my first
born child.

YSMERRA
It's been five minutes... Maybe if you didn't forget the *Toe
Jam*, the Come To Spell would work faster. Anyway, you're
over a thousand years old, it's' extremely unlikely you're
having children.

PIP
That's why I'm betting it. Raise or Call.

YSMERRA
A single cursed tooth and a half-eaten biscuit. Try me.

PIP
...That oddly explains a lot about your dating history.

YSMERRA
I once was engaged to a vampire.

PIP
It was a coat rack. In the wine cellar. You
were drunk. You made me officiate the
wedding.

YSMERRA
He was very tall. Great listener. Great
cheekbones. I can't remember why it
didn't work out.

CHAPTER 6
The Druid

A howling gust of wind swept through the room. Reagan's hair whipped wildly around her face. Heart pounding, she rushed to the window, fighting the wind to force it shut. Her trembling hands finally managed to latch the lock, but something felt... wrong. That had never happened before. She felt a prickling unease at the back of her neck, as if unseen eyes were watching.

Suddenly, the candles began snuffing out one by one.

Reagan's breath caught as her gaze locked on each flame, her pulse quickening with every extinguished light. The shadows crept closer with each fading glow, the room shrinking into darkness. She wondered what would happen when the last one went out.

The final candle sputtered, the flame clinging desperately to life before it vanished with a soft hiss, and complete darkness fell over the room.

Her breath hitched when she felt it. A massive, unseen presence rushing past her, brushing the edge of her arm.

One by one, the candles reignited on their own, their flames roaring to life, taller and fiercer than ever before. Shadows danced violently across the walls, casting jagged shapes that seemed alive.

In the center of the room, Kayleth sat giggling and clapping his tiny hands, blissfully unaware of what was unfolding around him.

The symbols on the floor pulsed with an otherworldly glow, illuminating Kayleth's innocent face.

Ghostly figures emerged from the shadows, swirling with malicious intent. They encircled the room like predators sizing up their prey. Then, the shadows began to merge and darken until it was no longer ethereal.

From the depths of the darkness, a figure stepped forward with unearthly grace.

The Druid.

Draped in flowing robes woven from midnight and starlight, his presence was both mesmerizing and terrifying. Long ice-blonde hair cascaded past his shoulders like a waterfall of moonlight, framing a face carved with regal perfection yet shadowed with menace.

There he stood, quietly, for a few moments just staring at Reagan. His eyes were piercing and locked onto hers.

His voice smooth like velvet, yet laced with an underlying menace. "Well, well… a dark elf dares summons me?"

The druid's eyes narrowed, a glimmer of intrigue sparking within his depths, mixed with an apparent annoyance.
"What do you want?"

Under the weight of the druid's gaze, she could barely get her words out.
"Are you... Zarriq?"

He lifted his chin slightly, as though basking in invisible applause. His response was deep, silky and dripping with power, arrogance, and theatrical pride.
"Ruler of Balderon, yes."

He glanced at the sigil on the floor, then looked back at her. His eyes glinted with dark amusement.
"I presume you wish to make some sort of trade? You've placed your brother in the center of these symbols. Is he not a sacrifice for your ritual?"

His voice dripped with unsettling charm, each word smooth and mocking, laced with a confidence that made her stomach twist.

Reagan looked at Kayleth sitting calmly inside the circle. Her heart dropped. She hadn't even thought, hadn't even realized.

The symbols. The placement. The intention they might suggest to someone like him.

She scrambled to speak. Her voice trembling with panic and protest.
"No! I didn't mean to. He's my brother! I would never—"

Zarriq quickly interrupted her. Lifted a finger, wagging it back and forth with maddening leisure, like a parent shushing a child who'd broken a rule. The interruption wasn't loud, but it landed like a slap. Firm and absolute.
"Ah ah ah... But you did."

Each syllable held weight, settling into the air like a warning. His smile deepened as he stepped closer, savoring her desperation.
"He belongs to me now."

He reached down to pick up Kayleth.

She lunged forward, snatching Kayleth just as Zarriq reached down. A word tore from her throat, raw and instinctive, as she lunged forward.
"NO!"

Her fingers grazed Zarriq's. Her arm brushed against him. A fleeting contact that sent a chill down both their spines. For one breathless second, they were inches apart.

Zarriq stiffened. He narrowed his eyes slightly, caught off guard. There was something inside her. Some deep, dormant magic that he couldn't sense before. Until now. It wasn't just the magic that stirred him. It was something else.

It hit him in silence. His magic whispering secrets to his bones. A jolt behind the eyes, as if something unseen had dragged part of him away momentarily. It *distracted* him. Unsettled him. His expression didn't break, but a flicker of tension passed through his posture like a ripple beneath still water.

Reagan saw Zarriq pause. She took that second and quickly moved. She stepped back, slid Kayleth gently behind her with one arm. Her other hand hovered, ready to reach for a blade if she had to.

She said low and razor-sharp, a warning.
"You can't have him."

His gaze lingered on her. No longer amused. Not quite angry. Just... watching. Measuring.

He stood there. Dark. Unreadable. Then he finally spoke. "You're a tribal elf... I've never seen one so young. Tell me, why don't you have soul-fire markings on your body?"

Confused by his curiosity but compelled to explain, she replied. "We don't get them until we're eighteen."

Kayleth seemingly unfazed by the tension, wandered toward the bed and climbed up. He didn't sense any danger in the room. He reached for a book on the alcove nearby and began flipping through the pages, humming under his breath as his small fingers traced the drawings.

Reagan's eyes were following him to make sure he was okay. "The markings show up with our powers during a ceremony. Then we are branded with ink specific to our tribe, powers, and duties."

He rolled his eyes, irritation tugging at the corners of his mouth. He huffed, clearly unimpressed with the simple-mindedness of her tribe's ways. He shifted, his boots tapping softly against the floor as he wandered across the room, eyes scanning her desk with faint interest. His fingers brushed over the objects strewn across a collection of neatly arranged books and a few worn trinkets.

He said almost to himself, as though it was the answer to a question she hadn't asked yet. "Ether."

Reagan's brow furrowed in confusion.
"What?"

He dragged his gaze from the desk to her.
"Ether magic. That's what you're going to have."

He turned back to fiddle with more delicate trinkets on her shelf, his fingers brushing the smooth surfaces of small, ornate figurines.

Reagan's confusion lingered. "What's that?"

His eyes narrowed, a flicker of impatience passing over his features. "Don't they teach you anything in school?"

She answered slowly. Still cautious.
"We don't really have school. We mostly focus on combat training. Once our magic is revealed, we get paired with an elder who teaches us about it."

He paused, considering this. His eyes glinted as he reached inward with his magic. Then, for the briefest flicker, his irises blazed with light as his magic stirred beneath the surface.

The tribes had long suppressed the wild bloom of magic in their young. Not with shackles, but with omission. Centuries ago, elven children were taught to wield their gifts as soon as they could walk. By five, power surged through them like wildfire.

But with power came chaos. Toddler tantrums turned to tremors. Teenage defiance sparked duels. Homes became battlegrounds. The sacred grounds grew volatile, unruly, and dangerous. A royal decree had ordered the suppression to preserve the tribes and maintain order.

Zarriq shrugged, as if none of it surprised him. His fingers idly touched the trinkets on her shelf. His eyes growing distant. "Ether magic is... controlling energy. The air. The wind. That can allow you to tap into dimensional travel. Telepathic communication."

His voice had a touch of awe now, as though he'd realized something about her he hadn't before. He started to smirk, his gaze flicking over her with new curiosity. He scratched his left brow, his long nail brushing his skin. A thoughtful gesture betrayed by the sparkle in his eyes.

He turned his attention to the bookcase, reading titles, fingers grazing over the binding columns. Then his eyes stopped on a small, delicate object. A tiny trinket with her name engraved on it. He leaned closer. He said the name slowly, testing it.
"Reaganna."

She flinched at the sound of it. Only her parents called her that. Hearing it now, from *him*, made her skin crawl. She corrected him, her voice just a little sharper than she intended. Not rude. But clipped. Controlled.
"Reagan, actually."

He was more curious than he let on. He didn't turn. Still studying the room. Then asked "How old are you?"

She didn't know what game he was playing. Her eyes stayed locked on him, watching for a shift in his posture, a flick of his hand, anything that might hint at what came next. She wasn't sure if she

was still afraid... or just fascinated. Either way, she kept her voice steady.
"Seventeen."

Something in him shifted. His demeanor quickly changed.

He whipped around so fast his cape flew with him.
"I have a son your age... A prince... Handsome... and in desperate need of a princess."

He smiled, waiting, expectant, as if that alone should make her swoon. He paused for her reaction. She gave him none.

His grin faltered. For half a second, he looked genuinely confused. Then, with a flourish, he tried again, arms opening like he was painting a picture in the air.
"Why don't you come to my realm? Meet my son. You don't like it here anyway. You'll be a princess. You'll be adored by everyone you meet. You'll live in a castle..."

Still nothing. Reagan's expression remained unreadable. Cool, cautious, almost bored.

Zarriq blinked, clearly surprised that she wasn't at least *pretending* to be impressed. His face fell, just a little. But he bounced back quickly, smoothing a hand through his hair, pasting on another charming smile like a stage magician yanking endless scarves from a hat, hoping his next flourish might finally win an applause.

He leaned in slightly, eyes gleaming.
"Time moves differently in my realm. A moon there is about a week here. Your parents won't even know you're gone. Just see if you like it. Get to know the prince and the land."

She said nothing, just kept staring at him like she was trying to figure out if he was insane, delusional... or just used to getting his way.

The idea was both alluring and terrifying. A castle, a prince... it all sounded too perfect. Was she walking into a trap... or the perfect escape?

Something in her had softened just slightly, like she was no longer just enduring his offer, but actually considering it. This is why she'd called the druid in the first place. For help. To escape.

Her voice was quieter now, not defiant, but thoughtful. A shift. "What about my brother? I can't go without him."

Zarriq's smile widened. Not warm, but sharp and knowing, like a predator watching its prey finally step forward. His gaze flicked toward Kayleth, lingering there just a second too long. His eyes lit with a glint of something darker, a private knowledge he didn't share. When he looked back at Reagan, the smile was still there but it had twisted.

His voice was honeyed. He said smoothly. "Bring him along. I can't very well separate the two of you. If you wish to return, I'll bring you back."

Reagan's heart thudded once. Loud and hard. She didn't move. The possibility was real now. For the first time, she could feel the shape of another life forming in front of her. A castle. Freedom. Power. The chance to escape.

She took a half-step forward... then stopped. Something inside her reeled.

She asked, her voice cautious now. "What if I do like it? And want to stay? What about my parents? Won't they think we ran away or were kidnapped by enemies? That could cause a lot of problems for my tribe."

Zarriq crossed the room, closing the distance between them. The temperature dropped slightly as he stopped just inches from her. He said, low and cold. Not a threat. Not a comfort. Just truth. "I can make it so your parents forget you ever existed."

A chill ran through her. Yet... the weight of her unsaid thoughts suddenly didn't feel so heavy. She looked down in contemplation.

He reached out, his hand rising with eerie calm. His thumb slid beneath her chin and lifted her face back up, forcing her to look at him until her eyes met his again. There was no tenderness, only control.

Zarriq's gaze bore into hers. His tone was soothing, and dangerous. Each word landed with weight, not invitation but prophecy. "It would be as if you two had never been born. "

He let the thought settle between them. Then, slowly released her chin.

But instead of letting his hand fall to his side, he simply shifted, turning the motion into an invitation. His fingers opened, palm facing up between them, offering her something far more than just his hand.

She didn't move. Not yet. Her eyes flickered from his hand to his face, searching, weighing.

He tilted his head slightly, voice soft but coaxing. He urged, extending his hand.
 "Come."

The word was gentle, but it carried weight.

He saw the hesitation in her eyes, the flicker of worry that hadn't quite left her face.

So he leaned in just a touch, his voice dropping into something smoother, more persuasive.
"Just a glimpse. While we're there, you can tell me all about the problems that trouble you here, and how I can help. I prefer a more proper setting when conducting business anyway."

With a hesitant breath, and a dangerous siren song in her ears, she took his hand. Then called her brother over.

Kayleth, clutching his stuffed animal tightly, rolled onto his belly and slid off the bed. He sprinted to Reagan's side and slipped his tiny hand into hers.

Together, they would carve their own destiny. Not the one written for them. Not the one expected of them. Theirs. By choice. By will. By fire.

They stood there, three figures, hands clasped together, the floor quivering beneath their feet. Magic answering to the call.

Cracks splintered across the wooden floor like lightning striking in slow motion. A groan echoed from below. Deep, splintering, and wrong. Something was waking.

Through the tiny cracks of the wooden floorboards, phantoms born of ash and fog erupted, shrieking softly as they spiraled upward. Encircling them like vultures in a storm.

The boards gave a final shudder then crumbled like brittle bone. The floor vanished beneath their feet. For one breathless second, they hovered over an abyss.

Then, with a thunderous rush, the phantoms surged, and dragged them down.

I

YSMERRA

Either there was something else in those eel puffs… or that shrub is desperately trying to get my attention.

PIP

Why does it feel like there's an *awful* lot of moths in here? I've swatted three and wrestled one out of my tea in the past five minutes.

YSMERRA

That's because you left the portal door open, you mildew turnip goblin.

PIP

I did not! I *distinctly* remember saying, *"Ysmerra, did you close the swirly death vortex?"* And you said, quote, *"Probably."*

YSMERRA

This is no time for pointing fingers. They're being drawn to the snacks. Fetch The Chick Wand.

PIP

The invisible chicken that eats moths? Absolutely not. It never listens. And we can never catch it afterwards. What about The Bane Candle? *That* repels moths.

YSMERRA

Yeah, but it smells like spoiled rat pudding and attracts starving ghosts. No thank you.

PIP

Too late. I lit it... It's luring them. Now what?

CHAPTER 7
Welcome To Balderon

Swallowed whole by fog and shadow, they plummeted through an abyss of swirling mist. The air around them hummed, charged with unseen forces. The fall threatened to stretch into eternity. A blinding burst of silver and violet split the void, and in an instant, they landed.

Not with a crash, but a hush. A seamless shift, like stepping through a veil.

The phantoms unraveled and dispersed, revealing the world around them. Something so vast and wondrous, the most impossibly beautiful and breathtaking landscape of the kingdom grounds.

Reagan stood, enraptured, pleasantly overwhelmed by the sheer unfathomable magnificence surrounding her. Slowly, she took in all the splendor and majesty laid before her.

A divine, otherworldly meadow, with dazzling blue trees, silver leaves, and flowers that cast an otherworldly glow, their petals shifting colors as if breathing magic. The very air shimmered with drifting motes of silver light. Crystal-winged fireflies floated lazily through the air.

Zarriq placed his hand on Reagan's shoulder.
"Welcome to Balderon."

Her gaze lifted to the heavens, which were just as if not more mesmerizing than the terra itself.

Three moons hung in the twinkling night sky. Hazy purple bands of light entwined the stars. Swirling light rivers of green, blue, and pink stretched across them. Three planets gleamed in the distance.

Zarriq followed her gaze.
"It's always night here."

She turned to him, eyes wide with wonder and disbelief.

He hesitated, clearing his throat. For the briefest moment, an emotion, something like unease, flashed across his face.

Then, smoothly, he continued.
"In this realm, the sun is but a forgotten myth. Instead, an eternal twilight drapes the sky, bathing this world in luminescence."

Kayleth clung to Reagan's leg, wide-eyed and innocent, giggling as a red deer approached. The creature pressed its nose to Kayleth's face, earning another delighted giggle before it trotted away into the night.

Zarriq urged, his voice smooth as silk. "Come."

Reagan tore her gaze from the sky, reluctant to move. But when Zarriq beckoned, she followed. Her feet drawn forward by wonder, and something deeper she couldn't name.

They walked toward the castle, following the moonlit pathways. With each step, she felt her heart race with excitement and anticipation.

The castle was more exquisite than any tale she had ever read. Made of dark stone and shimmering white marble, crimson vines curled around massive pillars of wide balconies and terraces, draped in sheer linen, overlooking the moonlit courtyard.

As they crossed the stone bridge, Reagan peered over the edge.

Beneath them, swans glided across the dark waters, drifting like phantoms upon the lake's glassy surface. She lifted Kayleth in her arms, whispering for him to look.

The castle loomed ahead, its towering gates open, welcoming, as if beckoning her into a life woven with power and mystery.

At the foot of the grand staircase, Zarriq swept out his arm, gesturing for them to step inside first. His lips curled into a knowing smirk as he leaned in, his voice like a whispered promise.
"Let me show you what it means to live within these walls."

They eagerly stepped through the towering obsidian and stained-glass doors into the grand entrance hall.

Reagan took a single step forward onto the vast opalescent tiles that rippled with shifting colors.

Zarriq stood before them, he noticing their wide eyes tracing the vaulted ceiling. *Reagan* slowing down, whispering in awe.

He added, with the faintest edge of pride.
"You could wander these halls for months and still uncover only a fraction of the castle's secrets. The kingdom stretches just as endlessly... Let me show you a glimpse of the grandeur."

He turned with a graceful sweep, his cloak unfurling with a dramatic flair, and began walking down the grand hall like a slow-moving current.

Above them, the vaulted ceilings swirled with deep indigo, midnight black, and velvety purple, intertwined like the starry night. No torches flickered, nor lamps stood sentinel; instead, a constellation of luminous orbs drifted effortlessly, their soft radiance casting a dreamlike glow throughout the castle.

Zarriq turned to Reagan. With a gentle, almost wistful explanation, he said softly, like someone remembering a song no one sings anymore. A king defending a kingdom no longer at its peak.
"You must understand, this is a quiet, peaceful kingdom. The moons drift by in tranquil harmony, and the halls rest in a hush... Most of the rooms' uses have dwindled over time."

He continued through the grand hall with them following behind, passing dimly lit corridors. Sheer white linens billowing in the graceful archways. Walls of milky quartz crystal shimmered like flecks of frozen stardust. He continued down the hall without pausing, his steps unhurried, his attention seemingly elsewhere.

With a slight tilt of his head, he offered, aloof, mildly disinterested, maybe even slightly amused at himself for bothering to play host.
"...Feel free to venture as you please. I, myself, don't have a need to relive the past."

He drifted onward. He didn't slow, only adjusted the angle of his stride, waving his hand in the air. Half-bored with just a *hint* of irony and dry charm.
"The grand staircase leads to the east and west wings. The east wing holds the royal heirs' living quarters where my son resides. The royal apartments have every luxury. A sitting room, drawing room, writing room, visitor room...All the rooms. We'll arrange chambers for you both there. They're far more accommodating than the noble

apartments, though…The nobles' view is slightly better, in my opinion."

Suddenly, he halted and whipped around quickly, his cloak sweeping sharply behind him. His eyes sharper than before.
He said firm, final and not to be crossed.
"The west wing is mine…"

The words echoed for a moment, swallowed by the stillness of the hall. A long, ominous pause followed. Zarriq didn't move. He just stood there, facing them, eyes locked on some thought behind them. Then, slowly, awkwardly, he blinked, straightened, turned back around, and continued down another dimly lit corridor on their left. Through the archway and pillars, the space opened into the dining hall.

Kayleth hurried over to the floor-to-ceiling windows, admiring the view. They perfectly captured the lake, meadow, moat, and castle grounds.

Zarriq walked to the far end of the gleaming obsidian dining table with gold legs and stood behind one of the deep burgundy chairs, resting his hands on top. Glancing down the empty length of the table.
"This is where dinner is served. Breakfast, however, can be brought to your chambers each morning, if you prefer. Just talk to the steward, she'll arrange whatever you need…"

His voice trailed off, then without warning he shouted, obnoxiously loud.
"Morag?"

The sheer volume was nearly deafening, his voice bouncing off the crystal walls like thunder in a cave. Reagan flinched. Kayleth winced.

Then, as if nothing had happened, Zarriq returned to his usual low and deliberate cadence, like a nobleman narrating a bedtime scroll "And she'll assign you both a chambermaid to help with… things…"

He abruptly bellowed again, louder this time "MORAG!"

The shout seemed vaguely aimed at the ceiling, as if Morag might descend from the beams like a bat in an apron.

That sudden pivot from ear-splitting roar to calm-and-collected velvet voice, then back to castle-rattling bellow was slightly unnerving.

A small, flustered woman came rushing through the doorway, dressed in a dusky blue and cream garb with a bonnet perched atop her head. Her face was flushed. She wiped her hands on her apron as she stood awaiting Zarriqs orders.

His tone pivoting seamlessly back to that of a pleasant host. He gestured vaguely toward the young elves, the reason Morag's day was about to get significantly more complicated.
"Ah, Morag. This is Reagan and her little brother, Kayleth. They'll be staying with us for the week. Set up rooms for them in the east wing and assign them personal attendants, please. They'll also need clothes..."

She stood there rigid and expectant. Waiting for more instructions. Not moving.

He said, with the forced brightness of a plea rather than a dismissal. "That's all..."

Morag gave the world's most uncertain curtsy, then turned to leave but forgot which way she came, spun in a slow circle and scurried back through the doorway, nearly tripping over her own feet.

Zarriq exhaled heavily, closing his eyes as if the sight physically pained him. He turned his head away. Then, with a defeated groan, one hand lifted to his face, covering it completely. Clearly mortified by her demeanor.

Kayleth gasped as he spotted something through the window. He ran over to Reagan, tugging urgently at her shirt. She looked down at him, curious. He pointed to the sky and pulled again, trying to bring her to the window.

She walked over with him just in time to see a huge creature with enormous wings soaring through the air. Its emerald hide shimmered with rainbow undertones.

Her eyes widened in disbelief, glowing with excitement.
"Is that a dragon?"

Zarriq turned to the window, squinting as he looked across the room at the sky beyond the glass. His expression remained bored and unimpressed as if dragons were about as thrilling to him as furniture. "Oh that. Yes. That's Neshasa. We have two elderly dragons. Mildly domesticated. Peaceful. Perfectly harmless. Ferrim, the other dragon, is probably in their lair beyond the forest, enjoying his slumber. They were meant to be companions for my son, Martouf. To help with his loneliness."

His voice dipped quieter. His gaze turning distant. Lost in a memory that dimmed the light behind his eyes.
"Though, it didn't work out quite as I hoped."

He released a soft breath, tinged with disappointment. The words seemed to carry him somewhere else. The weight of it lingered just a second too long.

But just as quickly, his tone snapped back into polite host mode, crisp and composed.
"Moving on."

Reagan scoffed at how uninterested and unbothered he was by the sight of such a breathtaking, magical creature. She and Kayleth followed him out of the dining hall, through a corridor lined with tapestries, then ascended a marble staircase laced with silver ivy. At the top, they approached an arched doorway framed in crystal vines.

Zarriq stopped at the threshold. He didn't enter. Didn't even cross the frame. He just stood there, peering into the dim room with a stiff spine and a distant look. Like someone spotting a shadow from an old nightmare. His voice was hesitant.
"The royal library."

Reagan and Kayleth stepped inside. The chamber was towering, circular, glass-domed, and utterly magnificent. Bookshelves lined the walls all the way to the ceiling. A cozy reading pit filled the center of the room, with a circular couch nestled into its base. A massive stained-glass window stretched across one wall, reaching the ceiling and casting radiant colors across the floor.

Zarriq snapped, sharp and frantic. Warning them.
"Don't get too close to the books!"

Reagan and Kayleth froze.

Zarriq nervously laughed. Realized he was quick and brittle. Then cleared his throat. Forcing his voice back into something resembling calm.

"To encourage our son to read, my late wife, rest her soul, enchanted them. They whisper to your soul as an invitation, tempting you to open them. If you enjoy reading, it won't affect you. I won't go in there."

Then he turned briskly and began walking away, already smoothing his coat sleeve. He asked casually, but his voice almost cracked at the nervousness the books seemed to have over him.
"Tea?"

Kayleth scurried after him, but Reagan lingered.

She moved toward the shelves with reverence, her fingers trailing lightly along the vertical seams of the books, smiling on her way out.

THE
VERMIN
VANISHER

UNWANTED
FAMILIAR
REMOVAL
SERVICES

PIP
Can we just call pest control?

YSMERRA
Don't be ridiculous! Last time they sent a raccoon in a wizard hat.

PIP
That raccoon had excellent reviews. I thought he did a great job.

YSMERRA
I hexed their goat. We can't call them ever again.

PIP
You hexed a goat?! You're a monster. What's next? Puppies? Baby unicorns?

YSMERRA
Since you're concerned about the goat, why don't you go live with him?

PIP
...I tried. You don't think I tried? He has a whole situationship thing going on. I couldn't stay. It's complicated.

YSMERRA
Pity.

CHAPTER 8
The Enchanted Tea Room

Reagan took Kayleth's hand and followed Zarriq next door to the enchanted tea room.

Inside, a crackling fireplace dominated one wall. Its warmth casting flickers across an array of plush and cozy seating.

Kayleth immediately let go of Reagan's hand and ran to one of the larger sofas. He laid down, closed his eyes, popped his thumb into his mouth, and drifted into a soft little slumber.

Each arrangement was carefully curated, ensuring that whether one sought solitude or lively conversation, there was a perfect nook waiting.

Upon each table sat a magical tea set etched with shifting sigils. The sigil magic endowed the teapots with enchantments to always remain hot, to brew exactly what one desired, and to never empty. They refilled automatically the moment you were in need of more.

In one corner, a small piano played softly on its own. The ivory keys tapping gently like an invisible musician had stepped inside to perform just for them. The melodies were always perfect, as if it somehow knew the exact song you wanted to hear.

Light orbs floated above shifted color with the movements of the moon. Golden tones in the early hours, soft lavender when the moon hung directly overhead, and later a deep, magical blue to cradle the room into slumber.

Clear crystals dangled from the ceiling, casting rainbow-prismatic light patterns across the polished mahogany walls and floor.

One wall was a floor-to-ceiling window, but the view wasn't fixed. It shifted with your mood. A dancing waterfall. A gentle snow. A silent rainstorm. Whatever matched your spirit in that moment.

Zarriq sat down in a garnet tufted high-back chair near the fireplace, facing away from the flames. His posture was always perfect. Straight and tall, like a statue carved from purpose.

Gesturing for her to sit in the chair in front of him. He said softly. "Please."

The fire crackled violently behind him, the only sound in the stillness of the room.

Reagan eased into the plum-colored chair across from him. An almost meditative calm settled over her. The warmth of the cushion melted her tension, filling her limbs with a hush of comfort.

Zarriq raised his hand, summoning the translucent, saffron teapot. It bent to his will, lifting off the tray and gently poured into Reagan's cup—a green ceramic vessel, with pink and yellow lotus flowers.

She reached for the cup, wrapping her fingers around the serpent-shaped handle. Tiny emerald gems glinted in the serpent's eyes as she brought it to rest in her lap.

Zarriq waved the pot to his side, filling his silver-flecked porcelain cup. The glaze caught the firelight like constellations. He lifted the crescent-moon handle and saucer to his lips, inhaling first.

The flames surged behind him.

Then came his voice, slow and steady, wrapped in the fire's roar like they carried a heat of their own.
"Now tell me. What was so horrible about your life that you summoned me?"

Reagan aimlessly stared down into her cup, searching for the right words... and the courage to finally speak them. She hadn't told anyone. Not fully. But it had built within her, pressing outward, waiting to be released. And now, she was ready.

"Not as a desperate child seeking escape, but as one who has opened her eyes and seen too much...

My realm was forged in steel and blood. We war over land, over veins of metal in the land, over the smallest whisper of power.

From the moment I could stand, I was given a blade. From the moment I could read, I was handed maps of battlefields. We are taught only what is useful for war. Nothing more.

Knowledge beyond conquest is not given.

I know there must be more.

I have spent all my life training. For what? To earn a rank? To stand atop the bodies of my kin and call it victory?

Among us, there is no childhood. Only rivalry. We do not make friends; we make opponents. We are measured by our lethality. And yet, when I raise my blade... I feel nothing. No triumph. No glory. Just... emptiness.

It is not my war to fight.

And my brother, he will follow me. He will be shaped and hardened just as I was, until he knows nothing else.

I refuse to let my soul be swallowed whole simply because it is the way things have always been.

I don't know what I seek. I only know it isn't this.
I have no name for what I wish to become. I only know that I cannot become what they demand of me.

My parents are good. Kind. And yet... even in their love, I am alone. All I have is expectation. And duty."

Reagan finally looked up, at Zarriq.
"So I called for you, Druid. One who speaks to the land, rather than spills blood upon it..."

Zarriq raised a hand to scratch at his eyebrow. His gaze shifted slightly to the side, like he was buying himself a moment to think. His brow scrunched faintly, and for just a second, he looked down. Like the movement might shield him from answering. An oddly uncomfortable gesture for someone usually so composed.
"Yes, well... beliefs can change, when life changes."

Reagan tilted her head slightly, unsure if the remark was meant for her... or a reflection of something within him.

There was a shadow behind his words. A brush of sadness that passed too quickly to catch. He quickly shifted the conversation.
"Tell me about the book. How did you know how to summon me?"

Her grip tightened slightly on her teacup.

"How one such as I, raised in the confines of war, found her way to a ritual lost to time...

I have spent years slipping away to nearby towns whenever I could. They don't carry many books. Just a few, tucked away in corner shops. But I buy them all. Hoarding words like they might grant me wings. As if, somewhere between their pages, I could find a way out.

The most recent book I found, I read it on my journey home, as I always do, devouring the pages.

It was the story of a man named Ronan, crushed beneath the weight of misfortune. Misery followed him. Swallowed his family whole."

Zarriq stilled. His expression changed, his gestures quiet but telling. He knew the name. Knew it instantly.

Reagan continued.
"A name passed down in whispers. A legend more than anything else. One whose magic could heal even the most shattered souls. For years, people spoke of him as if he were some distant dream. Something impossible.

There was a man named Ronan, desperate and broken, who believed those stories enough to try.

He scoured ancient grimoires, found a ritual, a summoning spell buried in forgotten pages. He was certain it was myth. But the ache in his heart drove him to try.

And against all odds... it worked.

The magic he summoned was real. And the druid, *you*, wove his power into Ronan's life, lifting him from despair. Everything changed for him.

Ronan, forever grateful, chronicled the entire experience. The spell, the ritual, the symbols. So others who found themselves in that same darkness might have a way out, too.

I was drawn to that story. More than I should have been. Something in it whispered to me. It lingered in my thoughts, haunting me.

I didn't truly believe anything would happen. I thought it was all make-believe. Tall tales. But something inside me compelled me to try. And so I did."

Zarriq lifted his eyebrows with a look that hovered between amusement and contempt. He said flatly, with a touch of sarcasm. "And here you are."

He studied her for a moment in silence. Then almost reluctantly admitted "I... remember Ronan."

The name left his mouth like it didn't belong there. Like it was pulled from a part of him he'd long since buried. There was hesitation. Whatever that memory stirred, he shut it down quickly.

His voice leveled again. The softness evaporated. More polished now, more composed.
"Well, I can guarantee you, we don't have any wars here."

There was lingering moment of quiet hush. Only the sound of the crackling fire.

Until Zarriq broke the silence.
"In this corner of the galaxy, within this dimension, there exist but four realms. Bound together by fate.

We were once their rightful rulers. The King and Queen of Balderon, crowned in ancient power, were sovereign over all. It was their birthright.

But long ago... treachery took root.

One realm, dissatisfied with the Council's decrees, cast aside the treaty that bound us. They sought dominion beyond diplomacy. Their ambitions festered like a wound.

They turned their gaze to the farthest reaches of the universe, where cursed sorcery festers, where foul magic twists the very fabric of existence. There, they steeped their souls in corruption. Their greed devoured what little honor remained.

They returned no longer the people we once knew... but something monstrous. Their hunger for power knew no bounds. Through a rift torn in the fabric of reality, they led their armies into our peaceful lands and war descended upon us like a plague.

The sky burned. The rivers ran red.

In that senseless carnage... I lost my wife and her parents—The King and Queen...

They stole the crowns—the vessels of our realm's magic. Cursing our land and with them, they wrought their own abominations. Twisting that power, they bent the very essence of creation to their will, declaring themselves rulers of the four realms.

Usurpers. Defilers.

I would not let such desecration stand. With the last remnants of this realm's true magic, I forged a barrier. An unbreakable seal to ensure such ruin could never befall us again. The shield is absolute. Impenetrable. But I am its maker. It bends to my will."

Reagan looked down at her teacup, cradling it in her lap. With a look of vulnerability that doesn't beg for mercy, just understanding.

That look stirred something old and deep in Zarriq. With a flicker of compassion. He said softly,
"My son has that same look in his eyes. That faint sadness of searching for something that isn't there... Of not even knowing what that thing is. It breaks my heart not being able to give him the world, as if that would even make him happy. But you...maybe you could make his eyes sparkle with hope."

Those words pierced her in a way she wasn't expecting. She hadn't let herself think too much about the prince yet. But he had been there, lingering at the edge of her thoughts since the moment she arrived. The idea of him.

The wondering bloomed faster than she could stop it. She tried to stay grounded in the present, but her mind was slipping toward the meeting she knew was coming. There was a strange pressure beneath it all. Her hope curled quietly at the center of it all.

Rosy hues rising to her cheeks before she could stop it. Blushing. Embarrassed. She turned her face slightly, hoping Zarriq wouldn't notice.

Her gaze landed on the window, wondering what scenery the enchanted glass would conjure for her. At first, the window appeared softly frosted, as if veiled in a delicate breath of winter.

Then, like snow melting, the haze began to lift. The frost dissolved in spirals of light curling away from the center. What she saw wasn't a dreamscape. It was the actual view behind the glass—the castle grounds and the glimmering kingdom beyond.

That is exactly what she'd hoped to see. She didn't need a fantasy. This was already her ideal one.

Zarriq set his teacup down with a soft clink. A slow amused smile curled at the corner of his lips. His gaze lifted upward as if he was imagining orchestrating a play and she just stepped onto the stage without realizing it yet.

He trailed off, savoring the moment.
"I believe it's almost time for the ball to begin. Our guests are already arriving…Yes. That would be the perfect place for you two to meet, mix and mingle. He'll be delighted someone his age is finally here… He is the last of his kind, you know. As far as children go… in this realm, he is the only one."

That gave her pause. Concern prickled at her thoughts. She asked slowly, carefully, trying to catch up to the implications.
"Your people…They're... dying out?"

He seemed reluctant to answer, as if revealing something precious and brittle, but didn't flinch or falter.
"Some. Yes. A problem I've been… attending to."

Then he looked at her. Not just at her, into her. With a smoldering, quiet intensity behind his eyes.
"And yet, a solution I may have very soon."

He said it with the weight of someone who had already made sacrifices, and wouldn't hesitate to make more.

He held the moment. The gaze. Savoring the idea. The final piece in something he'd been building for far longer than she could guess.

But before she could unravel the meaning behind it, he was already moving, already shifting the moment elsewhere.

With that same unnerving grace, he stood, and extended a hand toward the doorway with a smile.
"Shall we?"

She let go of the warmth of her seat, moving toward where Kayleth slept soundly. Gently, she lifted him into her arms. He stirred, his head falling to her shoulder, still half tangled in the quiet haze of his dreams. Holding him close, she walked slowly toward the door.

As one foot crossed into the hall, she felt it. From behind, Zarriq's hand settle lightly on her shoulder. She didn't flinch. Didn't turn. She simply paused, gaze fixed ahead.

It was a rare gesture of peace.

She felt that. Somehow.

Zarriq stood close, his voice low and even, laced with a softness that hadn't been there before.
"My son's happiness means everything to me. You can ease your mind, knowing I would never do anything untoward to either of you… not when it could risk destroying his spirit."

She turned and looked up at him, into his eyes. She could feel it. The deep love he has for his son. The safety in his presence. There was no menace in him. Just a man hollowed out by grief. She didn't have to think. She knew.

She nodded once. Her voice soft but certain, and whispered back.
"I know."

GREMLIN
GRUB WAGON
CURSED
CURRY
TACOS
DRAGON
DUMPLING
SURPRISE
SNAKE
SAUCE
OPEN

YSMERRA

Who's ringing the doorbell? We're clearly busy.

PIP

It's probably the Gremlin Grub Wagon. Ooh, I could
go for some Cursed Curry Tacos and a Mandrake Shake.
We should get extra for the Ghosts.

YSMERRA

We are not feeding them haunted street food or anything else
for that matter.

PIP

Oh, so now we're terrible hosts?

YSMERRA

We didn't invite them. This isn't a Bed & Breakfast.

PIP

You accidentally conjured a talking turtle last month and
that thing still uses my bathroom. Did you know he built
a shrine for my missing sock...

YSMERRA

He leaves inspirational quotes on the mirrors. You
just leave hair... Ugh! Fine! One night. ONE...
Get me the Possessed Plantain Pudding, and
the Dragon Dumpling Surprise with extra
Snake Sauce.

PIP

I've had a banshee living in my closet for a
couple weeks now. I think she'll enjoy the
ghosts company.

CHAPTER 9
The Ball Room

Zarriq led them down the hall, toward a wide set of towering double doors. With a wave of his hand, the doors parted. As the doors swung open, a soft breeze met them, cool and fragrant, like night rain over wildflowers.

The floor was a vast expanse of mystical moss. Soft, cool, and cushiony beneath the feet. The moss grew in spiraling patterns, glowing faintly with blue bioluminescence, casting a low fog across the floor.

Grand marble columns. A wall of arched windows framed in sheer white curtains looked out onto vistas of fantastical landscapes bathed in moonlight.

Reagan slowed her walk, admiring the breathtaking room.

At the far end of the ballroom, a raised platform housed ornately carved throne chairs. Zarriq moved ahead to the platform and stood in front of his throne.

Kayleth wiggled from Reagan's arms and ran up the steps to follow Zarriq, climbing into the throne beside his. He sat proudly, swinging his legs as he looked out across the ballroom.

Reagan approached and stood at the foot of the dais.

Zarriq placed his thumb and forefinger on his chin, giving her an appraising look.
"That's not really proper ball attire, is it? Let's get you into something more fitting for a princess... To meet the prince."

With two fingers he drew a sigil in the air, glowing briefly with silver fire. Golden threads of light spiraled through the air, unfolding across her like a whisper, weaving themselves into fabric around her. The space around her shimmered, light gathering like mist, swirling at her feet. Stardust transformed her clothing into cascading layers of silk and lace, until it became a breathtaking ballgown born from magic itself.

She gasped softly and looked down, running her hands over the sparkling gold fabric. Her hair was now twisted up and crowned with a delicate golden filigree tiara adorned with moonstones, and golden leaves.

She half-smiled in confusion and wonder, unsure what it all looked like. She walked slowly over to the mirror above the fireplace.

Every detail was exquisite. The dangling crystal earrings. The embroidered gold sequins. The starlace wrapped around her feet, glowing like distant constellations, and trailing stardust with every step.

Behind her, Zarriq clasped his hands together, looking quite pleased. He turned to Kayleth.
"And for the little prince…"

Zarriq snapped his fingers and made a small, swirling gesture. Gold light spiraled around Kayleth like playful ribbons. His clothes shimmered, shifted, then turned into regal attire.

A long black waistcoat paired with fitted black pants and gold filigree embroidery on the shoulders and cuffs. A crisp white shirt peeked beneath a black vest and tie. Atop his black hair rested a silver circlet adorned with ruby-red jewels.

He hopped off the throne chair and spun around, arms out, laughing, the hem of his coat flaring around him as he twirled. He did it again, and again, like a miniature whirlwind of velvet and joy.

Zarriq smiled to himself, clearly enjoying this soft, mischievous moment as he watched Kayleth twirl.
"Even the tiniest of things, can still look regal."

The doors behind the dais opened. Palace staff entered, some holding silver trumpets and golden horns, others holding baskets of flower petals. They lined up on either side of the door and throne platform in ceremonial formation.

A string quartet entered the minstrel's gallery, already tuning their instruments.

A flurry of palace staff came through the service doors, dressed in deep plum uniforms, carrying tables, chairs, and polished trays balanced effortlessly on their arms. Around the edges of the ballroom, they unfurled crisp white linens across long banquet tables, laying out a cornucopia of rich pastries, glazed fruits, spiced wines, roasted nuts, and braided breads. A feast torn from the pages of myth.

The main ball room doors burst open and herds of guests quickly filled the room.

The room came to life with laughter, voices, and the rustle of silk and satin filled the air. Gloved hands fluttering in animated conversation.

Each guest was dressed more lavish than the next.

Gentlemen in velvet capes trimmed in fur and clasped with gold. Their cravats pinned with brooches.

Ladies glided past in gemstone studded gowns and pearl-draped sleeves. Tiaras glinted from their coiffed locks.

Nymphs and dryads twirled among the crowd, their gowns spun from petals and leaves. Fairies flitted overhead in laughter, their wings glowing with gossamer light.

Reagan found herself slowly surrounded. Guests standing on either side of her, turned toward the dais. A hush fell over the ballroom as they humbly waited for the Zarriq to address them.

Zarriq stood with quiet majesty. One hand folded behind his back. He spoke with a steady calm of a king who didn't need a crown to be obeyed. "Lords and ladies, honored guests, I welcome you to this most splendid evening. Tonight, we gather not only in celebration but in the spirit of unity, revelry, and the enduring strength of Balderon. Your presence graces these halls, and for that, I am ever grateful. Please eat, drink, dance, and enjoy yourselves."

The whole room happily and graciously applauded.

One of the heralds stepped forward beside the door and announced loudly,
"His Royal Highness."

Zarriq beamed with a gleam of pride and exclaimed,
"My son is gracing us with his presence!"

He extended one arm toward the ballroom's main doors and announced with thunderous joy:

"It is with great pride that I present to you... the future of our kingdom. The heir to Balderon's throne. My son—Martouf, The Crowned Prince of Balderon!"

The room erupted into applause again.

The heralds played their trumpets and horns, their music regal and triumphant. Pages marched forward, tossing flower petals across the mossy floor in elegant arcs of color and motion.

Reagan stood at the very front of the crowd, center stage before the dais. Her hands nervously clasped, fidgeting as she waited with anticipation for the prince's arrival.

And then—Through the towering doors, Prince Martouf entered.

The pages moved before him, continuing to scatter flower petals in the air, the blossoms drifting and twirling around his every step.

Behind all the flowers being tossed in the air Reagan could see his jet-black hair swept neatly under a golden crown, adorned with massive black stones. The high stiff collar of his brass trimmed jacket was nearly brushing his sharp jawline.

Never did she think the prince would be so handsome, so charming, and so divine. In a moment of awestruck her heart fluttered. For Reagan, the prince seemed to be entering the room in slow motion.

She was nervous to meet him before, when he was just Zarriq's son, a noble heir in waiting. Now, meeting the very person who stole her breath away made her all the more nervous, anxious and excited.

The applauding, the inaudible chatter, the horns and trumpets all turned into a beautiful melody, a captivating love song that only she could hear. She was wide eyed and breathless watching him being adorned with flowers.

Prince Martouf walked toward the dais, regal and graceful. His chestnut brown eyes scanned the room, until they found her.

His gaze locked onto hers. Instantly. As if the world narrowed to only the two of them. He stopped mid-step. No longer heading for his throne. Instead, with unwavering focus, he stepped down from the platform and began walking toward her, his eyes never leaving hers.

Curious. Intrigued. Drawn.

Zarriq, seeing the spark ignite between them, lifted his hand and signaled the orchestra. The music swelled. The ballroom dimmed. The moss floor glowed brighter beneath their feet.

Guests began to dance in perfect harmony as the melody wove through them.

Martouf reached Reagan and stood before her, one hand placed neatly behind his back. With the other, he extended his open palm in graceful invitation to dance.

She broke into a wide smile, ear to ear, unguarded, pure joy. It was the first time she had smiled like that in… longer than she could remember. Maybe ever. She accepts by placing her hand in his, her fingers gently touching his palm.

Slowly, he comes in closer to her. Gently, his fingers caressed around hers as he adjusted his hand to clasp hers. Their palms found one another like a secret vow passed between them.

In a poised stance, they gazed into each other's eyes, their movements align, and they begin to dance with effortless grace.

From his throne, Zarriq watched with admiration. Leaning back, he propped his elbow on the armrest, with a satisfied expression on his face.

As dancers twirled, wisps of silver mist coiled around their feet. Ribbons of light lingered, curling in elegant shapes before dissolving into the glowing moss below.

Above it all, sparkling dust unfurls upon the ballroom like a mystical rain. The dust warm and soft, leaving them covered in a glittering, almost dreamlike shimmer.

The walls were enchanted with illusions. Each song transcended the room to a different time, place and landscape. With the start of each song, the partitions would gently fade as if it was merely a veil between worlds, melting away. Revealing a vast expanse of new scenery.

One moment they were bathed in the rose-gold glow of a sky at dusk. Wisps of pink clouds drifting all around them, casting a warm glow through the room. During another song, with the seamless grace of a page turn they were surrounded by the tops of tall towering buildings giving the illusion as if they were dancing on the roof. The next, they were surrounding by snow and descending from the ceiling, phantom snowflakes that disappear as they touch the floor.

The ceiling matched the mood of the music, and the walls new landscape to provide accompanying ambience. Falling stars, rose petals, glitter, bubbles, and other enchantments to fully immerse the dancers in the fantastical world that surrounds them. Pulling them deeper into the magical romantic night waltzing between worlds.

Kayleth, too, was swept up in the magic. He climbed down from his chair on the dais and wandered onto the dance floor, mimicking the guests with cheerful little spins. He waved at strangers, danced in circles, and laughed in delight.

From afar, Zarriq watched him, half-smiling. He kept a careful eye on them both the little one and the young couple. But Kayleth wandered further. For a moment, he vanished from view. Reagan noticed first. Her smile faltered. She began to glance behind her, scanning the crowd for her brother.

Zarriq caught her concern and snapped his fingers toward one of the nearby pages. The page darted into the crowd in search of the boy. He quickly returned with Kayleth in his arms.

Reagan exhaled in quiet relief. She gave Zarriq a small, grateful glance. To which Zarriq responded with a theatrical bow of his head. Then, Reagan truly began to imagine what a good life there might feel like.

Small bubbles of light begin to drift through the air, swirling around guests playfully. But none of it could distract Reagan or Martouf. Not the magic. Not the scenery. Not even the passage of time. For they couldn't take their eyes off each other.

Watching Kayleth from afar, Zarriq was reminded of when Martouf was that age. If his wife hadn't been taken so soon, they might have had more children. His heart softened. Slipping down from the dais, he scooped Kayleth into his arms and began to dance with him. Reagan and Martouf noticed, sharing a quiet laugh between them.

After twirling through countless melodies, Reagan gently took the prince's hand and, with a breathless smile, whispered a request for a moment beneath the open sky.

With fingers lightly entwined, she guided him through the open glass doors, stepping onto the white marble veranda, where the night air greeted them like a lover's embrace.

Zarriq caught sight of them slipping away from the ballroom. His gaze darkening with intrigue. With Kayleth still in his arms, he drifted toward one of the glass windows facing the balcony. His movements unhurried, deliberate. He pulled a chair from a nearby table, flipping it around to face the glass. Lowering himself into the seat, with Kayleth on his lap. He draped an arm over the backrest, his fingers idly tapping as he watched them with quiet curiosity.

PIP

Okay. The ghosts are all tucked in for the night.
Room 2 ghosts need extra pillows. Room 4 wants
chamomile tea, and Room 3 wants a fern.

YSMERRA

I'm not running a Haunted Inn. You get them that
stuff... You know you're not supposed to make eye contact
with them right? Also, under *no circumstances* should you
accept any gifts from them.

PIP

Why? What happens if I do? Is that... like a metaphor? Or a
warning?

YSMERRA

When were you going to tell me you had a banshee hiding in
your midsts?

PIP

What??

YSMERRA

Do you have *any* idea how dangerous banshees are?

PIP

She seems fine. She knits little mittens for the
mice. Bakes heart-shaped sugar cookies and leaves
fresh rose petals in my shoes for "protection." She
even made me a friendship bracelets out of
spider silk.

YSMERRA

She's protecting her food. You know they eat
elves right?... Little ones. With red hair...
Oh, would you look at that—it's exactly
time for me to go water my ficus. Good luck,
soul sponge... And If she tries to brush your
hair, RUN!

CHAPTER 10
The Balcony

Blossoms dangled from the vaulted ceiling, their petals mystically aglow. Reagan drifted toward the white-carved railing. She took in the breathtaking sight before her. Endless rivers of silken stardust coursing through the sky, and in the distance, a grand city of ivory towers and sapphire spires resting beneath the celestial glow.

She didn't want to leave Balderon. Everything felt too enchanting, too perfect. Her heart swelled with the promise of a new life, one that shimmered with wonder.

The dashing prince stood beside her. At the same moment, their eyes met. A spark passed between them. Neither could find the words, yet there was no need. A breathless, nervous laugh escaped them both as they glanced away, bashful yet brimming with the quiet wonder of a story just beginning. They stood in silence, the air between them humming with unspoken thoughts.

Reagan stared out at the scenery. Her breath caught somewhere between wonder and disbelief. It was too much, too vast, too beautiful. A smile touched her lips, gentle and awed. She whispered, almost to herself.
"It's so beautiful here."

Beside her, Martouf didn't respond right away. He hadn't been looking at the view. He had been looking at *her* and the way the light caught her hair. There was wonder in his eyes too, but it wasn't for the sky or the trees or the distant spires. It was for her.

The words escaped him before he could stop them. Low, unguarded, not meant to be heard. "So beautiful."

He hadn't meant the scenery.

She felt his gaze then. Her heart fluttered. She pressed her lips together, fighting the giddy urge to smile too widely.

A breeze lifted the sheer drapes, carrying the scent of night-blooming flowers as she wandered toward the far end of the veranda. A white marble bench rested in the corner, half-hidden by trailing wisteria, and she motioned for him to join her.

From the ballroom, behind the veil of glass, King Zarriq watched. With the faintest magical motion of his hand, the chair beneath him glided soundlessly across the floor, granting him a clearer view.

Prince Martouf and Reagan sat upon the marble bench and turned towards each other, eager to speak. Hoping to share a world of questions lingering on their lips, the quiet secrets of their hearts, dreams yet unspoken, the hopes they held for the future. But the moment their eyes met, the words escaped them. Time stilled, and in the hush of that fragile moment, conversation was forgotten and lost to the quiet wonder of simply looking at one another.

Inside the ballroom, Kayleth climbed down from Zarriq's lap and wandered over to the dessert table, helping himself to whatever looked most enticing.

Zarriq's attention still fixed on Martouf and Reagan. He extended his arm, fingers outstretched. In an instant, the wine glass from the nearby table swiftly grazed across the surface before landing firmly in his grasp. With his other hand he waved their echoed voices into the glass, creating a listening vessel to hear their conversation. He presses the opening of the glass against his ear.

Reagan finally fought through the tight knot in her chest and mustered the courage to speak. The words didn't come easily. As if even *speaking* required swimming through something heavy and unseen. But she pushed through it. Something inside her resisted. Like a weight pressing against her lungs, making it hard to form thoughts into language. Her throat felt tight, her mind clouded. She clenched her hands to steady herself, focused on the sound of her heartbeat, and forced her way to the surface of whatever held her back. Her lips parted.
"Do you... like it here?"

A small victory. One that no one would notice. But it had taken everything.

He hesitated. His eyes drifted toward the floor.
"It's..."

Torn between giving the polite answer and the true one. Honesty overtaking hesitation.
"Lonely."

He immediately winced, mentally kicking himself. *Lonely? That's what you lead with? Brilliant. She's going to bolt. Congratulations, you've just terrified the most beautiful girl you've ever seen.*

Her fingers tightening slightly around the hem of her sleeve. She admitted softly.
"I'm lonely in my world too."

Her words hit him like a stone to the chest. His pulse stuttered. She understood. Not out of politeness, but out of knowing. He turned toward her, his heart thudding a little too loud in his ears. In a quiet, encouraging tone, with a kind of gentle urgency and nervous hope.
"So stay…"

He reached for her hand, hesitant, terrified she'd flinch or pull away. But her fingers met his, and he interlaced them slowly, and he looked into her eyes.
"…with me."

Praying his voice didn't sound as shaky as he felt.

She smiled. Really smiled. And nodded, as if the question had been on the tip of her own tongue too. She said softly, the weight in her chest easing.
"I'd like that."

For a moment, he forgot how to breathe. His brain scrambled for what to say next.

She said yes! Say something normal. Something smooth. Or anything. Anything but just sitting here grinning like a lovesick fool.

Martouf's royal upbringing had prepared him for many things, but not for small talk with a young lady. His social graces were more refined in the courtly sense. All his years of royal isolation were showing. He shifted in his seat, visibly uncertain.
Although having a hard time, he managed to blurt out something.
"You…"

Then paused, brows furrowed as though he was searching for a question that wouldn't sound stupid.
"Hungry?"

Already regretting the words that came out of his mouth. Feeling embarrassed.

Hungry? That's what you go with? She just agreed to stay with you and you're offering snacks? Just go jump off the balcony now. You're done.

But she smiled so dearly at him. Looking at him like he said the most wonderful thing in the world and shook her head.

His heart lifted. He perked up a little, encouraged.

Okay. She's still smiling. That's good. Maybe you're not completely hopeless.

Getting more confident now. He pressed on.
"Thirsty?"

She laughed and shook her head again. Still smiling at him like the world around them had melted away.

Two smiles. Yes!

His chest warmed with pride. He was starting to get the hang of this. Maybe. Kind of. He offered, grinning.
"Tired?"

Her laughter grew fuller and her eyes lit up with sparkle.
"No."

That did it. She laughed. Really laughed. A full, bubbling sound that made something inside him unravel in the best way. Even for Reagan, she had never known the simple pleasure of a friendly conversation. In her world, talk meant strategy or orders. Bonding was foreign territory. But here, even their halting words felt like a language of comfort. They didn't need constant conversation. The silence between them was enough.

They sat together quietly, hands still gently intertwined. Neither of them moved much, as if afraid the smallest shift might break the stillness between them.

Reagan, without saying a word, rested her head on his shoulder.

Martouf's heart practically jumped out of his chest. He stared straight ahead, fixed on one spot like it had all the answers. *Okay. Stay still. Breathe normal. Don't freak out.*

Then, softly, suddenly she asked,
"Are you happy?"

The question cut through him like a whisper in a cathedral. He blinked, caught off guard. He looked at her in the corner of his eye. He felt there was so much she couldn't possibly understand about his life. Happy? That was a loaded question. Too long, too complicated to answer.

I want to tell you everything, What it's really like. But I can't. I don't want to ruin this night.

He wanted to tell her everything. What it was really like. The truth of the world he came from. The heaviness of it. The ache that never quite went away. But he couldn't. Tonight was too gentle. Too quiet. Too beautiful to fracture with sorrow. He swallowed the words, tucked them away where they always lived, and offered something simpler. Something honest.

There was a pause. Not uncomfortable, just long enough to feel real. The words slipping out a little raw, a little awkward.
"Not really... You?"

She let out a slow breath, soft and tired buried inside it.
"No. That's sort of why I'm here. I thought it would make me happy."

He turned his head slightly, enough to let her know she had his attention. He said softly with a calm certainty that felt heavier than it sounded,
"It will."

Surprising even himself with how certain he sounded. All he could think was, *Please don't leave.*

From his table inside, near the grand arched windows, Zarriq sat quietly, listening. Then something shifted, just enough to pull his focus tighter. Zarriq's brow furrowed, the flicker of concern unmistakable as it broke across his composed expression. He stood from his seat slowly, but with purpose.

He called Kayleth over, who was hovered near the dessert table like a tiny connoisseur, taking a single bite of nearly everything, perked up, cheeks full of pastry. Crumbs trailed behind him as he scurried forward, hands sticky with sugar and pride. He darted ahead of Zarriq and bounded toward the couple on the veranda.

Behind him, Zarriq followed at a measured pace, stepping out onto the veranda, his eyes sharp with intent.

Reagan lifted her head from Martouf's shoulder and reached out to Kayleth, smiling as she embraced him.

Zarriq stood just beside them. With an expression of effortless apology. One hand pressed lightly to his chest. A gesture half formal, half theatrical, as if to say he truly regretted the interruption. His voice was warm and disarming.

He was requesting Martouf's presence for a simple matter, nothing urgent. Promised to return Martouf as swiftly as a raven's wing in a storm. His hand brushed her shoulder gently, comforting, and reassuring. There was something so fatherly in the way he leaned in.

The ball, would continue well into the early hours. There would be no shortage of magic or music. No shortage of nights like this. In fact, he said with a soft laugh, there would be so many balls she'd grow tired of them eventually.

Martouf met her eyes with a flicker of regret in his features, gave her a small, apologetic smile before getting up, then stepped away with quiet obedience.

Ysmerra's *Come To Me* spell had been weaving through the night for some time. Quiet, unseen, patient. Waiting for the right moment to thread its will. And now, it found its opening.

Zarriq gestured toward the garden. The hedges were particularly lovely tonight, he noted. Suggesting Reagan wander among the moonlit paths and stroll beneath the stars while they stepped away. But the suggestion wasn't quite his. That thought, the gentle nudge to guide Reagan toward the garden, had been quietly, deliberately placed into his mind. A soft suggestion, born of blood magic. A direct result of Ysmerra's *Come To Me* spell.

Before Reagan could reply, he scooped Kayleth into his arms, earning a squeal and a smear of icing down his sleeve. Though Zarriq didn't seem to mind. He promised to watch over Kayleth as if he were his very own. That Kayleth would be safe and well cared for. They could be a different shape of family. One not born from duty, but chosen. Strange, imperfect, but whole in its own way. Zarriq gave a wink as he turned. A little flare of mischief beneath the polish. Then he turned toward the ballroom, Kayleth nestled against him like he belonged there.

Reagan watched them leave. They stepped through the open glass doors that led back into the ballroom. Just as they passed through, a breeze stirred the air, sending one of the sheer white curtains billowing outward like a ghost reaching into the night. The curtains slowly drifted back inside. And they were gone.

She turned toward the garden, unaware she was being led. Right toward the portal. Nestled away in a quiet garden. A cottage, veiled by bloom and stone. But something else was watching. Listening... and waiting. Far more powerful, strategic, and terrifyingly in control than Ysmerra. It had tolerated her involvement thus far. But only while her intentions aligned with their desired outcome. Soon, they no longer will. And when that happens, it will take back control.

PIP
Do you have any cauldrons?

YSMERRA
Nope. Go Fizzle! ... Where did you get that scarf?... Got any Ghouls?

PIP
Go Fizzle! The banshee made it for me. It's a protection charm... Got any eyeballs?

YSMERRA
Go Fizzle!... Wait! Did you feel that? That shift. She's close!

PIP
Or it could be just another one of those inter-realm evangelists. Going portal to portal, on a levitating bicycle, with white tunics and glowing name tags.

YSMERRA
No. It's her! Go put the kettle on. Make sure your ghosts have enough drinks and snacks. I don't want them wandering out of their rooms... And get rid of that banshee!

PIP
I thought you're not suppose to feed ghosts after midnight.

YSMERRA
Thats Gremlins, not ghosts! Now go! It's showtime...

CHAPTER 11
The Cottage

To Reagan's left, a staircase led down to the enchanted midnight garden. She descended the steps, her feet meeting a path of polished obsidian tiles. Large blue glowing mushrooms sprouted along either side. Ahead, an archway of roses parted, beckoning her into a twilight grove spun from breath and bloom.

Large butterflies with twinkling wings fluttered around ruby trees with white feathered leaves, while glass bell-flowers chimed in the breeze.

A lane of lilies led to a grand golden gazebo alit by veiled violet vines. In the center stood a fountain, casting soft enchanted whirls, where ghostly fish danced, and glistened like moonlit pearls.

At the garden's far edge, a narrow stone path led to a charming ivy-cloaked cottage. Its stained glass windows aglow, framed by flower-laden baskets brimming with boysenberry blossoms.

From the doorway, Reagan saw an old woman waving. It was Ysmerra, who had been awaiting all night for Reagan's arrival. Waiting to lead her into the portal.

Ysmerra called out, her voice sweet but pitched oddly high. Cheerful with a frantic energy tucked beneath it.
"Over here!"

Reagan grinned at the warm welcome as she walked up the path.

Ysmerra motioned frantically. Hands fluttering like birds.
"Come in, come in, come in!"

Ysmerra took a hold of Reagan's hand and leads her inside. "You're right on time, dear."

The cottage opened into the most darling large open space. Every surface was adorned with vases overflowing with fantastical floral arrangements. The walls were crisp white, the furniture a delicate sage green. Every cabinet, drawer, and knob was etched with floral designs.

Ysmerra gave Reagan's hand a delighted little pat as she led her deeper into the cottage, her voice bubbling with amusement."These *Come To Me* spells can be so finicky. I was beginning to think they had you all tied up with ribbons and rose petals. But look at you. You wobbled your way here just fine."

Reagan followed, eyes wide with delight at the whimsical décor.

Ysmerra floated ahead of her, motioning toward a pair of cushioned armchairs by the fire. Both draped in soft pink throw blankets, like something out of a grandmother's daydream. Her words lilting like a lullaby.
"Come, sit child. Let's have a look at you."

Reagan settled into the chair without hesitation, the cushion sighing beneath her. She glanced at Ysmerra, who hadn't sat down at all.

Instead, Ysmerra leaned over her, tilting her head, inspecting the fabric. Then plucked something invisible from Reagan's shoulder and rolled it between her fingers like a thread. With dainty fingers she held it up to the light. It shimmered faintly then vanished.
"You're already fraying at the edges."

She gently cupped Reagan's cheek. Her palm warm, her thumb brushing just below her eye.
"But that's alright. Nothing that can't be stitched back together."

She let her hand fall, then turned gracefully toward a small round table beneath the window. A porcelain tea set sat atop it, impossibly ornate. The cups rimmed with gold.

Ysmerra glanced back over her shoulder. Her voice was lighter again now, chipper. As if they were about to have a lovely chat.
"Tea, dear?"

Trying not to seem impolite, Reagan ignored the old woman's strange ramblings, choosing instead to admire the ambiance of the room. She replied graciously.
"Yes, please."

Ysmerra stirred the tea with a spoon made of glass, whispering a soft incantation as the liquid swirled. She grinned, all warm wrinkles and knowing amusement, before lifting the teacup and carrying it toward Reagan.

Reagan sat completely calm, her eyes dreamy and distant.

Ysmerra leaned in, peering closely at Reagan's vacant face. She waved a hand slowly in front of her eyes, as if dusting off a shelf.

Reagan didn't even blink. Her eyes were open, but no one was home. Not even a flinch. Reagan's gaze remained soft and unfocused, fixed somewhere beyond the room. Her eyes like glass marbles left in the sun.

Ysmerra cooed, tilting her head with a smile too wide to be innocent. Watching Reagan with a kind of twisted affection. Like she's both a precious porcelain doll and a trapped bird.
"Oh, you're thick in it, aren't you? Dripping like a sugar-dipped peach. Just sittin' there all soft-eyed and dim."

Chuckling to herself, she walked to the fireplace, opened a small glass box on the mantel and scooped up a handful of enchanted moon dust. She stepped directly in front of Reagan and without warning, blew the sparkling powder straight into the girl's face.

Reagan sputtered, coughing violently as the dust clung to the back of her throat. The rest of the powder drifted down over her skin, shimmering in opalescent flecks.

Ysmerra, entirely unbothered, pressed the teacup into her hands. "There you are, little moth. Drink this. Go on then, sip. Let's see if you remember the taste of truth."

Reagan downed the tea quickly, desperate to soothe the tickling in her throat.

Ysmerra lifts a single finger, tracing a symbol in the air. The symbol ripples over Reagan. Then the Ysmerra quickly walked over to an armoire and opens it.

After Reagan sips the last drop of tea, before she even removes the cup from her lips, she feels something, and for the briefest moment, she sees something else. A flickering glimpse, but it's gone. She wants to explain what she saw, but the words won't come.

Her thoughts moved like molasses. Heavy, slow, disconnected from her tongue. Something wasn't right. She knew it. Felt it. Not just in the powder on her skin, but deeper. In the bone-deep dissonance between what she saw and what she felt. Words formed in her mouth, but melted before reaching air.

And in the next moment, those thoughts vanished. Everything was lovely again. The cottage glowed with golden warmth. The air shimmered with soft floral perfume. The fire crackled with just the right amount of cheer. Reagan smiled faintly. She felt relaxed. Safe. Admiring the flower arrangements again. How charming they were, how perfectly pink the petals seemed.

Ysmerra fumbles about in the armoire drawers, shouting back at Reagan.
"You're looking at me like I'm speaking in riddles. That's just your poor, tangled-up brain hearing everything through rose-colored cotton wool."

She finds a silver enchanted hand mirror in the armoire and turns around. "That's the glamour's doing. But it will pass."

The word drifted through the air... *glamour...* but it landed in Reagan's mind like a lovely trinket, not a warning. She smiled softly, thinking it sounded like something from a fairytale. She tilted her head slightly, and echoed it back. Her tone light and pleasant. Admiring the sound, not questioning the meaning.
"Glamour?"

Ysmerra said softly, her voice suddenly gentler, almost like the hum of a lullaby.
"Hush now, little one. No need for fear. You are safe with me."

She placed the mirror before Reagan with great care, turning it ever so slightly until the reflection caught just the right shimmer of firelight.
"Now, deeply look at yourself... Closer... See with the eyes beneath your eyes."

Reagan leaned in slowly. Looking into the mirror. Searching. Her face appeared, but not quite as she remembered it. And it smiled before she did. The face blinked back, but the timing was off, like a puppet learning its strings. Her own gaze stared at her, glassy and rose-tinted. The irises glowed faint pink, soft as cherry blossom, but wrong. Wrong in a way her spell-fogged mind couldn't quite grasp.
"My eyes!... They're..."

Ysmerra interrupted, grinning knowingly, glinting with ancient knowledge.
"Yes. Rose-colored lenses."

Reagan stammers unable to form words and struggling to speak. A dozen thoughts surged forward. Panic, confusion, recognition. But they all collided and dissolved in the same place. Her throat tightened. Her mind fought to process it, to hold onto something real, but everything inside her felt smudged.
"I don't understand…"

But before it could settle, it was brushed away. Replaced with something about rose petals and tea and how lovely the fire looked.

Ysmerra winced slightly, lips twisting in a smile that was equal parts amusement and pity. Like she'd just watched someone walk into a glass door and they tried to pretend it didn't happen.
"Ooof! My cotton web kitten. Nothing but singing birds and mist in that little head of yours. But we'll sort that out, won't we?"

Then quickly walked over to the kitchen cupboards, rummaging through the drawers, pulling out strange objects, muttering under her breath, and throwing things over her shoulder.
"Where in the seven blinking moons did I put that blasted silver thread? Can't go unraveling knots without thread. That would be madness... Ah! No, wait. That's just an old sock."

She pulled it out, turned it over like it might reveal a secret, then tossed it over her shoulder with a soft thump. The sock landed on a crystal vase, which teetered but somehow didn't fall. She moved to the next drawer.
"Hmm. Cupboards full of trinkets, drawers full of nonsense, and yet the one thing I need is always off gallivanting in the ether."

She shoved the drawer closed with her hip and opened another. This one filled with an absurd array of magical oddities: vials glowing in unnatural colors, a frog wearing a monocle, feathers that twitched of their own accord.
"Teas, powders, bones, keys. No, not that key. That one opens the door to yesterday. Hah! Here we are. No, wait, that's just a biscuit. Why do I keep biscuits in my spell drawers?"

She sniffed the box, made a face, then hurled it at the sink. At last, she pulled out a fluorescent vial and squinted at it, holding it up to

the light like a jeweler inspecting a gem. The liquid inside shimmered between lime and fuchsia.
"No, no, this one turns your ears into fox tails. Funny, but not useful."

She turned to Reagan with flourish, the vial pinched between two fingers like a gemstone at auction. She asked, voice lilting with mock curiosity.
"Unless you'd like to hear better?..."

Reagan just blankly stares at her. Eyes glazed like a bakery pastry. Ysmerra could've tossed the vial at her face and it might've bounced off without a flinch.

Ysmerra's smile froze for a heartbeat, hopeful, then confused, then disappointed. "No?"

She sighed loudly and dropped her arm in exaggerated disappointment, letting it hang limp like a wilted flower. Then shoved it back in the drawer. She slowly closed the drawer with a huff. "Pity."

She was smiling again by the time she opened the next drawer. Finally finds the silver thread and holds it up victoriously. Then gathers mugwort, lavender, yew bark, and crushed topaz dust, tossing them into the fire. Before adding the silver thread, she says, "I've got oodles of this thread."

And then tosses it in. The flames gets larger and turn a deep purple and blue. The smoke causes Reagan's eyes to water, uncontrollably. She keeps wiping them, but they keep dripping. Once her eyes stopped watering, she gave a sigh of relief.

Then, without warning, she sneezed. A sharp, involuntary jolt that made her head drop forward and her hands fly up to cover her face. And in that moment, something strange and impossibly delicate *pulled free*. When she pulled her hands away, something glinted at the edge of her vision. A long silver thread spilled from her chest like spun moonlight. It shimmered as it uncoiled, alive, and impossibly long. Her hands hovered midair, palms open near her collarbone, too close to the thread, too afraid to touch it.

Reagan stared at the thread protruding from her, horrified and mesmerized all at once. Her mind scrambled for a rational

explanation. No words made it past her lips. They dissolved on her tongue before they could reach her throat.
"What the—"

But then... In the next breath, her thoughts changed. She wasn't concerned about a thread at all. She was sitting in the most darling little cottage. Enjoying a chat with old woman about herbs and stars and what color flowers meant in different realms. Reagan smiled faintly. Everything felt soft. Peaceful. She had the strange sensation she'd forgotten something, but the thought fluttered away before she could hold it.

Ysmerra gasps in excitement at the sight of the thread.
"There it is!"

She sits in the chair next to Reagan, and scoots it forward so that their knees are almost touching. She grabs a hold of the thread and starts tugging.

Reagan thought the old woman was simply scooting closer to hear her better. That maybe her hearing wasn't what it used to be. Reagan didn't see the thread. All she saw was the old woman seemed to use her hands a lot when she spoke, gesturing with enthusiasm as if caught up in some long story. Reagan thought nothing of it. Just simply listened. Her words a soft blur of pleasant nonsense. Never noticing what those hands were really doing. She saw a smile. And heard laughter that wasn't there.

Ysmerra gets comfortable in her chair, knowing unraveling the thread will take some time. She starts speaking to Reagan in a soft calming voice.
"This thread was spun from the sheddings of a silver furred celestial beast. A creature known to only appear on the longest night of the year, during the Winter Solstice. The thread must be spun by a blind monk, using looms carved from the wood of a frost blossom tree, beneath the light of a blood moon. If anyone looks directly at the fur, they will be entranced by its shimmer and forever see what the beast sees."

Her fingers paused at a knot in the thread. Sensing a shift, she reached for a pair of golden garden shears and snipped it clean. She tossed the piece into the fire. It burst into a white spark and vanished. She continued pulling the thread from Reagan's chest.

Ysmerra's expression darkened with quiet sorrow. She could feel the emotions stitched into the girl's heart, woven tight with longing, loss, and loneliness. She deeply understood her and empathized with her. Her own eyes burned. The emotion wasn't hers, but she felt it. For a moment, their grief overlapped.
"They wrapped you up in pretty words and prettier lies, didn't they? All whispers and waltzes, all ribbons and reverie…all sweetness you poor thing…pity none of it was real."

She cut another section loose and tossed it into the flames. A tear slid down her cheek. She wiped it away with the back of her hand, unable to stop it. She sniffled, almost fondly.
"Soft edges and golden light shouldn't have to be just a dream… What a horrible ruse…It's a lovely trap, I'll admit. They always are."

Ysmerra took her last pull. She finally reached the end of the silver thread. Strands of light began to peel away from Reagan's body, fine as silk, golden as starlight. They drifted into the air and dissolved like mist.

The threads of illusion. The layers of lies. Gone.

Ysmerra had undone them all. Subtly, steadily, piece by piece. The dust, the tea, the fire, the thread. It had all been part of it. Every odd, enchanting moment had been a step toward this.

Reagan gasped loudly, as if surfacing from underwater. A sharp, shuddering breath. She clutched her chest. Something inside her shifted. Opened. Her entire body jolting with the force of clarity. Her thoughts snapped into focus like glass clearing of fog.

Then, her vision was overtaken. She saw it. She saw it all.

The Druid King, Zarriq…moments before they arrived in Balderon. His hand weaving a spell over her and Kayleth. The shimmer of power wrapping her and brother in a grey fog. Pink iridescence covering their eyes. A Glamour Spell.

Then glimpses. Real glimpses of the realm as it truly was, without the veil of the spell.

Nothing was real. Just smoke. Mirrors. Silk and strategy.

Her brows furrowed, trying to focus her eyes into the vision. And realization struck.

She shouted in disbelief,
"WHAT!"

Her eyes snapped open, only to find *nothing* looked the same.

Horror erupted across her face. Eyes wide.

Her eyes darted from corner to corner. Her mouth opened, but no scream came out. Her entire expression fractured with disbelief.

BANSHEE
I made you another gift. Slippers. I stitched
them myself... May I brush your hair?

PIP
NO!!! Look... you're amazing. Really. I mean,
your voice could curdle milk, your presence makes
mirrors cry, and you haunt a hallway like nobody else.
But Ysmerra said I can't keep you. I'm gonna have to
take you back to the graveyard where I found you.

BANSHEE
But you're mine. I marked you already...

PIP
You don't want to eat me. I have an ulcer. I'm gluten-
sensitive. My blood type is lemon juice. I have a hangnail.
There's no nutritional value here. I'm like haunted trail
mix.

BANSHEE
I think you look delicious!

PIP
Okay, BUT... I've got athlete's foot... I have a
wart that sings sea shanties. My kidneys are
technically pickles. My toe hair has knots.

BANSHEE
Did you say pickles? I HATE pickles. The
look, the smell! The way they taste. They
make me SICK!!!! You're diseased! Fowl! I
revoke my claim. Don't come near me...
I'll show myself out.

PIP
That was a little rough.

CHAPTER 12
Inside Ysmerra's Manor

Before Reagan stood a massive hearth, a cauldron as wide as the fireplace itself bubbling ominously. The walls, once adorned with flowers, were now lined with jars. Each one labeled and filled with preserved organs, strange creatures, or unidentifiable remnants. Bundles of herbs and twisted bones hung from the ceiling. A full apothecary cabinet stretched the length of one wall, its drawers labeled in runes.

She leapt to her feet, panic thundering in her chest. She slowly backed away knocking over a small table behind her with a loud clatter. Her hand gripped the nearby chair for support as her breath hitched and her vision blurred.

She squeezed her eyes shut, but instead of finding calm, she was assaulted with more visions and images. Raw, harsh truths. The cracks in the illusion splitting wide open.

Dizzy, she lost her balance and her foot caught on the chair leg. She hit the ground hard, hands splayed out, ears ringing.

The warmth in the room flickers. The air seemed to split around her. Her energy field being peeled away like layers of paint, revealing something vast and cold beneath. As the magic is working to completely rid her of the spell she can feel the parts gently being pulled away down to her soul.

She pushed herself up to her knees, trembling.
"What's happening?!"

Ysmerra appeared beside her in an instant, voice like a lullaby, and helps her stand up.
"There you are, my little lost thing."

Reagan grabbed her head as the dizziness starts to settle and she gets her bearings. She looks outside the window only to see the garden trembling and distorting. Flowers withering in fast forward. Roots shriveled. The entire world outside convulsed until it completely vanished into the darkness.
The illusions faded completely.

Her lips parted, slow to move. Cracked with disbelief. Her voice was quiet at first, like it didn't trust itself to speak. Reconstructing trust. Every word is a risk. Every breath is hesitant.
"What's going on?"

Slowly she turned. Her eyes found Ysmerra. She didn't speak at first. She studied her. Wondering who this savior in a shawl was. There was no shining armor, no radiant wings. This woman was the reason she could think again. She was filled to the brim with gratitude. Reagan had never seen her before. Had no idea where she came from or how she knew Reagan needed saving.

She wanted to know. Aching, pure and curious. She gently asked. The words slipped from her mouth like ink in water. Slow and spreading.
"Who are you?"

Ysmerra looked up, her hands floated through the air as if tracing unseen constellations, and her voice dipped into a melodic hum. Savoring every syllable like it was part of a performance.
"The winds whispered into a dying star, that fell to the lands in a sigh of smoke and moonlight, revealing that I shall forever be known as… Ysmerra. Seer, Spinner, Dream Mender, and on Tuesdays, a dreadful knitter. At your service dear!"

A smirk tugged at Ysmerra's lips, delighted by her own theatrics. Then bowed her head, just slightly, as if acknowledging the moment, the magic, and everything in between.

She had just delivered the most unnecessarily dramatic sequence of words Reagan has ever heard in her entire life. Clearly, she didn't get the memo that this was a serious moment. Reagan didn't say anything back. She wasn't even entirely sure if that actually happened at first. She blankly stared. The soul leaving the body type of a stare. No reaction. Just a system shutdown because of how utterly ridiculous that was and she is so done. Her brain had a lot to say, but she pressed her lips together tightly in restraint. Because if she did speak, it would have come out very wrong.
Ysmerra guided Reagan toward a tall mirror mounted on the wall.
"Oh, you poor, tangled thing. Come."

Turning her gently, and slid the sleeve of Reagan's dress from her shoulder.

There. On the back of her left shoulder. A red handprint.

Reagan let out a sharp hiss of a gasp. Raw and rattled. She recoiled like she'd been burned, eyes darting between Ysmerra and the mirror. Her fingers brushed the red imprint.

Ysmerra cooed. "No need to fret my little pet."

She bustled off, snatching a towel on the way, and plunged it into an enchanted, shimmering water filled basin then wrung it out with a snap.
"That red smudge? Merely the ghost of a grip that no longer holds. Your magic's stitched, snug, sealed and safe against theft and thievery."

She returned to Reagan's side, dabbing the cloth gently against the red handprint as if blotting a wine stain from the hem of a wedding dress.
"And all the while his hands were reaching, stitching, and tying knots in your spine… His touch was no kindness. He was leaving his mark on you. Binding you to a tether, to his leash, so he could tug at your magic and it would come fluttering right into his hands."

Reagan tilted her head, trying to unscramble the meaning of Ysmerra's words. She assumed the fluffy riddles and lullaby-language had been part of the glamour spell. Turns out the sing song silliness was real, and really how Ysmerra speaks.
Reagan asked. "Huh?"

Just then, a voice rang from across the room. Flat, unimpressed, and so sudden it cut through the air like a snapped thread.
"He tried to make you his familiar."

Startled, Reagan turned to see a woodland elf casually leaning in the doorway. Arms crossed, a faint smirk playing at his lips. As if he'd been listening for far too long and was delighted to finally be noticed.

Reagan was waiting for him to start juggling or play the flute.
She asked Ysmerra."Who is that?"

Ysmerra stammered and replied awkwardly. Closing her eyes and scratching her eye brow as though trying to summon patience from

another realm. With all the enthusiasm of someone introducing a wasp nest she said,
"That's … my assistant."

He announced himself, stepping fully into the room with the flourish of someone who believed introductions were sacred performances. With a crisp bow and a theatrical hand flourish, he declared:
"Quillory Alder Pipkin... "

He paused, waiting for applause. None came. Undeterred, he cheerfully, brushed some nonexistent dust from his tunic. Then strolled across the room.

At this point Reagan is beyond tired. The glamour spell has worn off, the truth is horrifying, and now she's surrounded by the most theatrical woodland misfits ever created. Her silent judgment was so pure, so viciously calm.

With the solemnity of a stage actor taking his mark, Pip lowered himself onto the nearest chair, propped one leg over the armrest, and gave a very serious nod.
"That's why the Druid lured you and your brother to his realm. He wants your magic."

Reagan looked at him, how perfectly relaxed he was lounged across the chair like a cat who knew it couldn't be scolded. Her gaze dropped to his leg draped over the armrest. She didn't say a word. Face impassive. Instead she turned her attention to the wall quietly reviewing her life choices that led her to this point.

Ysmerra rolled her eyes at his words. She didn't even look at him. She simply exhaled, long and sharp, like someone forced to share their soliloquy. She'd spent far too long spinning the perfect stage for this moment to let it be hijacked by fluttering sleeves and dramatic entrances.

Desperate to shoo him away, she gave him a task that sounded sacred, urgent, and entirely invented. She waved a hand at him with all the grace of a queen excusing a court jester.
"Pip, go fetch The Silver Eclipse of Eternity."

He rose slowly, as if the weight of destiny had just been laid upon his shoulders. With one hand clutching his chest and the other sweeping wide, he gave an exaggerated bow, dripping in theatrical flair.

He responded with the pinnacle of sarcastic obedience, voice tinged with mock reverence.
"Sure thing... your highness."

He tripped slightly on his own cloak, recovered with a flourish worthy of an encore, and struck a dramatic pose. Then, without another word, he spun on his heel and disappeared into the hallway like a man on a mission from the gods.

Ysmerra turned back to Reagan with the softness as someone handling a cherished antique. She dabbed the cloth against the red handprint like she was restoring a crack in fine bone china. Each motion slow and eerily meticulous. Her brows pinched in concentration, her lips pressed tight.
"The glamour spell. That made you dreamy, dazed and docile. Only seeing the beauty in everything, ears stuffed with honey. It makes one easier to control. You would have never noticed your powers didn't come in. You also saw what you wanted to see. The spell wove deep into the recesses of your mind. Finding your most inner wishes and deepest desires to help fill in the gaps and smaller details of the world... But you're unstitched now. Clean. Cut free. I burned the threads, cracked the spell, brushed the last of his dust from your bones..."

Ysmerra's hand froze midair with the cloth clutched inside it. She straightened with a slow creeping stillness. Her gaze drifted, distant now. No longer fixed on Reagan but somewhere beyond the room, beyond the veil.
"But your brother? Oh, dear. He's still in the hands of the Druid King, and the longer he stays, the tighter the weave..."

A flicker of worry passed across her face. Her eyes lifted, distant. The portal. The boy. The clock ticking in silence. Then suddenly she flung the cloth aside like it had offended her.

In one smooth, desperate motion, she *spun* Reagan around, and gave her a firm push forward. Half-guiding, half-hurrying, like a mother bird booting a chick from the nest. Her voice shifting from soft to *urgent* in an instant and tumbling out fast.
"Off you go, little starling! Fetch the boy as quick as lightening. No dallying, no dithering, no stopping to sigh at the scenery! Or lack there of. This portal won't gape forever. Bring him back before it snaps shut. Hurry little moth. Slip through the cracks, blend in with the dark, and take back what is yours."

Slipping an arm gently around Reagan's shoulders, walking her back to the ceremony room, where the portal door is. Her feet slapped the wooden floor as she ushered Reagan through the twisting halls with a flurry of muttered charms.

They made it inside the sacred ceremonial chamber. Only feet away from the portal.

Pip approached, cradling *The Silver Eclipse of Eternity* in both hands like a relic pulled from the depths of legend. Sleek, ancient, and deadly. Its silver blade shimmered like moonlight caught in still water. Blood-red rubies pulsed faintly along the hilt, like a heartbeat trapped in stone. He presented it to Reagan, reverently, with both hands.

Then Ysmerra turned towards Reagan. Looked at her dead in the eyes. "If he tries to spin his silver words around you, or reach for your magic again…"

Then she leaned in. Her voice dropped low, not just in volume, but in temperature. Cold, dark, and dangerous. "CUT HIM!"

Reagan slowly reaches for the dagger and takes it from Pips hands with a sense of dread. She brings the dagger closer to her.

Just then, the air shifted. A soft golden glow pulsed through the room, slow and rhythmic, like a heartbeat made of light.

With everything that had already happened, Reagan was unbothered and unsurprised by the glow. At this point, the entire house could've caught fire, burst into song, or sprouted wings and flown away, and she wouldn't have reacted or cared.

Whereas Ysmerra and Pip were very taken back. Especially Ysmerra who pressed her lips together tightly. She knew exactly what energy was attached to this magic and she was not thrilled about it.

The soft golden glow became stronger and brighter until it was so blindingly bright they had to shut their eyes. The whole room violently shuddered. The light finally faded.

Ysmerra opened her eyes, only to find the portal had been forcefully stripped away and Reagan was gone.

Pip opened his eyes and noticed the same thing. He looked at Ysmerra for her to explain, but she shook her head in defeat.

The being that clung to the wood beams, out of sight but watching and listening was finally making itself known... A breeze carried through the dimly lit manor, but it was no ordinary wind. It carried no warmth, no cold, just the weight of something powerful and unseen. The wind gathered in one spot in front of Ysmerra. A tall, prismatic form filled that space. Not wholly there, not wholly real. Their form flickered, shifting between states. One moment, dark as the abyss, the next, as radiant as the light of the stars. Rippling like liquid silk, too fluid, too perfect to be bound by the laws of flesh. Their voice, when it came, was both song and whisper, thunder and hush.

The entity's voice crashed through the manor like thunder cracking open the sky. A violent gust swept through the room, shaking the floorboards in a sudden, soundless quake. Shelves creaked. The walls groaned. The echo of its voice carried through the manner. The entity demanded.
"Enough!"

Ysmerra stood rigid, straight-backed, chin high. But her left eye twitched. Then the other. The corners of her mouth spasmed before smoothing.

Pip, as fast as lightning, ran behind a chair at the furthest end of the room peaking over the headrest.

A different voice spoke through the entity. This one, soft and sweet. More endearing. The kind of voice that might soothe a frightened child. Or lull someone into sleep.
"We can't let you interfere anymore. We understand you're trying to help but, they are exactly where they need to be."

The light within the figure shifted and another voice came from its core. This one more direct, assertive. Came across like a warning.
"Their parents will come to you for help in the future, as you are aware...but let them come to you *on their own*."

There was a pause. A stillness. Then, a ripple passed through the being. When it spoke again, the next voice was deeper.
"This needs to play out in a certain way. Future events depend on it."

Ysmerra stood tall. Too tall, the kind of posture that dared anyone to call her rattled. She was hovering between regal indignation and suppressed panic. She took one step forward, chin lifted in full ceremonial defiance. Refusing to relinquish control without a monologue.

Her voice, when it came, was clipped and strained.
"Just because YOU lot think it needs to play out a certain way doesn't mean it NEEDS to! This is all highly unnecessary. Who's in charge? I should like to speak with them at once!"

But the entity was already fading, dissolving into the same breath of wind that had carried them in, until the wind stopped and silence fell through manor…

Ysmerra stood there. Her chest was puffed, but her heart was trembling. She didn't win. They let her lose gracefully.
After trying so hard to perform strength and control. It was a *dignified defeat* with just enough humility, bitterness, and exhausted grace to make her feel powerless and tragic.

She sighed so deeply it could have deflated the walls.
"Pip! Come out from behind there. And fetch me my cane."

Pip scrambled out like a guilty cat, darted forward with her cane, quietly this time. No fanfare, no flourish, just a crooked, sheepish smile that said he kind of felt bad about it all.

She snatched the cane from him.

His smile was soft and pitying, which made her feel infinitely worse.

She left the ceremonial chamber in silence. Pip trailing behind her. She made her way to the parlor. A low-lit room heavy with incense and velvet. Where the silver-glow never changed and the furniture never asked questions. She dropped into her favorite chair by the fireplace.
"Pip, put the kettle on. If I'm to stay out of trouble, I'll need a very strong cup of tea."

This wasn't the first time she'd crossed paths with that group entity. The ones who spoke in borrowed voices. Who bent time and fate like cards in a game only they knew the rules to.

Ysmerra had learned long ago that arguing with them was like trying to bargain with a storm. They weren't gods, but they felt like they were. She didn't trust them. Never had. And yet, her hands were tied. They always were.

It burned her soul to be forced onto their timeline. To watch them maneuver fate like a chessboard with zero sense for the game they are playing. A patzer with no foresight, and all the grace of a drunken sailer betting his last coin. Then tipping the board over when things don't go their way.

But what choice did she have? They are a much more advanced race, and even her strongest magic doesn't come close to theirs... For now.

For right now, all she can do is wait.

Until help is asked for.

PIP

... umm just FYI there will be a slight delay on the tea. The kettle is... currently a goose.

YSMERRA

Of coarse it is....

PIP

I might have grabbed the essence of ghost giggles instead of owl dandruff. The jars were very close together. And a pinch of worm dust, but only because I thought it was ground frog nails. Honestly, it's the bog sprites fault. He alphabetized everything by smell.

YSMERRA

Naturally...

PIP

Anyway, she's laying golden eggs. Which apparently violates an arcane treaty with the Golden Realm. The goose is technically a currency-producing entity, which breaches thirty-seven inter-dimensional trade laws. I got a talking letter about it. Very rude tone. I'm now required to return the goose with a formal apology.

YSMERRA

I care less than a warted toad cares for sock etiquette. My concern has gone on sabbatical to the Misty Isles of Perpetual Indifference.

PIP

So you're not mad? Good! I was worried. Right! Don't worry, I'll sort this all out—be back in a jiffy. I'll make you the best cup of tea you've ever tasted! Promise! Don't go anywhere!

YSMERRA

Marvelous. I'll just sit here and twiddle my thumbs and commune with the void until you get back. May your scent be wildly appealing to every silver fang beast along your travels.

CHAPTER 13
The Ruins of Balderon

The whole room shuddered, and the blinding light faded.

Reagan opened her eyes only to see nothing. The portal was gone. The cottage had disappeared. In front of her was just miles of rubble, dirt, and desolate that stretched endlessly.

Her whole body froze in shock. Her jaw and heart dropped in awe. The dagger slipped from her fingers and landed soundlessly in the dirt at her feet.

The visions did prepare her for this sight, but to actually see it with her own eyes, to actually stand in it, was entirely different.

She didn't want to look. But slowly, her head turned to the right.

Towers were collapsed in heaps of shattered stone. The cities in the distance looked like they had suffered the same fate. Walls stood hollowed out, ceilings gaping open.

To her left, bridges severed midair like snapped bones, their remnants swallowed by the abyss below.

Where there were once luscious, overgrown trees and bushes were actually dead and bare. Curling like withered fingers in the lifeless soil. Everything looked like the aftermath of a horrible war and fire.

The world she knew, crumbled into a myth.

Nothing shimmered. Nothing glowed. Only darkness and despair.

She turned around, and behind her she saw the castle. In *ruins*. This felt like the ultimate punch in the gut.

She let out a little laugh at how ironic all this was.

The level of deceit used in the glamour spell deeply unsettled her. Not being able to see this. Not being able to fully think or speak. A chill wrapped around her bones, though there was no wind.

She sucked in a breath, but it barely filled her lungs.

In the distance, where she once heard faint, soft, pleasant music was now a ghostly, unsettling silence.

Then, all of a sudden, from the castle, she heard Kayleth squeal.

Her eyes snapped to the dagger still lying on the ground. She grabbed it, tucked it into the back of her dress, and charged down the path toward the castle. The tremble in her hands stilled. The quiver of uncertainty faded. She stood taller, straighter, stronger.

She couldn't think of herself anymore. Her little brother was helpless. He needed her. Knowing he was still in Zarriq's grasp. Still under his leash, under his spell, just as she had been, ignited something deeper than fear. The anger in her chest burned hotter. A smoldering fire that pushed away the last vestiges of panic. She didn't have time to think. She didn't have time for plans. All that mattered was reaching Kayleth.

Reagan stormed through the castle doors.

Everything was wrong. So different. Broken corridors. Everything reeked of ruin. But she didn't have time to mourn the illusion.

She headed straight for the ballroom. She pushed the doors open. The moment she stepped inside, she skidded to a halt.

The room shimmered with opulence. The mossy floor still glowed beneath crystalline shoes. Guests twirled and dipped, laughter tinkling like wind chimes. Music swelled from the gallery.

Everything stood perfectly intact, untouched by the ruin around them. It was all… the same. Unchanged. Exactly as she'd left it.

The air shifted as she crossed the threshold. Warm, perfumed, heavy with illusion. Her stomach turned.

The walls still flickered with living enchantments of skies and cities and snowfall.

Reagan pushed through the crowd, searching. Sprinting across the ballroom to the dais, but the thrones were empty. She ran outside to check the balcony, but they weren't there either.

Martouf was nowhere. Zarriq, gone.

She stood in the middle of it all, surrounded by silk and laughter, and felt like she was drowning in sugar water.

She turned to the nearest guest and touched her shoulder.
"Excuse me, madam. Do you know where King Zarriq is?"

The woman turned with a delicate smile, head tilted, dead eyes... and said nothing. Not a blink. Not a word. Just watched. Like a haunted doll.

Reagan's breath caught. Her face twisted into something between horror and incredulity. And took a quick step back. Slowly, she turned to her right, to the next guest. He was tall, broad-shouldered, and dressed in layered silks. She touched his sleeve.
"Sir? If you please, I'm looking for my brother."

He stood facing another guest, a woman in deep red velvet. Both posed like actors mid-conversation, expressions frozen, eyes vacant. Neither said a word. The man laughed suddenly, raising a jeweled goblet into the air in a toast. Still not acknowledging Reagan.

A couple danced behind her, and bumped into Reagan, causing her to stumble into the gentleman in front of her. His goblet tipped, wine splashed across his arm and the mossy floor. He didn't react. He didn't even blink.

Reagan's eyes flicked back and forth to the couple. Him and the woman stood there perfectly still. Smiling, looking at each other. Like mannequins.

Reagan grabbed the arm of the next woman who passed by. Her voice struck with the kind of command that silenced spirits.
"Where is Martouf and Zarriq!"

The woman stopped, tilted her head slowly, and smiled. But her pupils didn't move. Her skin looked too smooth, her face too flawless, her voice, when she finally spoke was not quite real.
"Are you enjoying the party?"

Reagan recoiled ever so slightly, and stared, thrown by the answer. Searching for logic in the nonsense.
"What?"

The woman repeated it. Louder this time. Her smile widened. Too wide.
"Are you enjoying the party?"

Another guest turned, and echoed the phrase.
"Are you enjoying the party?"

Then another. And another. Their voices overlapped, layered like a distorted chorus.

"Are you enjoying the party?"
"Are you enjoying the party?"
"Are you enjoying the party?"

Reagan backed away, heart pounding.

The echoing chorus fell silent. The guests blinked. Smiled.
And without missing a beat, they returned to their dancing. Gliding, spinning, laughing, as if rewound and set back into motion. A hiccup in the enchantment.

She walked toward one of the long banquet tables. Lavish, overflowing with goblets and trays of sweets. She stood over it, grasping the edge. Collecting her thoughts and catching her breath.

In a moment of pure anger and frustration, she let out a raw, roaring scream that ripped from somewhere deep in her chest. She heaved upward, and flipped the entire banquet table in one furious sweep.

Plates crashed. Goblets shattered. Desserts soared through the air. Wine spilled across the mossy floor. They landed with an undeniably loud thud and clatter...

But not a single head turned. Not even a flinch. The music played on. The dancers twirled with choreographed grace. Completely unbothered. Their smiles locked, eyes unblinking.

This wasn't a party. It was a puppet show. A fairytale on loop, spinning in place. It wasn't real. None of it was.

Reagan backed away, her hands trembling. Her chest rising and falling in panicked rhythm. The illusion was so detailed. So perfect.

Too perfect. She shoved through the crowd of smiling, soulless dancers. Faces blurred around her, all… for show.

She turned and fled the ballroom. She tore down the hallway, away from the ballroom, her breath sharp in her throat. The sound of music still trailed behind her like a hunter's lullaby. Soft, sweet, and utterly unnerving.

The corridor ahead was stripped bare. Chunks of ceiling were missing. She didn't stop. She tore through the hallways at a full sprint, hair whipping behind her, breath catching in sharp bursts.

Yelling for Kayleth over and over again. Her voice swept through the ruined corridors like the wail of something hunted.

She rounded a corner, ducked beneath a sagging archway, vaulted over a collapsed beam, screaming for him again. Louder. Rawer. Her voice hoarse and cracking, like it had been clawed out of her. "KAYLETH!"

Still nothing. She kept going, eyes wide with terror. Each step fueled by fear that she was already too late.

She kept shouting for him. Louder, harsher. Her throat burned. "KAYLETH!"

Down another hall, entire patches of the floor were missing, exposing beams and foundation below. She had to leap across gaps, slipping once and scraping her shin.

A sharp laugh cut through the silence. She froze.

She followed the sound to East Wing, peering into every room until she found them.

Finally, in one room, she saw Zarriq standing inside a grand nursery with a gaping hole in one wall. A towering, elegant ogress stood near the crib, her long braid adorned with ribbons, charms, and tiny glinting jewels. She gently bounced Kayleth in her arms. Arms marked with a row of horn-ridges beneath polished silver bands. Kayleth squealed again. Not in fear, but in delight.

When Reagan stormed into the doorway, breath ragged, eyes blazing, Zarriq turned to her with an easy grin, like she'd simply wandered in late to tea.

He said, delighted.
"Ah, there you are. What do you think of this room for the baby prince?"

He gestured broadly to the space, then to the ogress holding Kayleth. "This will be his private nanny, Grubella. And we'll get him the finest tutors."

Reagan's voice tore through the room, sharp and shaking with fury. "Let him go!"

She stepped forward. Her stance widened. Her hands clenched at her sides. Every muscle braced for the lunge, already calculating her next move. The words ripped from her throat, raw with rage and warning.
"Put him down. Now."

A second ogre appeared, stepping through the archway. This one far larger than the other. Massive. Intimidating. His arms were thick with muscle, body forged from stone and strength. Horns curved from his forehead. His steps were slow, his smoldering gaze locked on her.

A scream ripped from her before she could stop it. A reaction born of shock, and the sheer size of him. He was built like a weapon. She stumbled backward, heart slamming in her chest.

As he neared, his lips parted, just enough to reveal the sharp curve of polished incisors.

There was nowhere to run. Nowhere to hide. And the look in his eyes told her plainly, he would not stop.

She backed into the corner near the doorway, trapped. Out of options. Panic pulsing, hand trembling, she yanked the dagger free and pointed it at him.

He kept coming closer.

Without a word, Zarriq waved his hand, freeing the dagger from her grip. It shot across the room and lodged deep into the wall.

Reagan instinctively raised her arms to shield herself, expecting pain, a hard blow or *something.*

Zarriq's voice called out sharp as a crack of thunder.
"Stop!"

He walked calmly to the ogre's side, resting a hand on the creature's broad shoulder. He looked back at Reagan with an expression caught somewhere between concern and amusement, as if her reaction was entirely unreasonable.

He said with a slow breath and tilt of his head,
"Well surely you're not afraid of *the prince*"

PIP
I don't think I've ever seen you in the kitchen
before.

YSMERRA
Well, you were gone so long, I assumed you'd been
adopted by a lonely mountain maiden, who collects
small men and dresses them in tulle, like her favorite
little doll. I'm just making myself a cup of tea. It can't be
that difficult... Why is there a snake in the sugar jar?

PIP
The snakes name is Sugar. Honestly, it would be weirder if she
slept anywhere else. That's her legal residence. She gets mail
sent there.

YSMERRA
I see. And where, pray tell, is the actual sugar? You know, the
kind meant for tea, not serpents or minor deities on sabbatical.

PIP
In the tea jar, obviously. Basic pantry topology.

YSMERRA
Basic pantry topology?... There's a frog in here!

PIP
That jar is clearly labeled Earl Grey. It's not
decorative—it's his title. He's the Earl of the Lower
Pantry. His influence spans several shelves... The
"Tea" jar is in the southern pantry annex. Past the
spice corridor, and left at the pickling section.
The teas are guarded by a mole named Harold.
Don't look at him in the eye... Although that
section may still be a portal to the catacombs. I
have to check the moon chart.

YSMERRA
I didn't realize making tea would be a cursed
expedition involving border negotiations and a
map! I'm not dealing with your pantry
aristocracy and sentient creatures. I'll be in the
parlor room. Just bring tea. Normal tea!

CHAPTER 14
Zombie Bride

Zarriq suspects the glamour spell broke. The glamour spell also made his half-druid, half-ogre son appear to be an elf like Reagan. With a gentle nudge, Zarriq sent Martouf toward the nanny. His quiet way of cueing he'd handle this situation.

The druid king stood there, facing Reagan but said nothing. He simply stared at her. Unblinking. Unmoving. Studying her.

Then, he slowly, soundlessly stepped forward. Closer. His gaze locked on hers. He stopped just in front of her. Looking down at her. Then, he tilted his head, his gaze shifted past her shoulder. Confirming what he already suspected, his imprint was gone. "Well... I don't know how you undid the glamour spell but you did... And I see my tether was broken..."

He stepped back. Then exhaled. A long, steadying breath that felt too casual for the weight of what he'd just admitted. A tight smile ghosted his lips, meant to pacify, perhaps even charm. He said lightly, voice slick with forced optimism.
"This is great. This is all out in the open now."

Disgusted by all he did. She took a step toward him, eyes burning with anger. A pulse of fire behind every word. She yelled.
"You lied to me!"

Zarriq leaned in close to her, his breath ghosting just beneath her ear. His voice dropped to a whisper. Calm, quiet, and razor-sharp. A murmur meant only for her to hear. He spoke carefully. Just soft enough that Martouf, who was standing only a few feet away, wouldn't catch a word.
"Lower your voice or I'll cut out your tongue and feed it to Kayleth for supper."

Zarriq didn't want his son to know the truth. That he had cast a glamour spell on Reagan so she would see Martouf as handsome and desirable. A charm to help things... progress.

Martouf didn't know. He believed Reagan's feelings were real.

And Zarriq intended to keep it that way. He didn't want to break his son's heart.

He gave a slight gesture, directing Reagan toward the adjoining room, so Martouf and Nanny Grubella could't hear their conversation.

She reluctantly followed him. They walked to the far end, away from prying ears.

Zarriq stood before her, eyes narrowed, shaking his head as though trying to read a language he no longer understood.
"Was it so horrible? To be a princess? In a beautiful castle?"

Reagan blinked hard, as if the words themselves physically struck her. For a moment, she couldn't even respond. Staggered by how easily he reduced everything to pageantry. Her eyes didn't waver. Only betrayal simmering beneath the surface.
"None of it was real."

His jaw dropped as if appalled and offended by her answer, then returning with sharpened intent.
"For my son it was *very* real... Can you honestly say, you would have ever considered marrying him if I hadn't used magic on him?"

Reagan froze. Not from fear. Not even from shock.
But from the sheer *audacity* of his words. She was recalibrating. She'd just caught the sleight of hand in his argument. Fully aware he twisted this into something it wasn't.

Her voice stern with disbelief, disgust and outrage.
"That's not fair! I wasn't given the chance to know what was real because you made that choice for me."

Zarriq's voice cracked like a whip. Throwing her own words back at her, but turning them into a crescendo of righteous fury. His expression twisted. Half grief, half rage.
"FAIR!?"

He started pacing. Sharp, agitated strides like a storm building in a bottle. Injustice crushing him as he throws it all down. Every word struck with thunderous weight, each syllable edged in fire. Building in intensity. Echoing like a war drum until it explodes.
"It's not FAIR Martouf lost his mother! It's not FAIR our allies burned our lands, slaughtered our people—"

He turned, and in two strides, he was in front of her. Inches away from her face, voice rising.
"—KILLED MY WIFE!"

He inhaled deeply, as if calm could be summoned by breath alone. It couldn't. The moment clawed at his restraint. He turned away, pacing a few steps, trying to gather himself. Hands trembling slightly as he struggled to collect his thoughts before they shattered.

Now calmer, gentler. Trying to sound rational, but the cracks are beginning to show. The uneven breaths. The forced composure. Every movement too measured, every word too carefully chosen. It's painfully clear: he's trying, and failing, to hold himself together. "With the balance of magic lost in this realm, a lot of the creatures here are out of sorts... I want your magic and your brothers, to restore the land... *I can't* fix the castle. Not while the curse holds. You would be saving *my son* and *all* the inhabitants in this realm from the fog that fills their mind where the magic used to be... He is thoughtful, loyal and kind."

He turned his face toward her, slowly, disgust written plainly across it. His eyes, full of contempt, raked over her like something foul. When he spoke, his voice was calm but dripping with disdain "But I'm sure you didn't notice that. The look on your face when you saw him said it all. You were terrified. As if he was some sort of monster. A look I never want him to feel ever."

Reagan stood rooted, shoulders squared, chin lifted. Not in defiance, but in absolute clarity. Her eyes didn't waver, blazing with betrayal, as if she were seeing him for the first time.

Her voice came low, but it was filled with fury barely restrained. Then, louder. Fiercer. Final.
"He's not the monster. YOU ARE!"

He strode toward her so fast it was a blur, fast and sudden. Rage flashing across his face. His hand shot up. A faint glow coiled around his fingers. Magic. Alive. Brewing. Crackling like heat lightning just inches from her face. The threat hovered there, one heartbeat away. Waiting and eager.
"For the way you looked at him, I should pluck your eyes out!"

Reagan instinctively lifted her hands, shielding her face. Because in that moment, some part of her couldn't be sure if it was an empty

threat. She gasped, her voice catching mid-sentence. Sharp. Fear-laced. Not groveling, not dramatic, just a choked, instinctive plea. "NO! *Please* don't!"

Zarriq's fingers twitched as if tempted, then paused.
He exhaled, smoothing a hand through his hair. His tone leveled, but the undercurrent of venom still pulsed beneath every word.
"Very well."

He didn't look at her. Maybe because if he did, he wouldn't be able to keep the facade from cracking. Or maybe because he didn't want to see the disgust still written on her face.

Instead, he adjusted the cuff of his sleeve, as if this conversation were a mild inconvenience, not a storm tearing through the room.
"He'll probably forget about this in the morning anyway. He is a man of few words. The glamour spell made it difficult for you to form words yourself because you were so happy and smitten and fulfilled. Doesn't he deserve to have that?"

A small part of her wavered. She didn't know Martouf. Not truly. Not without magic clouding her mind and twisting her heart into someone else's idea of love. Reagan never got the chance to get to know him.

For a moment, she didn't respond.

The words sat there, rotten and wrong. And yet, laced with just enough warped logic to make them dangerous. Twisting truth until it resembled kindness. Manipulation disguised as mercy.

Her voice came quiet. Not weak, but fragile in a different way. Like someone walking across cracked glass, trying not to fall through. Reluctant but honest.
"Of course he does… But, he deserves to be loved for who he is."

Zarriq scoffed. There was a bitterness now, subtle but cutting. His lips curled. Not in mockery, but something closer to exhaustion. The kind that comes from holding onto too many losses for too long.
"Like an ogre? Yes well, Ogres in general are a dying breed. So many realms were at war with them. So many died. An evolved female ogre with a good pedigree. I've looked."

He trailed off. And then, he looked at her. "The way you flinched at the very sight of him, I will not stand for it."

Zarriq's shoulders dropped, the fight drained from his posture, and slips into soft desperation. Like a king on his knees. Pouring honey over poison. Pitching a dream while barely holding it together.

His voice softened. Each word was spoken as if it were a gift.
"Let me put you back under the glamour spell. I wont make it as strong this time. I can create a dream world for you here. You can have anything you want. I'll create it just for you."

Even if she played along... even if she stayed... she wouldn't be herself. A princess-shaped mask trapped in a dream spun from someone else's will.

And Martouf would never really know her. He'd never know what was real and what wasn't. There'd be no truth between them, just a hollow fairytale replaying forever.

Reagan stared at him, a million thoughts colliding in her head. Her throat tightened. Terrified at even the mere thought of it.
"I don't want to be a prisoner again in that dream world."

Genuinely baffled. His brow furrowed as he began to pace again. Slow and agitated like the truth had slipped through his fingers and he couldn't figure out why. Adding mockery to mask his desperation.
"How is this any different than those books you read to escape your reality? Spending countless hours caught up in some fantasy of another world and another life."

He stopped just in front of her, lifting his hands, palms up, fingers slightly curled, as if presenting her with an invisible treasure.
"I'm offering you that fantasy. You can be the architect of that fantasy."

To her it felt more like a gremlin merchant peddling snake oil. Her eyes flicked to the floor, then back up at him. Uncertain and tired. She wrapped her arms around her waist, trying to hold herself together.
"I... don't know…. I just want to go home. You said if I didn't want to do this we could leave…"

His brows lifted. He tilted his head ever so slightly. Then he gave a small, nod. "Yes…well…"

His eyes drifted across the room, absently, as if thinking aloud...
Then, locked onto hers again. Cold and steady. He paused. It was
quiet. Too quiet. The air went still. Like the castle itself was holding
its breath.

With a soft shrug and a voice so calm it curdled the air, he revealed.
"I lied."

Those words came down on her like a guillotine. Her heart dropped
into her stomach She tried to breathe. The walls felt like they were
closing in. Reagan stared at him, stunned silent.

He chuckled. Quietly. Chillingly.

Looked at her like she was a child. Small, simple, and so, gullible.
So foolish for believing it.
"Like I was really going to let you leave."

The laugh that followed was sudden and sharp. Manic and echoing.
It rolled out of him bigger than it should've been.

Then just as fast, it stopped. He took a sigh of relief. Recomposed
himself with unnerving ease, like flipping a switch.

His voice dropping deep. Terrifying. With a serious cold authority
and bone-chilling gaze he threatened,
"Either give me your magic willingly and stay here, enjoy the fantasy
or I'll take it from you and keep you in a cage..."

For a moment it felt like the air got sucked out of the room.

He let out a soft chuckle. Light and amused. The kind of laugh you'd
expect over tea and cake. Not this. He's savoring this. The way he
watched her squirm. With a playful smile on his face he clarified.
"Just kidding about the cage part... mostly."

He tilted his head, mock-pity softening his grin.
"No. I wouldn't want my son to have to see the face of the person
who rejected him... I'll just send you the furthest edges of the realm.
I doubt you'd ever be able to find your way back."

It hit her all at once. A quiet, breathless understanding. The
realization had sunk in. She wasn't leaving.

That unbearable, suffocating stillness where hope had once lived. Gone. This was the cost of every choice she made. Every sign she ignored. And now, it was too late. She accepted her fate.

Now, all she could think about was Kayleth. What was Zarriq going to do with him? Put him under a glamour spell, keep him in a cage, drain him of his powers. Or something worse. She was almost afraid to even ask. Afraid to know the answer.

She reluctantly, hesitantly asked anyway.
"What about Kayleth?"

Zarriq's grin stretched slow and wide, he was amused, excited and savoring every word before he delivered it.
"We rather like him. We're gonna keep him. You see, I don't really *need* you. Although your magic would be fun and I would definitely take it, I don't really need it. I do however need your brothers though. He has earthen magic. Which is exactly what I need... "

He straightened. Hands clasped in front of him now. No more games, no more charm. The amusement drained from his features, replaced with cold expectancy. The final move. He's giving her a choice now, but it's not really a choice at all.
"So.... What's it gonna be? Zombie Bride or Swamp Hag?"

She stood frozen. The weight of his offer pressing against her chest like a stone slab. Her mind spun. To lose her thoughts. Her voice. Her will. To become some smiling, spellbound doll dancing in someone else's fantasy...

Her silence wasn't fear. It was grief. Grief for the version of herself she could lose if she gave in. But Kayleth would be there. He wouldn't be taken from her. He'd be safe. She could see him, hold him, even if she wasn't truly there. Maybe she could find a crack in the illusion. Maybe she could get them out later. Or maybe there would there be none of her left to save him.

Her lips parted, unsure. Thinking. Weighing all the possibilities quickly. She stammers.
"Well..."

Her weight shifting in her place as she thinks. She nervously fidgets with her hands. Twisting her fingers together as her eyes darted to the door, the floor, anywhere but him.
"I... I... "

Zarriq began to circle her. Slowly, deliberately. His boots tapping against the stone like a ticking clock. He's already won. Now he's just toying with her. Savoring the moment like a cat playing with a wounded bird.

He didn't look at her at first. Just let the tension coil tighter and tighter. Every step he took was laced with smug amusement.

He stopped behind her. Leaned in close. And whispered, low and playful—
"Wooop took too long!"

A strange pressure built in the air, like the moment before a spell detonates.

A tremor rippled beneath her feet. The ground bowed beneath her, and then it collapsed.

She tried to turn, but it was too late. She didn't even have time to gasp before the ground vanished beneath her with a violent shatter.

She dropped like a stone, swallowed whole by the waiting dark.

Her hands scrambled wildly, grabbing for anything— stone, the edge. But the gap was too wide. The drop too sudden. There was nothing to catch. Nothing to stop it.

His words still hanging in the air like a noose.

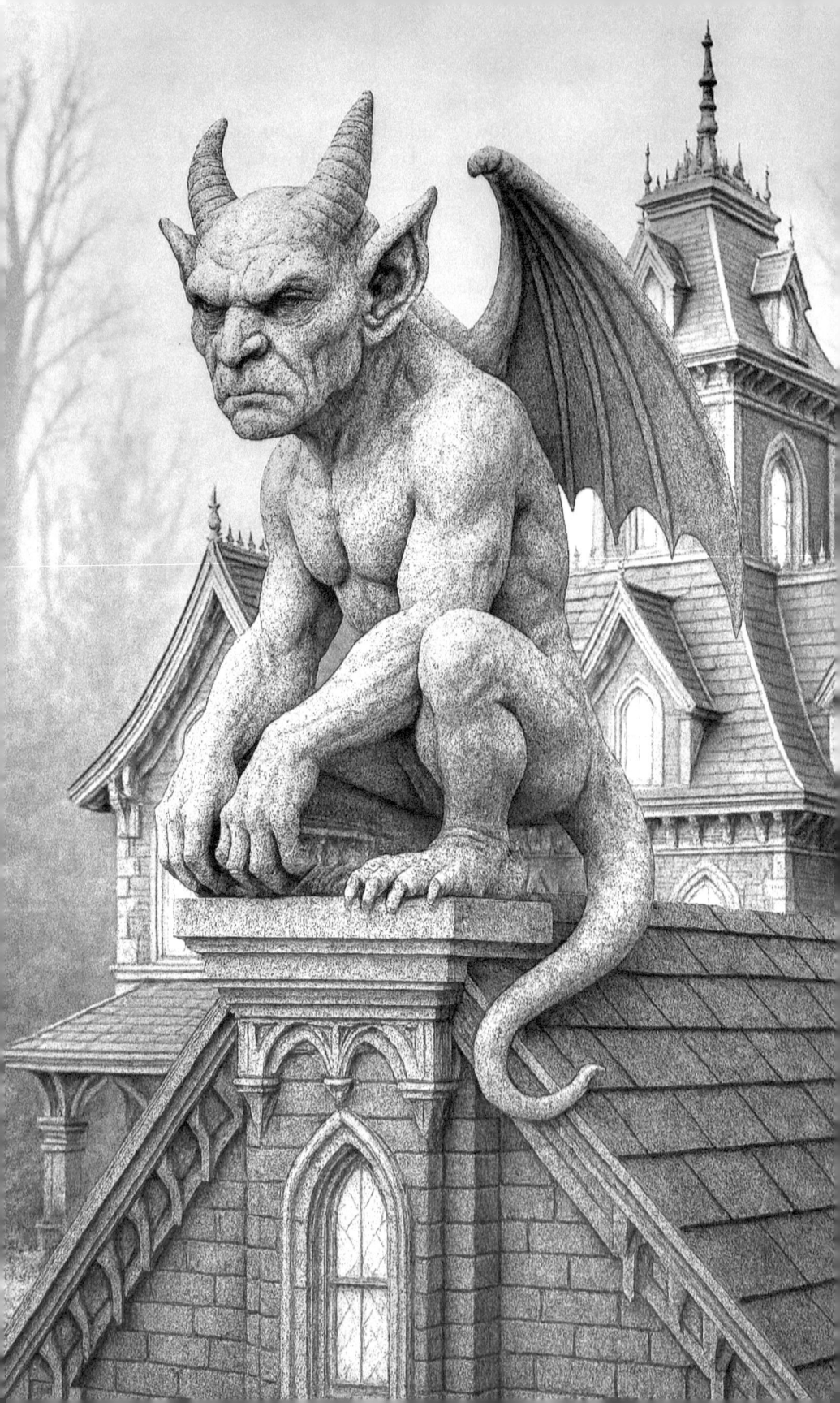

PIP

Tea has arrived! Mmmm. The scent of desperation and burnt sage. Must be a scrying day. Who are we spying on?

YSMERRA

The scrying mirror. Ah yes. I'm trying to locate Reagan, or at the very least confirm she hasn't been swallowed by something that speaks in riddles and smells of mildew. I'm not *spying*. I'm *monitoring*.

PIP

Right, of course. Monitoring. Like a concerned aunt... What in the nine flaming voids? She's falling... This is the longest falling sequence I've ever seen. Ooooh! I think I see something! Is that fog?

YSMERRA

No. That would be your breath. Would you kindly step back. You're steaming up the mirror like a bathroom vanity. This is a magical surveillance tool meant for serious— you didn't add anything weird to the tea, did you?

PIP

Define "weird"... Ooooh—What's this little ring here?

YSMERRA

The bottom of your cup. That's because you put your mug there. *Repeatedly*. How many times have I told you this is not a drink coaster. It holds the weight of prophecy. No amount of lemon juice isn't going to remove that... Now be a dear and hang it on the wall.

PIP

Shhhh. The villain's still gloating. Never interrupt a man mid-power trip. Mmm. Spiraling tendrils. Classic timeline purge maneuver. Very on-brand for lunatic kings. I'd give it a six for execution. A four for subtlety... Whats that growling noise?

YSMERRA

It's the gargoyle. He's teething again. Better fetch him some lava rocks soaked in mead. Otherwise he'll get quite cranky.

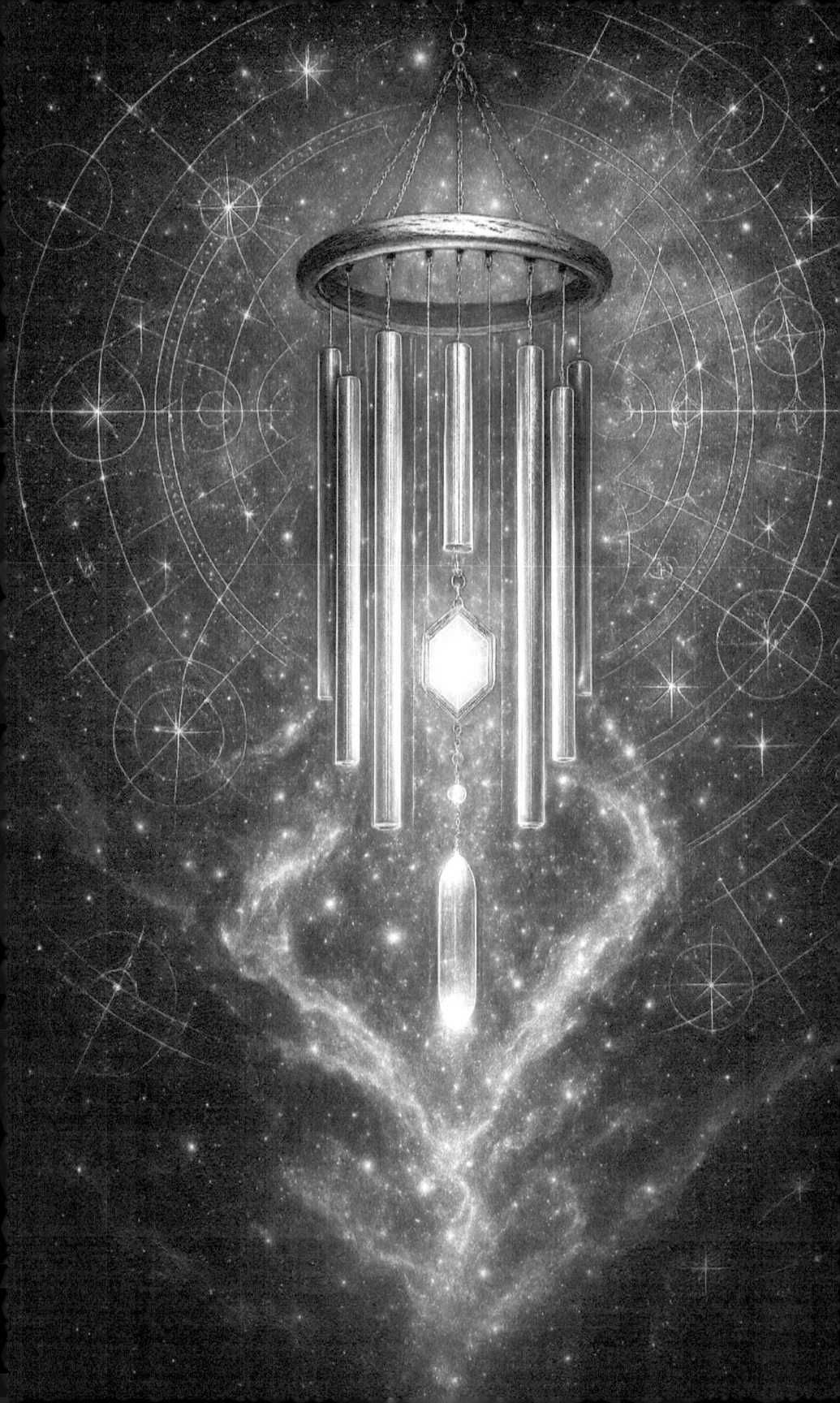

CHAPTER 15
Fate & Destiny

Reagan's world turned into a chaotic blur of crumbling rock and rushing air as she plummeted into darkness. Jagged walls of stone spiraled around her in an endless descent.

For a fleeting moment, she saw the Druid King standing at the top of the chasm. He lifted a hand, his fingers curling in a precise, malevolent motion. Tendrils of magic, midnight laced with gold, spiraled from his palm. They twisted and writhed through the air, following her into the abyss.

The magic caught up with her, weaving around her like invisible chains. Her body jerked as an overwhelming sense of loss struck her, deep within her soul. A strange, pulling sensation flooded through her—the unraveling of her life.

As she fell through the tunnel, the magic worked in reverse, erasing every interaction she and Kayleth had ever had with anyone since birth. Rewinding all events. Excluding them from it.

Somewhere, far above and unseen, the Druid King's magic spread like an infection through her world in Eldrannor.

In their family home, a faint ripple passed through Reagan's room. The soft sound of wind chimes rang from nowhere, though no one was there to hear. Her journal vanished from the desk. Her boots disappeared from their spot by the door. Her favorite scarf faded into nothing, leaving behind only a faint scent of lost memories.

Slowly, their rooms transformed. In Kayleth's room, the shelves emptied, the walls left bare of his carefully drawn doodles. His toys dissolved into dust and floated away with the wind.

Kayleth's room reshaped itself into a training area. Wooden racks filled with weapons, and an open space cleared for sparring. His childhood treasures and the remnants of his dreams were gone.

The magic that had already begun erasing Reagan's space now accelerated, clearing every inch. The space that was once filled with her essence and life, softened into a tranquil chamber for meditation. Perfectly placed candles appeared along the windowsills. A simple cushion replaced the bed. The shelves that once held Reagan's books were now filled with carefully arranged crystals.

Their parents attended a tribal meeting deep in the heart of the sacred grove. A vast clearing encircled by towering Blackwood trees, their trunks etched with symbols of protection and unity. At the center, a great bonfire crackled.

Elders, draped in ceremonial robes of deep indigo and moss green, sat atop wooden thrones arranged around the fire. Warriors and council members stood behind them. Their postures proud and resolute. Every member of the tribe was present. An unspoken law that none would miss a meeting held under the full moon.

Their parents, Valla and Arithel, stood near the front, their presence commanding but humble. Valla's long black hair was braided with dark feathers and small silver charms that jingled softly as she moved. Arithel's sharp features and unwavering gaze radiated a warrior's presence.

The meeting had begun as usual, discussions about patrols along the borders and trade agreements. Yet beneath the mundane, a ripple of Zarriq's magic wove its way through the assembly and through the grove, as if a sudden wind had swept through.

Memories began to unravel. The joyous birth of Kayleth—gone. Like a leaf swept away by the wind. The first time Reagan had reached for her mother's hand—faded into nothingness. Laughter, bedtime stories, tears... every precious moment vanished as if it had never been.

Zarriq had erased it all...

Fate and destiny stepped in and helped pave the way for new memories that blossomed.

Valla rose in ranks within the tribe, chosen as an Elder's apprentice. With shadow magic flowing through her veins, she became a master of darkness itself, using it as both a shroud and a weapon. It was a power that earned her the respect of even the most seasoned Elders.

She harnessed the ability to walk through shadows, using them as portals, weaving nightmares into reality, tethering shadows to control and manipulate objects or people, and manifest hauntings. Her reputation grew as one unafraid to wield fear itself as a weapon. She fully immersed herself in the tribe's traditions, ascending in power and influence to fill a hollow ache in her soul. A void that not even the tribe's deepest rituals could fill.

Arithel, no longer a father, now walked the line between light and shadow as a Dusk Warden. A protector of the tribe who specialized in espionage, assassination, and reconnaissance in enemy territories. Tasked with eliminating threats before they reached the tribe's borders. He embraced the most perilous missions the tribe had to offer, slipping into enemy camps and forbidden lands without hesitation.

With his illusion abilities, he could create mirages, alter his appearance or blend into his surroundings like a chameleon. He could even erase or change his characteristics from someone's memory, making it impossible for an enemy to recall his face.

With his quiet, watchful demeanor masking his deadly precision, Arithel became a ghost in the night, an unseen force that struck fear into the hearts of all who opposed the tribe. He embraced the role with relentless dedication, driven by an emptiness and longing he didn't understand.

Their lives were rewritten in seconds, and the weight of these new memories settled upon their shoulders.

The magic rippled through the grove, unnoticed by the others. The meeting continued, but the world had changed.

The children were forgotten… but a space always remained open for them in their parents' hearts.

YSMERRA

Standard spell for a memory displacement curse.
Mildly illegal. Redecorating your child's old bedroom
into a gym. *Tacky!*

PIP

I signed up to assist in minor enchantments and potion
upkeep. How did that translate into full-time chaos
containment and undead pest control.

YSMERRA

It's your fault she escaped the magical containment room. Honestly,
who feeds a troll cheesecake? That's the oldest trick in the book!
She's acting like a gremlin on its fourth espresso, just wrecking
absolute havoc... And there goes the china cabinet. Why is she
targeting *my* collectibles? Would you get that troll under control!

PIP

She's like a cursed pinball. I'm not going in there without a net, and
a tranquilizer dart.

YSMERRA

Why don't you set a trap? Use banana bread. Irresistible to forest
trolls. Put it in the center of the hallway. When she grabs it, the
chandelier drops a net... Or! We prop up a laundry hamper with a
stick, tie it to the curtain cord, bait it, and when she crawls
in—*snap!*

PIP

OR... and hear me out! What if *you* use your magic to
freeze her, and I calmly put her back in the magic
containment room?

YSMERRA

I suppose...

PIP

I'm gonna to start charging hazardous work pay.

YSMERRA

If you insist. However, toenail clippings are the
only currency I'm authorized to dispense at this
time.

CHAPTER 16
Swamp Hag

At the bottom of the chasm, a blinding radiance of magic awaited her. The wind whispering secrets in her ears as she plunged through the dark and shadows. The light surged up to meet her, like moonlight blooming in reverse. Reagan slammed into it, with all the force of her fall. Her starlace slippers twinkled faintly as they fluttered off her feet. For one impossible breath, she felt weightless, undone. Torn apart by magic before being stitched back together.

Then the light yawned open with a sigh, and spit her out like a bad secret, straight into mud.

The impact knocked the breath from her lungs. Cold, damp ground pressed against her back. She laid there, stunned, staring up at the black sky. Thin, jagged clouds streaked across twinkling stars. The air smelled of rotting plants and stagnant water.

She sat up, scanning the bleak swamp around her covered in mist and moss. The swamp stretched endlessly, like a festering wound, shadows slithering across gnarled tree roots half-drowned in sludge pools.

Every decision, every step that had led her here felt like a slow-motion disaster.

The Sigil.
The Incantation.
The Glamour spell.
The Tether.
The Confrontation with the Druid King.

And now, this place. A forsaken corner of the realm. No one to turn to. No way back. No plan.

Reality wrapped its cold fingers around her throat, squeezing until it hurt. Desperation, anger, and regret burned inside her chest, boiling over until she couldn't contain it anymore.

Reagan let out the loudest, longest scream she had ever known. A raw, guttural sound that tore from the depths of her soul. Her throat burned as the sound bounced off the twisted trees and stagnant waters, shaking the silence of the swamp. It was a scream born of helplessness and fury, of shattered dreams and crushing regret.

The scream finally faded into ragged gasps and left her hollow. Defeat wrapped around her like the damp mist hanging in the air. Her body trembling from the force of it, every ounce of energy spent.

She just sat there.

This waking nightmare had stripped her of everything.

The minutes stretched on as her mind drifted, too numb to form coherent thoughts. Eventually, exhaustion won.

Maybe if I just sleep....Just a little... then I'll be able to think... I'll figure something out.

The silence was absolute. No birds. No animals. As if death had already come and gone, and taken her with it.

A lump rose in Reagan's throat. Her voice sounded hollow, even to herself.
"This... isn't real. This can't be real."

But it was. It was all real. Too real.

She tore off several long pieces of her gown, twisting them into rough cords. Her hands moved mechanically, even as panic threatened to swallow her whole.

She stood slowly, her legs unsteady. The ground was damp and soft beneath her feet. Her *bare* feet. It took her a moment to register the sensation. She looked down. Her starlace slippers were gone. Gone like everything else. She hadn't even felt them slip off. She scanned the swamp around her but they were nowhere in sight.

The soft mud squished between her toes. The ground squelching with every step.

Finally, she found a dry patch of land beneath a towering tree. Using the fronds and twigs scattered around her, she built a crude shelter. The swamp offered little in terms of resources, but it was better than nothing.

When it was done, she sat beneath it, knees pulled to her chest, wrapping her arms around herself.

The events flashed through her mind.

And now… no one even remembered she had existed.

Tears slid silently down her dirt-smeared cheeks.

I'll find a way back. No matter what it takes. I'll get him back. I'll get him home.

The darkness closed in around her, but even here, in the outer edge of the realm, her defiance burned bright.

Overhead, the moon was veiled by a thin, smoky mist, casting an eerie half-light over the shelter Reagan had built.

Reagan closed her eyes, and just for a moment, imagined her mother beside her. Her chest tightened just at the thought of her. But she spoke anyway.

Her voice raw and cracked. She whispered,
"Mother."

The word alone nearly broke her. She hadn't allowed herself to say it since arriving here. The sound was almost foreign on her tongue, but now it poured out of her, desperate and aching.

She began in a voice as fragile as moth wings, the words trembling from her lips.
"I'm sorry. I messed up. I didn't see the danger until it was too late, and now I don't know what to do."

She drew in a shaky breath. The words catching on the edges of her grief.
"I miss you. I miss home. I don't even know where home is anymore."

She laid down, curling onto the rough, cold ground. She felt herself starting to rise emotionally.
"I'll find a way back. I'll get him back... Somehow."

Her words floated out into the swamp, carried by the night's breeze. For a moment, the weight on her chest seemed lighter. Speaking the words aloud, even if no one could hear, made her feel a little less alone.

As sleep began to pull at her, she whispered once more. "I'll try. No matter what it takes."

Her makeshift shelter barely kept out the swamp's damp chill. Her eyelids growing heavier with each slow breath. The plan could wait until tomorrow. For now, all she wanted was to forget, just for a little while.

Meanwhile, in Eldrannor, the tribal meeting continued beneath the full moon. The bonfire crackled, sending embers spiraling into the night sky.

Valla stood just beyond the firelight, her hands raised in quiet concentration. Her magic cast outward, sending a magic veil of darkness around the gathering. It wrapped the sacred grove in concealment. From a distance, should any outsider look upon the grove, they would only see darkness.

With her eyes closed, letting the magic move through her, she extended the reach of her shadow magic, higher and wider. Letting it seep into the forest like smoke seeking every corner.

Then, something slipped through. Uninvited. Unexplained.

A vision bled into her mind like spilled ink. Haunting, vivid, and wrong. A girl's face, tear-streaked cheeks. Voice trembling. Sorrow etched into every word.

And then, just as suddenly, it let her go.
Her eyes snapped open, heart pounding as if she'd been jolted awake from drowning.

Her breath came in short, sharp gasps, and her heart pounding against her chest. The vision lingered in her mind like smoke, refusing to dissipate.

Those words... Valla could still hear them.

I'm sorry. I miss you. I'll get him back.

The girl in the vision felt... familiar, as if Valla had known her once, long ago, but couldn't place her.

She glanced around the vast clearing of warriors, council members, and the rest of the clan. No wide eyes. No startled gasps. No signs of unease. No one else had felt it. No one else had seen it. Only her.

A distant breeze rustled the Blackwood trees beyond.

She dismissed it, quietly. Regrettably. Half-heartedly.

With one last glance at the moon, she let her eyes fall closed and returned her focus to the cloak of shadow.

But the girl's words stayed with her, haunting the edges of her thoughts.

The
SWAMP
INN

ACCEPTS
PAYMENT IN
LOCKS of HAIR

PIP
This is getting out of hand. Shouldn't we intervene?

YSMERRA
Absolutely not! We're observers. Mysterious. Aloof.
Like decorative owls.

PIP
Even decorative owls serve a purpose. They keep away the
snizzlebeaks. Can't we do something. Just a teensy ambience
upgrade. We could charm the swamp. Less 'doom nap' and
more 'enchanted slumber'.

YSMERRA
Oh sure. Let's just conjure up a goblin hotel. The Swamp Inn.
Room service, continental breakfast, and accepts payment in locks
of hair... We cannot risk drawing the attention of those Cosmic
Nosey-Parkers. They already warned me not to "interfere". I don't
want another visit from them.

PIP
We just need to do it under the radar. Nothing to attract their
attention. Small enough to where the they could miss it if they
weren't looking close enough.

YSMERRA
Hmmm something the Sisterhood Of TheTraveling Snobs can't
see. We could adjust the weather. No wind, no chill.
Just a gentle a spring night. Enchanted firefly night
lights. Velvety moss sprouting beneath her like a secret
mattress.

PIP
Come on. They couldn't spot a dragon in their
teacup if it belched fire and sang show tunes. We'll
be subtle, tasteful, and completely untraceable.

YSMERRA
Truth be told, that League of Un-extraordinary
Grumblesnouts do have the observational skills of
a damp cabbage... Alright you talked me into it.
Fetch me a pinecone, three angry buttons, and
my travel wand. We've got some ambiance to
finesse and some overblown egos to ignore.

CHAPTER 17
The Kapre

Reagan stirred in her makeshift tent. Her limbs felt sluggish, her dress stained with mud, and a film of dampness clung to her skin. But she had slept. Deep, dreamless, and heavy. Now, there was only one thought on her mind—

I have to get him back.

Her brother. Kayleth. She dragged him into this. She made the mistake, and he had paid the price. There was no giving up, no surrender to despair. Even if it took years, she would find a way back to the castle, and find a way home.

Reagan pulled herself to her feet. Her determination hardened like iron in her chest. She picked a direction. The one that felt least oppressive, and began walking.

The swamp stretched endlessly before her, its dark, brackish waters broken by patches of mud and gnarled roots. Hours blurred into each other, and her legs began to ache. Then, in the distance, a shadowy outline appeared. A thick forest of trees, their bark dark and twisted.

She drew closer. The trees were enormous. Colossal trunks. Branches knotted and twisted into one another so tightly forming a canopy so dense not a sliver of the night sky could peek through. The forest was shadowed, damp, and ominous. Reagan hesitated, but with no other options, she stepped inside.

The air changed immediately. Heavier, more oppressive. And there was something else.

Cigar smoke.

It was faint at first, but the deeper she went, the thicker it became. It clung to the air, mingling with the damp scent of the trees. The sensation of being watched prickled the back of her neck. Every so often, just out of the corner of her eye, she thought she saw flashes of yellow glowing, predatory eyes hidden within the shadows.

Her steps quickened, but the feeling only intensified.

And then she saw, perched high on a thick branch...

A *Kapre*.

A forest trickster. Watcher of the deep woods. Muscles corded and taut beneath his bark-like skin. His hair fell in wild, tangled locks around his shoulders, and a thick cigar was clamped between his sharp teeth. Yellow eyes, slitted like a cat's, followed her every move as he exhaled a slow, lazy plume of smoke.

He didn't move. Didn't speak. Just watched her.

Her pulse hammered in her ears as she walked past him, forcing herself not to break into a run. Another Kapre appeared on a different branch, then another and another, all silently watching her walk past. Smoke curling from their cigars.

The deeper she went, the more disoriented she became. It was as if the forest twisted and turned around her, the path disappearing beneath her feet. Her thoughts became muddled, slipping away before she could fully grasp them.

She stopped, clutching her head. "What was I doing?"

The sound of laughter broke through the trees. It was rough, guttural, and filled with amusement.

A Kapre snickered from the shadows.
"Got another one."

Another Kapre chimed in.
"Poor thing's all turned around."

They laughed even louder, the sound echoing through the forest until it felt like the very trees were mocking her.

Then, with a heavy thud, one of them dropped from his perch onto the ground in front of her. He was taller than any man she'd ever seen, towering over her with ease. His yellow eyes gleamed, but there was no malice in them. Only curiosity and a hint of mischief.

He barked, glancing up at the others. His voice was deep and carried a syrupy drag of dripping sap.
"Enough! Knock it off. You've had your fun."

The others groaned in disappointment but obeyed, fading back into the shadows.

The Kapre turned back to Reagan. He said, with a slow drawl that gave him a kind of lazy charm.
"We like to play pranks on the ones who wander in. Make 'em lose their way. Bit cruel, but there ain't much entertainment around these parts."

He gave her a lopsided grin.
"You look half-starved and worn out. Why don't you come inside? I'll fix you somethin'."

He gestured toward the trunk of the massive tree he had leapt from. There was a towering wooden door, seamlessly blended into the bark. He pulled it open, revealing a descending winding staircase. Reagan hesitated, but her hunger gnawed at her stomach, and exhaustion weighed heavy on her limbs. She followed him down the stairs.

At the bottom, the space opened into a vast underground cavern, lit by soft, warm lanterns hanging from the ceiling. The walls were lined with carved wooden shelves, and the furniture looked like it had been chiseled from the very wood of the forest itself. Despite the roughness of the materials, the space was cozy and inviting.

The Kapre grabbed a plate of food and a pitcher of water from a nearby shelf and set them down in front of her. Reagan didn't wait for an invitation. She devoured the food.

The Kapre watched her with amusement, puffing on his cigar as he whittled a piece of wood. Gesturing with his knife, he said,
"That's quite the dress you got there. Fancy. Don't see that kind of thing 'round here."

Reagan swallowed the last bite of bread and wiped her mouth. "I... came from the castle."

The Kapre didn't seem surprised. Only confirming what he already suspected.
"Figured. Only ever seen three other girls with dresses like that. They had the same look in their eyes too. Lost. Desperate."

He leaned back, then, casually, too casually, he added.
"Run-in with the king, I take it?"

Reagan's heart skipped a beat. She froze mid-bite, eyes snapping up to meet his. With her mouth still half full of food she blurted out, "Three other girls?"

She hurriedly swallowed her food, wiping her hand across her mouth. Her voice was tight and urgent.
"Who are they? When did they come? What happened to them?"

The Kapre smiled again, but this time it was softer, almost sympathetic.
"Finish your drink. Then I'll take you to them. They don't live far from here."

Reagan guzzled down the rest of the water. She hadn't realized how hungry and thirsty she'd become until it was all gone. Her fingers trembled slightly as she set the empty cup down on the Kapre's rough-hewn table. Her body aching but her mind buzzing with renewed energy.

She wiped the corners of her mouth and looked up at him.
"Okay. I'm ready!"

The Kapre gave a slow nod, set down the piece of wood he was whittling on the table nearby, and led the way back up the wide staircase carved into the base of the tree.

Reagan followed closely, her pulse quickening with each step. She couldn't shake the hope growing inside her. Hope that maybe, just maybe, the girls he spoke of would have the answers she desperately needed. Answers about the druid king. About her brother. And perhaps even about a way back to the castle. Her thoughts churned as they reached the surface. Never in her wildest nightmares had she considered that she might not have been the only victim. All this time, she'd believed her suffering was singular, that the Druid King's cruelty had been aimed solely at her. But now, the possibility that he had banished others gnawed at her mind.

And if these girls had survived here, had found a way to keep moving forward, maybe they would know something she didn't. Maybe they could help her find her brother. Maybe, for the first time in this forsaken realm, she wouldn't have to do this alone.

The Kapre walked silently through the dense forest, the twisted trees looming over them. Reagan's heart thudded harder with each step.

They finally stopped at the boundary where the trees met open ground. The landscape beyond was desolate. There was a shack standing crookedly on a patch of uneven ground. A clothesline swaying gently in the wind, strips of cloth fluttering like ghosts in the breeze.

The Kapre stopped, rested one long hand on the trunk of the nearest tree, the bark cracking slightly under his grip, cigar smoke curling into the air between them. His golden eyes watching her closely. He said,
"This is as far as I can take you. I'm bound to the trees and shadows. You'll be on your own from here."

Reagan swallowed hard. Unsure of what to say. Eternally grateful. Taken back by his help and kindness to a stranger. Her expression was a tangle of disbelief and quiet, aching gratitude.
"Thank you... for everything."

He gave her a half-smile and nodded. Easy and unhurried. The kind that came without ego or effort. Just kindness and decency, baked into his bones.
"I hope you find what you're looking for. And if you ever need me... you know where to find me."

With that, he melted back into the shadows, his hulking form disappearing into the darkened forest like he'd never been there at all.

Zarriq's magic erased Reagan and Kayleth from existence. No one remembered them. Not even their parents. Their memories were rewritten in seconds.

But memory is stubborn, and some whispers cling tighter than magic intends.

Valla and Arithel returned home from the tribal meeting in silence, the kind that hums with lingering magic and thoughts left unspoken.

Once inside, Valla moved on instinct, boots clicking softly down the stone corridor. Valla wasn't thinking, she was *remembering* without realizing. She didn't even know where she was going. It was muscle memory walking the path like it had done a thousand times, but one she didn't consciously remember.

At the end of the corridor she arrived at the door of her meditation chamber. It had always been her meditation chamber—at least, according to every memory she had.

It used to be Reagan's bedroom. Before Zarriq erased her from existence and removed every trace of the girl Valla once called daughter.

And yet…

Valla's body remembered.

Her mind might not recall ever having a child, but her instinct still did.

She used to stop by that room every time she
came home. Just to peek in. Just to check on her.
That muscle memory still lived inside her,
moving her feet before her thoughts could catch
up.

Her hand lifted to the door. She knocked twice, then
opened it.

Her eyes scanned around her meditation chamber. Quiet.
Calm. The scent of dried sage and lavender filled the space.

Valla froze in the doorway.

She couldn't remember why she had come to this room,
and for the life of her, she couldn't understand why she
knocked!

Suddenly aware of how odd this was she slowly backed
into the hallway. She pressed her fingers to her temples
and took a sharp breath. She cleared her throat, too
forcefully, like she could cough out the ghost of a
memory, and turned toward the kitchen. Thinking
maybe a cup of tea could clear her mind.

But she couldn't shake the feeling that
something was missing. Like a word caught
on the tip of her tongue.
Or that strange tension when you know
you've forgotten something, but you can't
remember what.

The sensation lingered, nameless and
heavy,
haunting the edges of her thoughts.

CHAPTER 18
The Shack

Reagan could still feel the Kapre's gaze on her. She took a deep breath as she crossed the boundary between the gnarled, ancient woods and the clearing beyond.

The shack seemed even smaller and more fragile up close, its weathered walls barely held together. It stood crookedly on a patch of misshapen ground. It was made from rough-hewn wood, with patches and cracks barely held together by vines.

Beyond it, the sky was a dim, eternal twilight, and in the grayish light, she could see someone moving in front of the weathered dwelling.

A girl, no older than Reagan, was bent over a bucket of murky water, wringing out a tattered cloth and hanging it on a sagging clothesline. Strands of her auburn hair had come loose from a messy braid, clinging to her cheek as she worked.

Her dress, or what was left of it, had once been beautiful deep crimson silk now faded to an ashen pink. The bodice torn and reworked into a crude vest. The bottom of her dress was ragged, repurposed into a skirt that hung unevenly past her knees.

She hummed under her breath, a haunting melody that matched the sorrow in her worn appearance.

Two more girls emerged from the crumbling hovel.

One carried a basket full of foraged herbs and wild fruits. Her long brown hair tied back with a cloth band. She wore a pale green dress that looked like it had been ripped and re-stitched a dozen times, the faded color barely visible beneath layers of grime.

The third girl carried a broom, sweeping away dead leaves and dirt from the shack's entrance. Her attire had once been a rich shade of violet, but now it was no more than scraps and rags, tied around her waist to form a tunic. She brushed a hand across her forehead, blue eyes gleaming with quiet amusement mid-conversation.

Despite their ragged appearances, they were all talking and laughing quietly. Their companionship offering some small comfort in the desolate landscape.

The girl at the clothesline suddenly paused, her hands stilling over the damp cloth. Her gaze lifted, and she locked eyes with Reagan.

For a long moment, neither of them moved.

The other two girls noticed the silence and followed her gaze. Their conversation fell away like leaves from a dying tree. They froze, the basket and broom dropping to the ground with dull thuds.

Reagan swallowed hard as she walked closer, her pulse a steady thrum in her ears. Her feet felt heavier with each step, as if the weight of their unspoken pasts pressed down on all of them.

When she finally reached them, the girl at the clothesline stepped forward first. Her eyes held a kind of pain Reagan knew all too well. Without a word, she reached out and took Reagan's hand. The skin of her palm was rough and calloused, but her grip was steady and grounding.

The others followed, each taking Reagan's hand.

They didn't speak. There were no questions, no accusations. Just an understanding. A silent acknowledgment of shared suffering.

The girl in the green dress gave a small, tentative smile that faltered, and didn't quite reach her eyes.
"You came from the castle, didn't you?"

Reagan nodded slowly, her throat too tight to speak.

The girl tightened her grip. Not just in reassurance, but like she was making a vow. Almost mournful. She'd said it before. Hoping she'd never have to say it again.

Her voice, when she spoke again, it came softer.
"Then you're one of us now."

Reagan opened her mouth to speak, but no words came. She didn't know how to explain herself. Didn't know how to ask the questions swirling inside her head. Instead, she let her eyes meet the girl's, silently pleading for understanding.

The girl seemed to see it. The raw, aching grief buried beneath Reagan's exhaustion.

She turned slightly toward the shack, tilting her head toward the door.
"Come inside."

Reagan didn't argue. She let the girl lead her toward their crooked home. The other two still holding onto Reagan to reassure her she was safe.

She hadn't come looking for them, and yet somehow, they had always been waiting.

Later that night, not long after they'd returned from the tribal meeting, the house had begun to settle. It was the first night without Reagan and Kayleth. The first night Zarriq's spell had quietly rewritten their lives. Valla had already wandered toward what had once been her daughter's room, drawn by instinct more than memory.

And now, just an hour later, Arithel found himself standing outside another door. One he used to open every night without fail.

The room that used to be Kayleth's.

Every night, Arithel would go there to tuck him in. He'd check underneath the bed for ghosts and monsters. Peering into cubbies and wardrobes with mock seriousness while Kayleth giggled.

Then told him a bedtime story. Usually something ridiculous, embellished, made up on the spot. He never left until Kayleth was fast sleep. Then, and only then, would Arithel quietly slip away, closing the door with quiet care.

That deep longing he couldn't place, that routine he didn't even know was tucked away somewhere deep in his heart, that led him to this room at this exact hour.

He stepped inside.

Now it was a weapons chamber. The air smelled faintly of oiled leather and wood polish. Freshly cleaned, recently used.

He didn't usually train this late. He wasn't sure what he was looking for. Or why he was even in there. It wasn't habit. It wasn't boredom. It was something else.

He reached for one of the training swords, giving it a small spin in his hand.

Then picked up another weapon. A short-bladed dagger. It felt unfamiliar. Weighted wrong. He set it down.

He crossed the room to the far corner, just beside the bench where the practice armor was kept.

He turned, scanning the space like he'd forgotten something.

He walked slowly back toward the door, pausing before he crossed the threshold. Looking back, staring at the room. Looking for something he couldn't quite name.

Then he stepped into the hallway, closing the door behind him.

Gently. Carefully. Quietly.

And he couldn't understand why he closed it that way.

CHAPTER 19
Calla, Evra, Sorrel

The inside of the shack was small, even more so than it had appeared from the outside, but it was filled with small comforts. A patchwork quilt draped over a rickety chair, a pot simmering on a tiny wood stove, and shelves lined with dried flowers and roots.

One of the girls closed the door behind them with a soft creak. For a moment, no one spoke. They all just stood there, staring at each other, with unspoken questions and shared pain.

The girls guided Reagan to a low, rough-hewn table in the center of the room. A dim lantern, cracked but still functional sat on the table, casting light over their worn faces.

Reagan lowered herself to the bench slowly, her exhaustion and nerves spilling into trembling hands that she kept tightly folded in her lap.

Across from her, the three girls sat, their gazes sharp with curiosity and a hint of sadness.

Reagan's eyes scanned the girls before her. Each carrying their own story like a stone tied to their hearts.

The air in the shack was still, as if even the walls held their breath, waiting.

The first to break the silence was the girl who had led Reagan inside.

Calla.

Tall and sharp-featured, with long brown hair. Her eyes, amber and fierce. She carried an air of quiet strength.

Calla had been just a child when the druid king came for her. Nine years old, living on the outskirts of a once-thriving village. She spent her days running barefoot through the meadows and climbing trees with her brothers. She was wild and free. Her world untouched by the dark politics that loomed over the land.

But that peace shattered the day Zarriq arrived.

He came without warning, astride a black mare that seemed to blend with the shadows. His eyes swept over the village like a hawk searching for prey. When they landed on Calla, he smiled. A cruel, calculating twist of his lips.

He declared her a "perfect match" for the young prince. But her purpose was not what one might expect for a girl her age. She was meant to be a companion, a friend to his son, who had lived most of his life isolated in the castle, with no one to connect to.

The prince, cursed at such a young age, was plagued with strange magic that kept him alone in a world of silence and sorrow.

The druid king had no intention of giving up the throne to his son. He had no intention of letting the prince inherit the weight of the crown, especially with the curse hanging over him. But a playmate, someone to share his son's lonely world with, that was something Zarriq could offer.

To Calla's parents, the druid king offered things no one could turn down. Riches beyond measure, fertile crops that could grow in the harshest of winters and droughts, and power that would elevate their status. The offer was too good to resist, and they gave their daughter away with hopes for a future filled with prosperity.

Her parents, caught between awe and fear, did not dare refuse. Zarriq made it sound like an honor, a gift, but Calla soon learned the truth.

In the castle, she was expected to amuse Prince Martouf. They played games, simple at first. He'd show her his favorite toys and she would smile, pretending to enjoy herself, though her heart ached for home.

Until one moon they were racing each other through the halls. Martouf chased her, but when he repeatedly couldn't catch up to her speed, he wailed.

Zarriq appeared moments later. He didn't speak right away, just shook his head slowly. Then lifted his hand and wagged a single finger back and forth, clicking his tongue in that same rhythm. Tsk tsk tsk. His gaze burned through her, not with rage, but with disappointment. He gave her a cold, calculating stare, like she'd failed some unspoken test.
"Disrespect."

He picked up Martouf, and turned his back on her, already walking away. Done with her. With a flick of his wrist over his shoulder, he sent back a pulse of magic, wrapping around Calla and transporting her to the farthest edge of the realm.

She was too young to understand it fully then. The years hardened her, taught her how to survive. Now, her eyes held a determination forged in suffering.

Evra was smaller than the others, with freckles dusting her pale skin and auburn hair tied back in a loose braid. Her eyes, wide and bright, gave the impression of someone who had once been endlessly curious, but now saw too much of the world's cruelty. She leaned across to hold Reagan's hand.

Evra was from a family of noble stature, and a long line of refined lineage.

For the druid king, such qualities were paramount in his search for Martouf's next companion. They had lived quite well in a coastal village. Her mother wove tales that could make even the stormiest of nights feel warm. Evra grew up surrounded by imagination and hope. He saw Evra's beauty and claimed her for Martouf.

Her parents were thrilled, as they had already been scouting potential suitors in town. They saw the offer of marriage to a prince as an unparalleled opportunity.

When Zarriq arrived with promises of wealth and prosperity, they eagerly accepted. The increased wealth would elevate their noble status, expand their land holdings, and assist in arranging more prestigious marriages for their other children. He paid them handsomely, more than they could have dreamed, effectively sealing the arrangement.

For Evra, the prospect of becoming a princess was a dream come true, and she was whisked away with grand visions of her future in the royal court.

At thirteen, Evra was taken to the Balderon, unprepared for what lay ahead. When she first saw Martouf, she gasped. Not from fear, but surprise. He looked nothing like the noble figures she had imagined, and nothing like his father, Zarriq. Martouf was broader. Taller. Horns crowned his brow.

The sound of her gasp echoed too loudly in the grand hall. Zarriq, standing nearby, didn't ask for an explanation. He assumed disgust and passed judgment in the same breath.

Before she could utter a single word in her defense, she was surrounded by magic, searing and soundless, and a flash of blinding light. When it faded she was surrounded by a vast swamp. Decay stretched around her in every direction.

Now, her eyes held an old sorrow. She had lived with the weight of misunderstanding for too long, and it had carved lines into her soul. Her words carried the depth of a hundred unspoken stories.

Then, there was Sorrel, the last of the trio. She sat apart from the others, her posture rigid and her expression unreadable. She had long blonde hair. Her blue eyes, sharp and wary, flickered toward Reagan but never stayed long enough to invite conversation. Sorrel was like a closed book, its pages bound too tightly to reveal its secrets.

Her story was the most recent of the three.

At sixteen, Sorrel had been chosen because she was "practical". A trait the druid king valued above all else this time.

She hailed from a mountain village, known for its hunters and survivalists.

Sorrel could track a fox through snow without leaving a trace, and build a fire with nothing but frostbitten twigs and a flint scraped raw.

The druid king took her not because she was beautiful, but because she was agreeable. He believed Martouf needed someone who would endure without complaint. Someone who understood the situation in its entirety beforehand and was willing to participate.

Her first dinner at the castle was also her last. Not because she was disrespectful, and not because she passed judgment. In fact, she was very polite, very respectful to Zarriq, Martouf, and all the castle staff.

The problem was her silence.

At dinner, she stared at her food, stared across the room. Every once in a while, she'd glance at them and smile, then take a bite and chew while looking away.

The silence stretched too long. It was awkward and uncomfortable. Zarriq, ever watchful, deemed her unsuitable.

She disappeared from her chair before the meal ended.

Sorrel still hasn't forgiven herself for that night.

Now, the three girls sat in the shack, survivors of the druid king's cruelty.

Reagan saw her own pain reflected in their eyes, and for the first time, she understood that she wasn't alone in her suffering.

But understanding didn't bring comfort. It only deepened her resolve.

PIP
How was your meeting with The Entities of
Mild Concerns and Strong Opinions? I told you
filing that complaint was a good idea! What did
they divulge?

YSMERRA
The usual cosmic rubbish. Apparently Kayleth is destined
to prevent or lead some future war of global magnitude.
Save the toddler, save the timeline. I stopped listening. It
was all sanctimonious drivel... Anyway. What did I miss?

PIP
Reagan stumbles upon a hut with three forest girls who
act like they just stepped off the set of *The Craft*. It was
like a coming-of-age horror novella meets trauma
bonding. Valla and Arithel, just had their brains
scrambled like mystical eggs, courtesy of our king
druid daddy Zarriq. They're wandering into rooms,
and questioning the furniture. It's giving: 'We forgot
our child and replaced them with throw pillows.'

YSMERRA
...That can't be right. Why do I feel like
your interpretation of events is so dazzling
wrong. Either way, I lack the stamina to
correct it. Turn the mirror back on.

Welcome back, boils and ghouls. Tonight's tragic tale is brought to you by suspicious memory loss, and enough swamp aesthetic to make Shrek weep into his mud bath. Stay tuned because someone's going to lie, someone's going to cry, and someone's definitely going to eat a mystical mushroom they shouldn't. Back to the show my little night creepers...

YSMERRA
You added The Mistress of Midnight commentary to my scrying mirror!?... Ahhh that actually explains your upside-down theatrical retelling of events. Turn her off!

PIP
I like her. Or we could change the commentary to an enchanted turnip with a flair for drama. He's really good too.

YSMERRA
Fine. Let the vegetable narrate.

PIP
I think you're really gonna like him. He does voice overs.

CHAPTER 20
The Warning

Silence hung heavy over the table. Steam curling from their untouched mugs. Until Calla spoke again. She leaned forward just slightly, her voice low and comforting.
"Tell us your story, Reagan. How did you end up here?"

Reagan's gaze dropped. Her hands fidgeted in her lap beneath the table. The memories surged. Shards of broken glamour, lies spoken with syrup cruelty, and the wrenching disappearance of her brother. She spoke haltingly at first, but the weight lifted with each word, and the girls listened in tense silence.

Calla's expression twisted, her brows drew together in a subtle crease as if something sour had touched her tongue. She tilted her head a fraction, like trying to hear past the words, trying to make sense of a truth too cruel to grasp. She sat back slowly, as if what she'd just heard had physically struck her chest. Her words dragged out, thick with disbelief.
"A glamour spell? He put you under a glamour? That's… horrible. You must have felt like you didn't even know who you were."

Reagan pressed her lips together and looked away. She couldn't meet their gaze, didn't want to see the horrified looks on their faces. She slightly shrugged her shoulders.
"I didn't... Now I'm just trying to find my way back, to find my brother."

Calla shook her head grimly, the words leaving her mouth were dripping with sympathy.
"None of us were put under a spell like you."

Each of their faces were filled with sorrow and regret, each of them held captive by memories they could never change.

Evra's expression etched with quiet empathy. With the slow, fluid grace she always carried, she leaned forward, elbows resting lightly on the table and reached across the wood to gently take Reagan's hand. Her fingers were warm and steady, a silent tether in the storm.

Evra's voice was soft, every word wrapped in comfort.

"None of this was your fault."

The dim shelter they now called home wasn't much, just scavenged comforts patched together, and fragile peace, but it was *theirs*. The kind of quiet life you cobble together when everything else has been torn away. They made a life for themselves there. It wasn't much, but they found small things to hold on to.

The offer was there—a place to stay. A chance to stop running. A small space in their quiet world carved just wide enough for one more soul.

Reagan straightened. Spine rigid with determination. Her chest rose once, deep and steady. Then she met Calla's eyes, gaze unwavering. She leaned forward slightly, as if that truth anchored her. She spoke urgently almost franticly but her voice didn't shake, it rang with clarity.
"I have to go back. I have to find my brother."

The girls exchanged uneasy glances, but it wasn't just uncertainty that passed between them. It was something heavier. Unspoken. And they were waiting for someone else to say it aloud.

No one did.

Reagan shifted slightly, suddenly aware of how still the room had become. She could feel it, the tension, the weight of some knowledge she didn't yet understand. The silence stretched too long, and no one looked at her.

Calla's eyes locked with Evra's. Then Sorrel's.

A silent conversation passed between them, quick and loaded. Still, no one volunteered the words.
Finally, Calla let out a sigh of surrender. Slow and strained. She didn't look at Reagan right away. Instead, she stared at the crack between two floorboards.

When Calla finally did speak, her tone was filled with dread.
"Reagan… the lands beyond here are just too dangerous… They're cursed."

The room fell silent.

Sorrel understood Reagan's longing, she recognized it all too well. But she also knew, from bitter experience, just how dangerous that longing could be.

She had tried once, too. Even someone like her, a hunter, a survivalist, someone who could read the land like a map, had barely escaped. Even she hadn't come back untouched.

For someone who rarely spoke, she knew this was the moment she had to. What she had been through wasn't just memory, it was a warning. One Reagan needed to hear before it was too late.

Sorrel didn't look at Reagan when she spoke. Her gaze remained fixed on the chipped rim of her tin cup. Her voice came low and firm, each word drawn from a place carved deep by memory. There was no drama to it, no embellishment. Just truth. Beneath the even tone was rage and fear that had dried into something harder.
"The magic out there festers. It warps everything it touches. Villages where people no longer wear their own faces. Towns where time coils back on itself. The ground breathes beneath your feet. Doors lead nowhere, and roads bring you back to where you started no matter how far you walk... I barely made it back alive."

Evra's eyes shimmered with fear. She lifted one of her trembling hands to her mouth, fingers curling against her lips, like she was trying to keep the words from spilling out. When she finally did speak, her voice cracked.
"We can't go with you, Reagan. We just... can't."

Her other hand still clutched Reagan's. Her grip tightening with quiet urgency
"Stay with us. It's not safe out there."

Reagan hesitated, just for a moment. She looked down at their hands, Evra's thumb brushing softly over Reagan's fingers. Reagan pulled her hand back gently and shook her head with an unyielding steadiness. The kind of resolve that couldn't be talked down.
"I have to try. He's my brother."

Reagan's resolve left no room for persuasion. And that truth settled like dust across the room.

No one argued with her. No one tried to change her mind. But they were filled with unspoken fears, heavy with the ache of things they wanted to say but couldn't, because deep down they knew they wouldn't reach her.

Calla's last flicker of resistance slipping away. She gave a slow nod, understanding etched into her face. It wasn't surrender. It was all they could offer, one final act of support.
"At least stay the night. Rest. You'll need your strength."

Reagan nodded, her throat too tight to speak. Despite their fear, they were offering her what little comfort they could, and she was grateful beyond words.

That night, the girls prepared a sleeping area for Reagan. It was a simple pile of hay and rags, softened with an old woven quilt. It was only one they had, and they took turns using it.

Reagan laid down, staring at the thin beams of moonlight cutting through the gaps in the walls. Sleep evaded her.

Her mind spiraled. Her thoughts ran dark and frantic. Survival felt uncertain and slipping further with each breath.

And worse, that she might never get to Kayleth, no matter how hard she tried.

Around her, the girls were all haunted by the same unspoken dread.

They slept in uneasy silence that came in fits. Restless and shallow.

When they woke, the goodbye hovered, unspoken, but already present in the way they avoided each other's eyes, and the hush between them.

They packed a satchel for Reagan, filled with bread, roots, and a flask of water. It wasn't much, but it was all they had to give.

When the time came to say goodbye, the girls gathered by the shack's door.

Sorrel stepped forward first. She handed Reagan the satchel with food and water.

"There's food and water in there. That should last you a few nights... I made the satchel. Took me five nights... I want you to have it. You'll have something to remember us by."

The satchel was simple but beautifully crafted. The outer layer was made of tightly woven swamp reeds. Tiny, decorative knots ran along the edges. The strap was braided from wild vine, softened bark, and a strip of fabric from Sorrel's old dress. It was worn from years of use, but still sturdy.

Reagan half smiled as she ran her fingers over the satchel's surface, tracing the careful knots and stitches. Tears slid down her cheeks, but she wiped them away quickly, not wanting to make things harder. Her voice was breaking as spoke.
"I'll treasure it forever."

Sorrel's eyes brimmed with tears that clung stubbornly to the edges. She wrapped her arms tightly around Reagan. Hugging her much longer than she intended. She whispered.
"Be careful."

And stepped back. Reagan looked at her and nodded.

Evra stepped forward next. Her noble demeanor never faltered, but her hands trembled as she clutched Reagan's.
"May you find your way back to your brother."

She stood on her toes to reach, her arms curling around Reagan's shoulders in a hug that felt both too small and impossibly big—all heart, all hope, all fear tucked into that brief, trembling embrace.

Finally, Calla approached. She rested a hand on Reagan's shoulder, her eyes filled with a mix of sorrow and determination. She said low enough to hide the hurt.
"Good luck."

She gathered Reagan into her arms, not rushed. Steady and warm, an anchor in the storm. Placing her hand on the back of Reagan's head meant to pass strength from one soul into another.

Then Evra and Sorrel moved in quietly, wrapping their arms around them both, reluctant to let go of the fragile bond they had formed.

As Reagan turned toward the gravel path, she heard stifled sobs behind her. She didn't dare look back. If she did, she knew she wouldn't be able to leave. Instead, she held the satchel tighter to her chest, took a deep breath, and forced herself to keep walking, each step heavier than the last.

Evra collapsed against Calla's chest, trembling. Heart-wrenching sobs broke free. Her cries echoed through the valley.

Reagan heard it and her heart splintered with every sniffle.

The girls stood at the doorway, watching Reagan walk away, until she disappeared beyond the hills.

After Reagan disappeared from view, the girls lingered on the doorstep for a long time, staring down the gravel path as if hoping she might turn back.

But she didn't.

Eventually, they returned to the shack, their steps slow and reluctant, heavy with the weight of parting. Each of them holding on to a single hope, a quiet prayer that, somehow, she would make it there alive, and find her brother.

Calla sat near the small window, gazing out, lost in thought.

Sorrel stayed busy making another satchel.

Evra clutched the blanket Reagan had used the night before.

The quiet between them stretched unbroken until the next night.

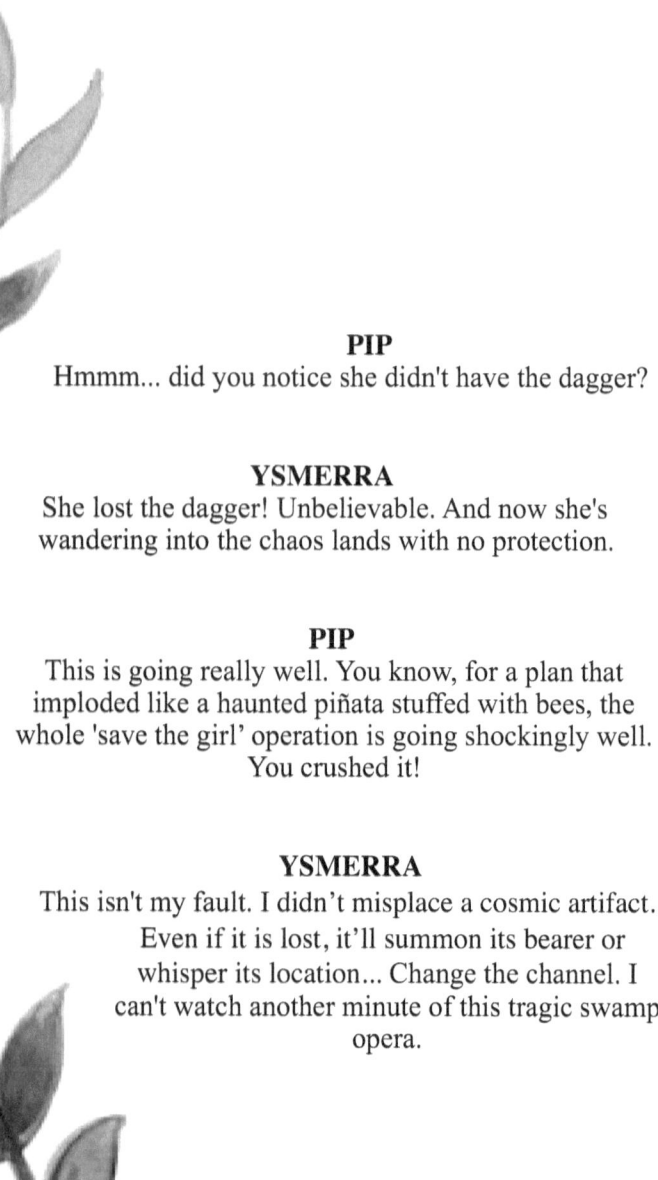

PIP

Hmmm... did you notice she didn't have the dagger?

YSMERRA

She lost the dagger! Unbelievable. And now she's wandering into the chaos lands with no protection.

PIP

This is going really well. You know, for a plan that imploded like a haunted piñata stuffed with bees, the whole 'save the girl' operation is going shockingly well. You crushed it!

YSMERRA

This isn't my fault. I didn't misplace a cosmic artifact. Even if it is lost, it'll summon its bearer or whisper its location... Change the channel. I can't watch another minute of this tragic swamp opera.

PIP

Losing a mystical weapon of destiny happens to the
best of us. Maybe it ditched her. You know how
enchanted weapons can be. Moody little buggers. Unless
the dagger *wanted* to get lost. Maybe it's on a journey of
self-discovery. A little dagger sabbatical.

YSMERRA

Stop flailing your aura about like a startled pixie. Can you
not sense the mood of the chamber? The air in here is
humming with displeasure!

PIP

Was that dagger the one that vibrates when it's near
betrayal or am I thinking of the cursed ladle…?

YSMERRA

No, that's your toothbrush... Actually come to
think of it, the dagger does that too. It's
sentient. Temperamental. Bonding with it
unlocks its secrets. Otherwise, it just glows
near forbidden bloodlines and warps time
when offended.

CHAPTER 21
The Hollow

A month had passed since Reagan left the shack behind, but it felt like years. The chaos territories had twisted her path in endless circles. It stole days, even weeks, dragging her along like a river running against itself and leaving her with no memory of how she'd even gotten there.

Her body ached from being dragged through terrain that fought back. Her feet were blistered from being hunted. Her dress was stiff with dried blood and dirt. She could barely remember what it felt like to be clean, safe, or still.

Most of the inhabitants in the chaos lands were not people anymore. They were something else. Some terrifying. Some trapped. Some lost.

Eel-like creatures coiled around peoples spines, whispering in their ears, puppeting their every move. Others were skeletons in robes that floated inches above the ground, every skull turning as she passed. Some, their minds were wrecked and muddled. Speaking nonsense or not at all.

The land took from her constantly. Her voice, when she tried to scream. Her sight, when she needed it most.

She hadn't had a decent night's sleep in weeks. The vines that once cradled her started strangling her. Shadows sprang to life and attacked her like she was trespassing. The faceless beings she'd encountered chased her through every dream. Arms outstretched and trying to grab her. Tall, antlered creatures rode past on horses, wearing those stolen faces like ceremonial masks.

And yet, she talked to her mom and dad every night, like a prayer. Keeping their spirit alive, and her hope strong.

It took everything she had just to keep moving. Because if she stopped, the chaos of this place would swallow her whole.

The chaos never stopped, only changed its scenery. And now, it had led her here, where the air was thick and foggy, suffocating with the scent of flowers.

Surrounding her was a lush meadow, overgrown with vines, towering shrubs, and flowers. Everything seemed alive and watching her.

Reagan was trying to find her way out when a sudden cry shattered the eerie stillness.

"Mommy! Mommy, where are you?!"

Barely visible beneath the fog, at the end of the winding path, a little girl stood in a white dress with a pink bow in the back, tears streaking down her face. She couldn't have been more than six or seven.

A strange, silent urgency inside Reagan flipped on. She stepped forward without thinking, and shouted to the girl before her brain had caught up.
"Hey! Are you okay? Do you need help?"

The little girl darted around the corner, vanishing behind the tall shrubs that lined the narrow trail.

Reagan bolted after her, but just as she thought she was closing the distance, long flowered vines lashed out across the path, tripping her. Reagan hit the ground hard, scraping her palms on the rough soil.

The little girl had stopped ahead on the trail and looked back.

Reagan scrambled to her feet, ignoring the sting of the cuts. She called out.
"I didn't mean to scare you. It's okay. I can help you."

Reagan walked toward the girl, following her deeper into the root-maze. As soon as Reagan got within ten feet, the girl dashed around another corner. Reagan rounded it, but a tree's branch swung down like an arm, slapping her across the face and chest. She staggered backward, dazed.

The Hollow didn't want her catching up to the girl.

It happened again and again. Every time Reagan got close, the Hollow found a new way to block her. Vines snared around her ankles. Shrubs closed in like walls.

She stumbled into a small clearing, with narrow paths leading off in every direction. She turned in a slow circle, trying to make sense of the winding paths. The girl was nowhere in sight.

An older gentleman in a threadbare suit sat at a small wrought iron table, sipping from a delicate china teacup. The table was neatly set with a teapot, and a three tiered serving tray filled with decadent delicacies like he had all the time in the world.

Behind him, barely visible through the mist and trees, stood a crooked old house. Its windows were dark and vines curled up the stone walls like claws.

Reagan almost didn't look at him. Thinking he was just another grumpy old man, the kind who yelled at kids for breathing too loud. She veered slightly, planning to pass without a word.

The gentleman's eyes were tired, but there was something sharp and calculating behind them. Like they'd been staring too long at something no one else could see.

He didn't look at her. Just sipped his tea, eyes half-lidded like he was commenting on the weather.
"You won't catch her."

Reagan froze mid-step. Not sure if she'd heard him right. Not sure if the words were meant for her, and if they were, what an odd thing to say. She cautiously asked.
"What? What do you mean?"

The old man stared into his teacup for a long moment before answering.
"That little girl...She's not real."

Still holding his cup close to his mouth. His eyes darted around the surroundings.
"None of this is. It's all a trick."

Reagan looked at him. Really looked at him. Her eyebrows burrowed. Taking in what he said.

Her eyes moved toward the edge of the clearing, where she saw a flicker of white fabric just between the trees. The little girl was there, walking down the path. The pink bow on the back of her dress bobbed with each step. Reagan's eyes darted back to the old man.

"A trick?"

His lips didn't move at first. Like he was contemplating his words. Then they just slightly twitched, like he'd seen this all before but was hesitant to admit it.
"This place...it plays with your mind."

His voice wasn't cruel. Just tired. Like someone who had already chased ghosts for too long. He set the teacup down with care. The china clinking softly against the iron tabletop. His fingers lingered on the rim.
"Pulls from your memories, your regrets, your fears. It shows you what you want, or what you think you've lost. And it keeps you chasing it... The longer you see the apparitions, the longer you spend chasing them, the more you believe they're real. The more you forget they were ever once gone."

She gave him a look sharp with confusion. Her eyes slowly flicking from his face to the trees, searching for something to anchor his meaning.

The old man laughed loudly, cackling like dry leaves underfoot. His head tipped back as if the joke were too good to hold in.
"Don't you see... you're chasing yourself. That's you!... Look closely."

Reagan hesitated, her feet rooted in place as dread dripped down her back, slow as poison. Slowly, she stepped toward the tree line. Through the shifting fog, the little girl on the trail stopped and turned around.

Then Reagan saw the little girls face.

It was her *own* face! Younger. Tear-streaked. Eyes wide and terrified.

Reagan staggered backward, shaking her head, and whispered.
"No...That's impossible."

The old gentleman didn't flinch. He didn't even look up. He simply lifted his teacup again and took another calm sip, as if none of it surprised him.

Before Reagan could gather her thoughts, a figure emerged from a different path. A man with wild eyes and a bloodless face, dressed in formal foppish finery. His clothes looked like they belonged in another century.

He walked towards her, one hand clutching his top hat to his chest, the other tapping her shoulder. His hand shaking in his fingerless gloves.
"Have you seen my brother? He just walked by here. He was just here a moment ago!"

Reagan's entire body tensed. Something about the man's presence itched beneath her skin. His desperation was real, but wrong. There was a strange hollowness behind his eyes, like whatever made him human had long since been scraped away.

She took a slow nervous step back.
"No... I haven't."

He let out a frustrated sigh, then turned and wandered past them without another word, disappearing into one of the paths like he'd never been there at all.

The old gentleman tilted his head slightly as he watched the man go. Then he looked back at Reagan with a tired smirk, and leaned in like he was reveling a huge secret.
"He's been searching for this brother for fifteen years... This kind of stuff happens all the time around here."

Reagan's stomach twisted. *Fifteen years.* That could've been her. Wandering forever after some phantom child. How easily she'd slipped into the trance, following the hallucination.

Her heart dropped. The Hollow hadn't just lured her in. It had nearly *kept* her. If that old man hadn't spoken... if she'd gone just a few steps further...

She glanced at the old man. Her mind now scrambling to understand why this unsettlingly calm, tea-drinking relic isn't affected. Her voice was uneasy, almost accusatory.
"Why hasn't the Hollow entranced you?"

The old gentleman let out a loud deep, throaty chuckle, hoarse with time, like embers in a dying fire. Then shrugged his shoulders as if the question was silly. Preposterous even.
"I have no one to search for."

His laugh lingered. Then, with a kind of soft, haunting grace, he turned toward the empty chair beside him, lifted the teapot, and spoke as if someone invisible was seated there.
"More tea, darling?"

He poured the tea into the other empty cup on the table, and tilted his head as if listening to something, or *someone.*

And then, he laughed. His laugh was so deep, so phlegmy and so unnerving. Each cackle rattled in the back of his throat.

Reagan's blood turned cold. She stepped back, slowly. She didn't wait for him to say anything else. She turned and walked away from the clearing, not stopping until the old man, his table and invisible friend were far behind her.

The Hollow didn't let her go that easily.

The path ahead twisted violently, roots snaked across the ground trying to trip her. Hedges shifted, blocking the trail, forcing her down another path.

It was guiding her. Herding her.

Then came the voices. Soft voices echoing behind her. A little girl's sob. Her mother's voice calling her name. The sound of her brother's laugh. But she didn't stop.

Flowering vines reached across her shoulders as if to embrace her. She struck them aside with the back of her hand.

In front of her, the fog thickened and pressed in from every side. Shapes shifted inside it. The fog parted just enough to see a figure step out.

Her little brother, Kayleth.

Smiling. Holding out his arms like he'd just found her.
"Reagan…"

His voice. His face. Perfect. Too perfect.

Everything in her screamed. Her throat clenched. She grit her teeth and pushed forward. She closed her eyes and walked right through him. He dissolved like smoke.

She kept walking, heart hammering, mind locked like a vault. Calm and focused, ignoring the rustling plants and distant cries that tried to lure her back.

She refused to play along. Refused to look back.

Eventually, the Hollow relented. The vines recoiled. The fog thinned.

And slowly, almost reluctantly, the path began to straighten before her, just enough to let her pass through.

Since the first night Reagan arrived in Balderon, she spoke to her parents before she went to sleep every night. Like a prayer.

She didn't know her ether magic had carried those whispers across realms, threading them directly into her parents' dreams.

Actual telepathic messages. Vivid and haunting.

The dreams always woke Valla with a fright, and the girl's voice clung to her like perfume. A girl with dark hair and bright eyes, searching for Kayleth.

That name sounded achingly familiar. Being lost and alone. The words never quite made sense. Though they never changed.

Always the same tone. Always the same urgency.

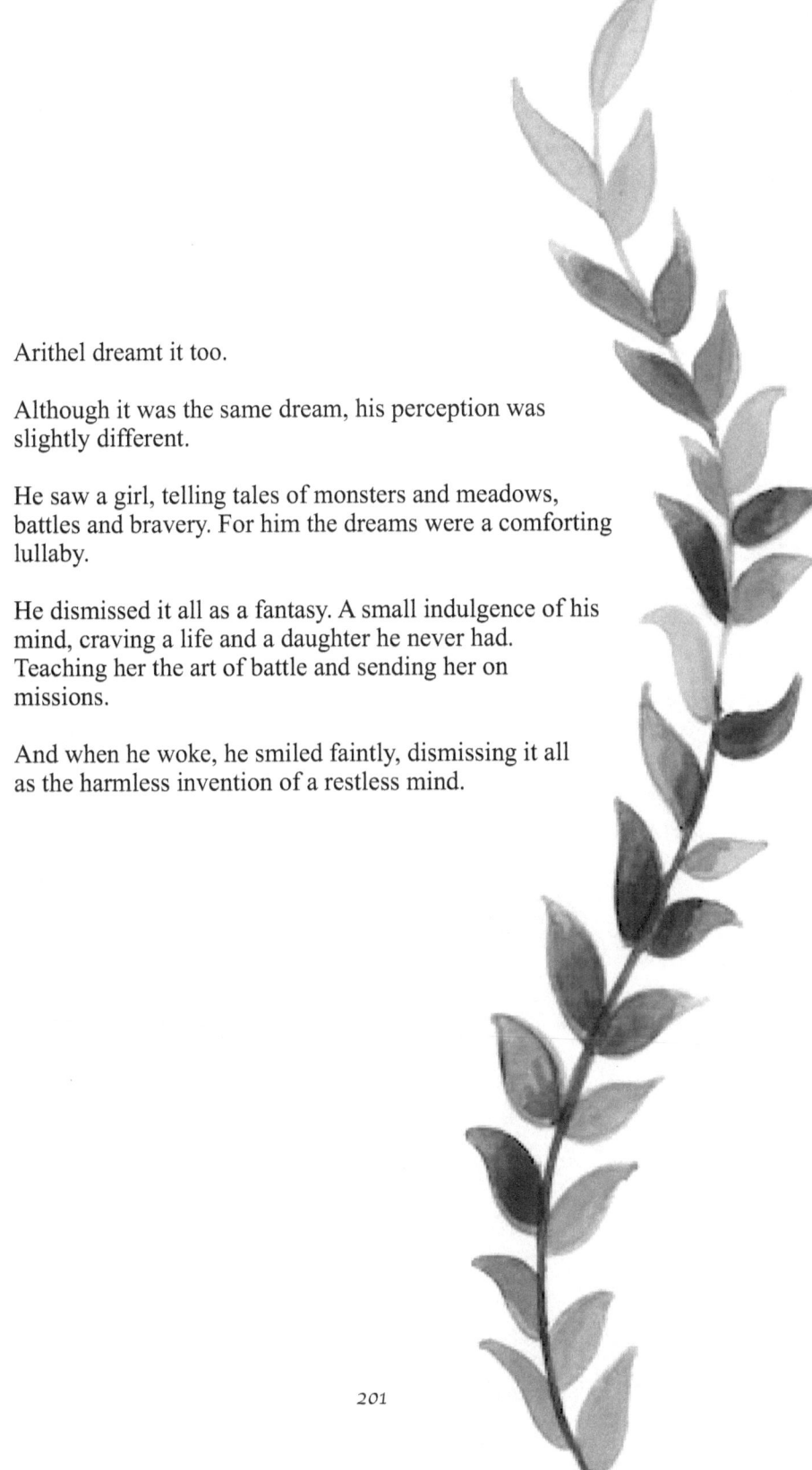

Arithel dreamt it too.

Although it was the same dream, his perception was slightly different.

He saw a girl, telling tales of monsters and meadows, battles and bravery. For him the dreams were a comforting lullaby.

He dismissed it all as a fantasy. A small indulgence of his mind, craving a life and a daughter he never had. Teaching her the art of battle and sending her on missions.

And when he woke, he smiled faintly, dismissing it all as the harmless invention of a restless mind.

CHAPTER 22
The Lagoon

Reagan stood at the edge of the foggy meadow, her feet crunching lightly on mossy roots as she stepped through a break in the trees. The forest suddenly parted, revealing a lagoon nestled like a secret.

The lagoon shimmered beneath pale moonlight, still and impossibly smooth. So clear it looked like stretched glass.

She narrowed her eyes. She didn't trust it.

Nothing this beautiful came without teeth. In the Chaos Lands, even beauty had a body count. Blossoms screamed, vines slithered, and seemingly lifeless stones would open eyes and lunge. Stillness was often a lie. Tranquility, a trap.

She would not be fooled by mirrors and moonlight. Her shoulders stayed rigid, every nerve prickling with suspicion. If this lagoon was alive, it was meant to lure her in.

She crouched low, snatching a smooth stone from the ground. Her fingers curled tight around it as her voice rang out, slicing through the hush.
"Come out from hiding, beast!"

She hurled a stone at the water with force. It skipped once. Twice. Then sank beneath the surface with a soft *plunk.*

She grabbed another rock and flung it at a nearby tree.

Nothing stirred. No angry faces in the bark. No vines shifting like snakes. Just the rustle of leaves and the hum of night.

She called into the clearing, her voice cutting through the calm.
"Hello?"

It echoed faintly off the lagoon's surface… and faded.

No answer.

She exhaled slowly, the tension in her shoulders loosening like a knot finally untied.

Kneeling by the water, she dipped her fingers in. Cool, clean and splashed her face. It felt so nice against her skin, startling in its clarity. It felt real.

The dried blood and grime clinging to her arms begged to be scrubbed away. She peeled off her tattered gown, dunked it in the water, and scrubbed furiously at the stains. Her fingers worked with quiet determination, wringing and dragging the fabric across stones until the worst of it faded.

When it was as clean as she could manage, she wrung it out and hung it over a low-hanging branch nearby.

She walked back to the lagoon and stepped in. Letting it greet her ankles, cool and velvety. It rose slowly past her shins, silk-wrapping her legs as she waded deeper. The thin fabric of her slip dress clung to her like a second skin, each step a quiet surrender to the stillness around her. She moved deeper, letting it swallow her until she was neck-deep.

Her gaze swept the shoreline.

Nothing. Just trees. Mist. Moonlight.

Still alert, she submerged herself for a moment, then quickly surfaced again, scanning the clearing.

Nothing. Another minute passed. Then another.

Finally, she let herself go. She leaned back, surrendering her weight to the stillness. Allowing the water to cradle her. She closed her eyes. Relaxed. Let her breath slow down.

Peace. A rare and precious peace.

Until a voice shattered it.

Smug. Teasing. Young.
"Will you be needing this?"

Her eyes snapped open.

In an instant, she surged upright. The water sloshed around her as she found her footing. Scanning the shoreline. Eyes sharp. Breath caught. Every instinct, ready.

At the edge of the lagoon stood a figure, roughly her age. He had dark hair, and a grin that was a little too pleased with itself.

His foot was propped up on a rock, extending his sword out before him in mock display. Her gown dangling from the edge of it. He twirled it once, the fabric fluttering in the moonlight.

Reagan held still in the water, muscles tense beneath the surface. Watching him with cold precision. Calculating. Assessing. When she spoke, her voice was sharp and commanding.
"Give. That. Back."

He waved his sword lazily in the air. Grinning like this was the most fun he'd had all week. The dress flowing with every movement.
"I think I'll keep it. Looks about my size."

He took the dress off the edge of the sword and held it up to his shoulders, allowing the dress to fall in front of him. Tilting his head as if genuinely considering the fit. With mock seriousness, he looked up, smiling faintly.
"What do you think?"

Reagan's expression ignited into something primal. Her body lowered just slightly, a subtle shift that promised violence. She glided towards him, cutting through the water like a snake slithering through tall grass. Silent. Inevitable.

Her gaze locked on his with a quiet fury. Every stroke brought her closer.

Her voice was low and lethal, barely containing the storm.
"Last. Warning."

He laughed. It was a short, boyish chuckle. Like he had no idea how close he was to regret.

The moment Reagan's feet touched the grass, she surged forward. In the blink of an eye her hand clamped around his wrist. With a sharp turn she twisted his arm, the sword slipped free. In the same motion, she pivoted low, hooked her leg around his, and flipped him clean over her shoulder in a seamless arc.

He landed with a thud, flat on his back in the soft grass. The gown was already in her hand, her foot pressed firmly on his chest, and the sword angled clean and sharp at his throat.

He looked up at her, mouth parted in amazement. Dazzled and wide-eyed.
"Wow! Where did you learn to do that?"

Reagan studied him for a moment. Assessing his threat level. *No tension in his limbs. Lean. Eyes not scanning, not calculating his next move. Just surprise. Cute. Very cute. Harmless... Amateur.*

She held his gaze a second longer then lowered the sword.
Stepped back and tossed the gown over her shoulder.
"What? Don't girls in your land know how to fight?"

He slowly stood, brushing off the dirt from his pants and casting a grin at her. His eyes still held that wide, stunned admiration, like he hadn't expected someone her size to drop him like a stone. "Not like that. Sure, the ogres have super strength, but they don't know tricks like that."

Reagan gave a small, triumphant smile and turned slightly, tossing her wet hair off her shoulder.

A long pause settled between them, neither one quite sure who should speak first.

Finally, he offered, "I'm Baylos."

She confidently flipped the sword in reverse, catching it by the blade, and handed it back him. Respectful in form, but the message was clear. That she could wield it better than he ever would.

She looked up him. Calm. Unapologetic. "Reagan."

They settled on a flat rock near the lagoon's edge, just within reach of the soft breeze drifting across the water. Reagan's gown hung nearby on a low branch, swaying slightly in the night air.

As the moon climbed higher in the forever-night sky, they traded stories in low voices, like they didn't want to disturb the peace the lagoon offered.

Reagan spoke of the Druid King, the curse, and the long, twisted path that had brought her here. Skimming over the worst parts, but never hiding the weight of them.

Baylos listened closely. His gaze lingered on her between words, watching her expressions and how her hands moved while she talked. He didn't interrupt, just listened, like every word mattered. He recognized the way grief lived behind her eyes.

When he finally spoke, his voice was softer, worn. He explained how he had been wandering the land alone since the war, having lost his family in its aftermath. He didn't offer details and Reagan didn't ask for them.

Baylos stood and wandered toward the lagoon, trailing a hand along the mossy bark of a nearby tree. He paused at the edge, staring out over the water.

Reagan tilted her head, watching him. She understood him. That kind of solitude left marks no one could see. It took a second for his words to settle in. She replayed them silently, piecing together fragments, trying to make sense of it. The weight of what he said hitting her in layers. Confusion. Sympathy.

She responded with softness beneath her curiosity.
"So... you've been out here by yourself? This whole time?"

He didn't answer right away. He nodded. His gaze still fixed on the moonlit surface of the lagoon.
"For a while. Yeah."

His words silenced them both. Not out of discomfort, but in quiet acknowledgment. Neither felt the need to speak right away. Like a river easing around a bend.

He reached up and grabbed a low branch overhead, his hand curling around it as he stretched. He was quiet, caught in something. Debating with himself, weighing risks and regrets.

Then, without looking at her, he spoke.

"I know every tree and shadow for miles. I can help you get through this part of the forest, and the next few towns."

Reagan tilted her head slightly. Studying him. There was something else. She could see it in the slow rise and fall of his chest. The tension in his jaw. Her eyes narrowed, not suspicious, just searching. "What about beyond that?"

His gaze dropped as he faced her, the branch still in his hand like an anchor. He shook his head. His eyes lifting to hers, not defensive, just honest. His voice was low and calm, but the truth behind it wasn't small.
"It's too dangerous. Even I'm not that brave."

The Chaos Lands were already horrific. For there to be a part even he wouldn't touch. She didn't know if that meant he hadn't ventured as far as she had, or if beyond this was even more horrific than everything she'd survived.

She didn't press him, but she saw it. Something deep and heavy flashed across his face at the mention of what lay beyond.
Not fear exactly, but something worse. A memory he kept buried behind the jokes and charm.

And that was what unsettled her most.

Whatever the truth was, she didn't ask. She took his word for it. Whatever he saw... it was enough. Enough to keep him rooted here, never pushing farther. And even though it wouldn't stop her, she respected the line he'd drawn.

There was a long pause. Then, he let go of the branch. He set down the weight of that memory and stepped back into the present.

He turned toward her again, this time fully, with a grin tugging at his mouth. He pointed at her and said,
"And you can show me some cool fight moves."

Reagan gave a faint smile, just enough to meet his in kind. A quiet truce between two people who had both seen too much.

Baylos stepped closer, closing the space between them. He held out his hand as he met her gaze.
"Deal?"

Relief surged through her. Company. Help. Someone else to carry the silence. The constant edge she'd been walking dulled quite a bit. But none of it showed.

Not in her voice. Not in her posture. Not even in her eyes.

She played it off like she was the one doing him a favor.
Like sure, if you really want to tag along... but deep down, she would've said yes a hundred times over.

She reached forward and shook his hand firmly. Calm and composed. Not a flicker of enthusiasm showing on her face.
"Deal."

They worked side by side to set up camp, stringing up their hammocks between the trees. No words, just the comfort of shared purpose.

Baylos stretched out in his hammock, resting one arm behind his head, his eyes drifting toward the lagoon.

Reagan climbed into her hammock and let her head fall back. The soft rustling of leaves filled the silence, mingling with the distant murmur of waterfalls. Stars twinkling faintly behind drifting clouds above her.

She blinked up at the sky, almost in disbelief. It was the first time in what felt like months she could actually relax.

Even in the peaceful stillness of an oasis, her mind wandered back the Druid King. She thought of what he said about Martouf. About how the bloodlines were thinning and dying out. That *he* is the last of his kind.

Reagan hadn't seen a single soul her age or younger in the Chaos Lands. She didn't sit up. Didn't twist to face him. Just laid there, eyes fixed on the sky, and let the question slip out.

Her voice broke the silence. Soft and hesitant.
"I didn't realize there were others my age out here. I thought... I thought there were very few. If any."

Baylos didn't answer right away. From his hammock below her, his eyes drifted upward, landing on the curve of the fabric above him. His expression wearied. It wasn't that he didn't want to answer. It just hurt to speak it aloud and he didn't want to share something she'd have to carry.

His gaze shifted, slowly turning away, letting the motion pull his thoughts somewhere distant.
"There weren't many children for a long time. I was the youngest in my village. There were a few older kids, but... most of them didn't make it."

Reagan's thoughts lingered on the words, *they didn't make it.* There was no hesitation. Just her honest desire to know him better. Curious and genuine. She asked.
"What happened to them?"

Baylos shifted slightly in his hammock. No tiptoeing, but instead a natural, easy comfort of two people getting to know each other.

That's what came with company. Questions. Conversations. Stories that reopened old wounds. And for him, it was worth it. The way she asked was so gentle, it made it easier for him to open up about it.

His voice dipped down a bit, as if pulling the story from a place he didn't let himself linger in.
"When the chaos magic struck, it spread like wildfire. The older kids who looked after me... they did what they could. One would go off for a food and supply run, but they never came back... It happened one by one. They either got swallowed by the chaos or lost their minds wandering into the madness... Eventually, I was the only one left."

Baylos regained his composure quickly. He brushed those thoughts away like dust. Deliberately lightening the tone, and steering the conversation back to the more casual curiosity the conversation started with.

He leaned back into the hammock, letting his voice find a lighter rhythm again.
"You're the first person my age I've seen in years. That's why I was so intrigued when you stumbled into my pond. I wasn't expecting anyone."

Reagan raised an eyebrow, lips twitching with the start of a smirk. Just staring at the stars above her, tone dry as dust.
"*Your* pond?"

Baylos chuckled. A soft, breathy laugh that seemed to surprise even him.
"Yeah. This area's one of the only places I've found that the chaos hasn't touched. It's been my hideout, really."

Reagan looked down, brushing her fingers along the edge of her hammock. Her voice dropped, laced with a quiet sincerity.
"I'm glad I stumbled onto your pond."

The quiet, the company, the unexpected comfort of not being alone. Baylos forgot how much he missed all of it.

A half-smile tugged at his lips. Slower this time, more genuine. It reached his eyes, softening something in him that had been tense for too long. Though still shadowed by the weight of memory.
"I'm happy to share it with you."

Reagan hadn't realized how much she needed this too. In her realm, there had been no companionship. No warmth like this. Here, under the canopy of blooming trees and rustling leaves, something had shifted in her.

She said like a secret she wasn't sure she wanted to share, almost bashfully.
"Thank you."

Eventually, they began planning their next steps into the unknown.

Baylos explained the nearby terrain and describing how the chaos magic lingered in certain regions. He spoke in detail. Where to go, where *not* to go, how to recognize when the magic was stronger.

They spoke like two people who had learned the hard way that planning wasn't always about survival. Sometimes it was about hope.

Eventually, their bonfire crackled its final embers, flickering in the darkness before dying into a faint, glowing hush. They were wrapped cozily in the slow rustle of trees overhead, the chirping of tiny creatures and the far-off sounds of a place that never truly slept.

In the first few days after the Druid King's spell,
Valla and Arithel's household should have settled
into the new rhythm of a smaller family.

And yet… something remained misaligned.

Valla was consistently making too much food for just two
people. When she set the table for dinner, she instinctively put
out four bowls and four glasses.

When Arithel wandered in, sometimes he wouldn't notice.
Other times, he'd see the two extra bowls, flash her a smile or
make a joke like,
"Expecting guests?"

She'd stare at the table like it had betrayed her. Then, with a
soft chuckle that didn't quite reach her eyes, she'd started
clearing the extras.

At the market, Valla found her hands reaching for things
she hadn't intended to buy. A jar of blackcurrant jam—
Kayleth's favorite. Two bundles of riverfruit—
Reagan's favorite.

She didn't register the strangeness of it, not even
when the shopkeeper handed over the goods
with a curious glance, noting how far she
strayed from her usual shopping list.

Not realizing the things she was buying
were for children she didn't even have.
Things in another life path she bought
every week.

Another evening, as the sun slipped low beyond the trees, Valla stepped onto the porch and, without thinking, she called out into the gathering dark that dinner was ready.

The words carried out across the empty air.

In the kitchen, Arithel paused, halfway to pouring a drink. He turned toward the door, confusion wrinkling his brow. When Valla came back inside, he gave a small, bemused smile and said,
"I'm right here."

She stared at him blankly. She didn't dare tell him she wasn't calling out for him. It concerned her that even she didn't know who she was calling out for, but she knew it wasn't to him.

She didn't say much at dinner that night.

Didn't speak of the hollow that gnawed at the edge of her thoughts.

Didn't speak of the strange emptiness that made the house feel too big, too quiet, too wrong.

She only ate in silence, wondering who exactly she had been expecting to come home.

Not even Zarriq's magic could erase love that deeply rooted.

It remained, senseless but enduring, like a song whose words had been forgotten but whose melody haunted the air.

GARGLEG

noun /'gär-gleg/
Subspecies: Anura Tenebris
(Order: Caecifera Nocturnus)

Classification:
Amphibian. Subterranean
parasite of the Chaoslands
ecosystem.

Habitat:
Dense, decaying forest biomes of the central
Chaoslands. Frequently observed near stagnant
water sources and decaying architecture. Avoids
direct light.

Physical Description:
Small-bodied quadruped with eight to twelve
locomotive appendages. Epidermis is smooth,
translucent grey to beige, coated in a viscous
secretion of unknown composition. Lacks
discernible ocular structures. Respiration is
cutaneous. Exhibits photophobic and thermophobic
tendencies.

Behavioral Patterns:
Non-predatory by biological classification, though
functions as a parasitic entity through prolonged
contact. Seeks sources of emotional unrest and
elevated adrenal response. Latches via adhesive
ventral pads that mimic leech-like behavior. Host
may experience physical lethargy, hallucinations,
spatial disorientation, and short-term cognitive
decline.

Feeding Mechanism:
Vital force through energetic siphoning. Prolonged
attachment results in psychological degradation
and breakdown of somatic regulation. Provoked by
vocalization, erratic movement, fear, anxiety and
panic.

CHAPTER 23
The Garglegs

There was no sharp dividing line between night and whatever came next, just a shift in the air, a subtle pressure that signaled time to move on.

Reagan stirred, blinking up at the flowers dangling above her. She let out a final inhale of peace, then heard a faint rustle of movement below. Baylos, already stretching, already awake.
The lull was over, and they readied themselves for the journey ahead.

They moved through the camp with quiet purpose, rolling up hammocks, and gathering their things. Then, they stepped forward, onto the path ahead. Away from shelter. Toward whatever waited in the wild unknown.

The safety of their hidden oasis seemed further away with each step they took, and the ominous landscape ahead drew nearer.

Soon, the lush undergrowth of the oasis gave way to the stark, decaying remnants. The path ahead cracked beneath their feet, guiding them toward a land unwelcoming and strange. The scent of rot choked the air, and the trees, once strong, now leaned with the weight of ruin.

Through the collapsed woodsy village, crumbled houses leaned precariously against splintered trees. Shadows crept in from every direction. Black ponds dotted the landscape, their surfaces rippling and burping as if something just beneath waited to break free.

Baylos walked a few paces ahead, his sharp gaze darting between the trunks of the trees. He suddenly paused, glanced over his shoulder, and whispered as quietly as he could.
"Breathe through your nose, and whatever you do, *don't* make a sound."

Her heartbeat quickened, but she nodded and fell in line behind him.

They moved with painstaking care, placing each step like a secret. The softest crunch of a leaf felt deafening. Twigs were treated like tripwires. Even the brush of fabric seemed too loud.

The oppressive silence was broken only by the deep, croaking sound above them. Large frog-like creatures clung to the gnarled branches of the towering trees. They had no mouths. Just blank, slick faces and countless sticky limbs that gripped the bark like they were fused to it. Each movement they made sounded like wet suction cups peeling away from wood.

Then, with a sudden slap of displaced air, one of the creatures launched itself from the shadows above. It landed on Reagan's arm, its sticky legs clamping down tightly with an unsettling squelch.

She froze in place, her eyes wide with revulsion. Its grip was unnerving. Its flesh cold and damp, and its suction tugging at her skin. She tried to remain calm, but the disgust was written all over her face as she turned her head sharply away from it.

Her fingers wrapped tightly around the creature's slick body as she tried to pry it off, but it didn't budge. Her frustration grew fast. She hissed through her teeth and tried again, shifting her grip, wrenching from a different angles. Nothing. It wouldn't budge.

Every failed attempt only spiked her urgency. She yanked harder, more frantic, her breath quickening. Its grip was as tight as iron.

Just then, another one jumped from the tree and landed squarely on her upper back. Panic surged through her veins, and her breath came in short, sharp gasps. Her heart thundered in her chest, loud enough to drown out the chirping.

Baylos felt something was off and turned around, his eyes widening at the sight. He rushed toward her, but before he could reach her, two more creatures latched onto her leg. They were multiplying.

Reagan's arms shook as she struggled to pull free, but her strength seemed to ebb away. Her vision blurred, and her knees wavered beneath her.

Baylos leaned in, his expression tight with concern. His face drew close. Close enough for his breath to stir the edge of her hair as he lowered his voice to a whisper meant only for her.

"Don't struggle. If you keep fighting, they'll drain you until you feel nothing."

That made her panic spike and her heart race faster. The creatures were feeding off her. Siphoning her, leeching her vitality, her clarity, her will. They were starving her.

The world around her shifted into a nightmare. Everything was melting and warping before her eyes, stretching, sliding, rearranging into something horrifying.

She blinked hard, squeezed her eyes shut, desperate to reset what she was seeing.

When she opened her eyes, standing before her was one of the faceless beings from her dreams. Her breath sharp and ragged, her body trembling as strength drained from her limbs.

A scream tore from her throat, raw and panicked.

The moment her scream tore through the air, Baylos reacted instinctively. His hand shot up fast, covering her mouth in a heartbeat. Firm and urgent, muffling the sound before it could echo further. His face was right beside hers.
"Shhhhhh....."

But it was too late. The forest responded. The trees shuddered. A deep, collective groan rising from their trunks. Branches creaked and trembled, shaking loose dried leaves that spiraled down like ash. The nearest black pond quivered. Its surface rippling as though something massive had stirred just beneath.
In the distance, a strange clicking echoed, followed by a low, rhythmic thump, like something woke up and was coming for them.

The creatures tightened their clutch on Reagan. Another one slithered up her back, cold and slick, wrapping around her shoulder like a wet vine.

She staggered, choking on a breath. Her hands clawing at them in desperation. Another dropped onto her from above and clung to her leg. Another clamped onto her arm. They were swarming her.

Their weight dragged her down inch by inch, as if the soil beneath her wanted to claim her.

Baylos released his hand from her mouth and looked around. The groaning slowly stopped. The clicking faded.

But something had shifted.

There was a presence watching them. He felt it. He looked back at Reagan. His eyes widened for the briefest second as he took in the new creatures clinging to her. He exhaled slowly through his nose and gave a small shake of his head, as if pushing the panic aside.

He ever so quietly whispered in her ear
"You *have* to stay calm. They sense fear. They're attracted to emotion... Breathe. Just relax."

Baylos? Her breath caught. His voice, his tone, it cut through the fog. It didn't match the thing standing before her. It didn't belong to the faceless being. And yet… it came from it.

Her mind scrambled, twisting, trying to make sense of the fracture.

She blinked hard, but the shape remained the same. Still warped, still faceless, but now she understood. It wasn't real. Her vision was lying. Her body was failing her. The creatures weren't just draining her strength, they were stealing her clarity. Her grip on reality.

The numbness spread. An icy wave flowed through veins, that made her limbs useless. She dropped to her knees.

He knelt down in front of her and gently wrapped his hands around her wound up fists.

He paused, took a couple loud sniffs of the air, and whispered to her with an exaggerated curiosity. His tone was light and teasing.
"Is that you? Or the Garglegs?"

She let out a shaky laugh, and the tension in her limbs began to ease. Her nerves quieted. Her fingers started to uncoil, one by one.

His face came back into focus. She looked at him, relieved and exhaled shaky.

Baylos gently interlaced his fingers with hers.

She closed her eyes. The darkness inside her mind was vast and swirling, but she latched onto her breath like an anchor.

Slowly, steadily, the air flowed in through her nostrils and filled her chest.

One by one, the creatures began to loosen their bind, and eventually let go. With a soft, sticky *pop*, the one on her arm leapt off. Then another. And another. With every exhale, with every ease of her tension more of them released and crawled back into the shadows, disappearing into the trees.

After the last gargleg released her from its hold, Reagan opened her eyes. She looked at Baylos and smiled.

Baylos leaned in and whispered.
"You had me worried there for a second."

He stood and extended a hand to her.

She was too weak to even whisper plus she was afraid her voice might attract more garglegs. She tried to make light of the situation. She raised a finger and pointed to herself and then gave him a thumbs up. A bold-faced lie, but it was all she could offer.

She was too weak to get up. She reached for his hand and let him pull her to her feet.

Baylos's grin widened slightly. He pulled her in close to him and whispered in her ear.
"You're a terrible liar."

Neither of them laughed.

He carefully slid one of her arms over his shoulder. His other arm wrapped around her waist, steadying her as she leaned into him. Helping her walk.

They took their first few steps, unsteady and slow. Reagan winced with every movement, her legs heavy and uncooperative, dragging more than walking. Refusing to let Baylos take on more than he had to.

Baylos shifted his stance, adjusting his hold to support her. He saw how much she was struggling and refusing to let all her weight fall onto him. He murmured low.
"Don't worry, I've got you."

Reagan wanted to stand on her own, but her strength hadn't returned. She quickly realized she couldn't do it on her own. Eventually, she gave in and fully leaned on him allowing him to carry her extra weight.

The world around her remained blurry, but his presence was solid and grounding.

They moved slowly through the broken village, every sound muffled by the eerie stillness. The dark forest watched from the edges of their vision. Silent, waiting.

Just as Reagan felt the grip of weakness begin to loosen, the path ahead shifted again. The cursed village was gone, swallowed by the trees behind them.

They pressed onward, step by step, into lands where everything seemed to possess a mind of its own. Chaos rippled through every corner. Strange obstacles appearing before them. Each more bewildering and more dangerous than the last.

But together, they kept walking.

Leaning on each other for strength.

And whatever madness the world offered next, they faced it side by side.

Valla could no longer ignore her dreams. The unease gnawed at her. She paced the length of their bedroom, unable to settle. She stopped every few steps to glance out the window.

She was convinced an enemy had infiltrated her dreams and her thoughts have been compromised. She retraced every recent interaction, every passing glance from a stranger, every innocuous conversation. Wondering who could have done this and what are they after.

Yet, even through her suspicion, something in the dreams felt different. There was no dark magic woven through them. No hand guiding the girl's voice. No whisper of menace in the air. Only a familiarity so painful, so intimate, that it unsettled her far more than fear ever could.

She sat down on the chair across the bed biting her thumb nail, trying to decipher the dreams. Searching for any hidden meaning, something she might have missed. She closed her eyes against the mounting dread, wondering if she dared bring it up to the council and what it would cost if she didn't.

For Arithel, his pleasant dreams began to twist into something unsettling. The girl's voice, once bright with hope, was now fragile and trembled with fear. Her tales of wonder, battle, and discovery turned darker, more dangerous, the landscapes shadowed by unspoken terrors and threats. The blood on her hands was no longer from victory.

Arithel awoke, his breath tight in his chest. He thought his imagination had taken a beloved fantasy and led it astray. He tried to shake the unease, but the cold tendrils of worry crept into his heart.

He saw Valla sitting in the chair across from the bed, her face lost in the dim light of their room. He asked if she was alright. She admitted she was having a hard time sleeping, but didn't explain why. He too admitted he was struggling to sleep but didn't mention the dreams.

Arithel settled back down, pulling the blanket over him, but sleep would not come easily. He tossed and turned. The girl's image lingering in his mind, her trembling voice, her growing fear. The dreams continued. But now, they no longer felt imagined, they felt like a warning.

CHAPTER 24
The Bazaar of Endless Paths

In the midst of desolation, a marketplace came into view like a mirage. The ground beneath their feet shifted from hard-packed dirt to an intricate patchwork of rugs. The air grew hot and thick with unfamiliar spices. Stalls stretched far beyond what should have been possible, twisting and folding into aisles that seemed to loop endlessly.

Smoke tendrils from burning incense cones swirled toward them, curling around their throats like unseen fingers, choking them. They gasped for air, frantic, waving and fanning the smoke away in a blur. The smoke flashed them a look of vengeance before floating back to its cones as if it wasn't finished with them.

Baylos looked ahead, eyes calculating the new terrain.
"Stay close. If we get separated, we might not find each other again."

They passed by awning after awning, draped in vivid, jewel-toned fabrics. Trinkets hung from thin cords, clinking like wind chimes. Lanterns glowing with mischievous grins. There was a cacophony of haggling voices and the occasional burst of strange laughter that seemed to come from nowhere.

Reagan took in the surreal scene. It was madness. And yet... oddly enchanting. Unlike anything she'd ever seen. And somehow, in a way she hadn't expected... it almost looked fun. She tugged at the torn edges of her gown.
"This place is insane."

Baylos side-eyed her then turned his head toward her. His eyes swept her from head to toe, slowly, deliberately. Then looked forward to the path ahead as he gave a faint shake of his head, lips curling into a smirk. "Not as insane as that dress."

Reagan whipped her head toward him, brows shooting up as her mouth parted in mock outrage. Completely taken back by his comment. "Excuse me?"

He gestured vaguely at her attire. The tattered, mud and blood streaked ball gown that had once been a gorgeous and shimmery gemstone beauty. Now looked like it had lost a fight with the wilderness and the beasts. "You're walking around in rags. You look like a lost princess who fell into a ditch."

Her eyes narrowed, her expression twisting into a look of exaggerated offense. She tossed a glance his way, deadpan, letting the sarcasm hang like mist in the air. "Ohh, well let me pull out my combat leathers from my magical storage pockets…"

Then began patting herself down. Tapping the tops of her thighs, her arms, even checking behind her back with a mock frown. She looked down at her empty hands. Her voice was dry as bone.
"Huh. How odd. I thought they were in here."

Baylos let out a low chuckle. He genuinely appreciated her humor and was impressed by her wit, even if it was aimed at him. His head tilted slightly, a crooked grin tugging at one corner of his mouth as he shook his head. "Let's get you some normal clothes before someone tries to barter for your royal hand in marriage."

He made a sweeping gesture, arm extended like a courtly escort. His voice dropped into an overly formal lilt, the sarcasm unmistakable. "After you, Your Highness."

They wove through the market, passing stalls that rearranged when they weren't looking. One moment, a stall had cages of tiny creatures with glittering wings. The next moment, it shifted to baskets of strange fruits, singing violet pears and peaches that blinked.

They reached a crooked little clothing stall nestled beneath a web of tangled lanterns. The vendor behind the stall was muttering to himself as he folded garments. His shadow was being oddly uncooperative, and moved in the opposite direction.

Baylos stepped inside first, brushing aside a beaded curtain that chimed softly as they passed through. Reagan followed, her eyes sweeping over the chaotic assortments.

Baylos turned toward her with an arch of his brow and the faintest smirk. His gaze drifting deliberately down to the torn remnants of her regal gown. He said dryly. "Something practical."

Reagan ignored his comment with a subtle lift of her chin. Her fingers glided across the hanging fabrics, scanning the racks. Her movements slowed with intent. Curating something that felt more like her.

After gathering an outfit, she turned to Baylos with the bundle of clothes in her arms. Her expression softened. Earnest now, with a flicker of unease behind her eyes.
"I like these... but I don't have anything to trade."

The merchant overheard and quickly dropped the garment he was folding. His lips curled into a knowing smile and leaned across the counter. He steepled his fingers, tapping them together with a slow, deliberate rhythm. Eyes alight with some deliciously wicked thought.
"No coin needed. A memory will do."

Slowly, she turned to face the vendor, eyes narrowing in quiet suspicion and intrigue. She took a cautious step closer.
"What kind of memory?"

The vendor grinned wider. He gave an exaggerated shrug, as if it were the fairest deal in the world. Lifting his hands in a grand, dismissive flourish. His voice dropping with a conspiratorial lilt.
"Nothing vital... A childhood moment. A forgotten sunrise. Something small. Something you won't miss."

Reagan stood across from the merchant, the strange marketplace buzzing around them, its oddities growing more apparent with each passing moment. She laid out the collection of clothes and boots on the counter then shifted uncomfortably on her feet.

The merchant leaned closer, his wrinkled face lighting up with a predatory gleam in his eyes. He sniffed her, able to smell what kind of life she had lived, the primary emotions that occupied her space.

Something flickered in his eyes. Recognition. Delight. He leaned back, fingers stroking his chin thoughtfully as he studied her. Then, his gaze drifted to the clothes she had chosen.
He tilted his head one way, then the other, as if weighing invisible scales. A soft hum of consideration escaped him.

Finally, with a sudden grin, he lifted his hand and pointed at the garments. "For all this, for you... a memory where you've experienced *fear* and *defeat*."

Reagan let out a dry, incredulous laugh. Half amusement, half disbelief. She looked at the merchant with a pleasantly surprised smile. "Fear and defeat? I've had plenty of that since I got here. I'd be glad to give you ALL of them."

Without thinking, Reagan reached forward to shake his hand. The merchant, already grinning, lifted his own to meet hers, fingers curling with eager anticipation. Their hands drew closer, breaths apart, fingertips nearly brushing, but right before their hands could touch—

Baylos shot forward, his hand snapping out to grip Reagan's wrist, halting her from the merchant's grasp. Stopping her in her tracks.

He leaned in, expression calm, lips twitching at the corner with dry amusement. His voice was low and casual, like someone pointing out a very obvious mistake.
"Wait!"

He laughed nervously, glancing at the merchant before meeting Reagan's eyes. His gaze softened, but there was a hint of concern in it. He spoke low and genuine in concern.
"You need those memories. You need to remember the fear, the defeat... all of it. It could be invaluable to you later. I know they sucked, but that's not what you give up. Not right now, at least."

A faint frown tugging at her brow. She hadn't really thought about it that way. Those moments of fear and failure, as crushing as they were, had shaped who she was now.

Baylos's gently let go of her wrist. He leaned an elbow on the counter, like someone who'd bartered in places like this far too often. His tone turned relaxed, low, instructional. As if he were explaining how to bluff in cards. "Give him something you won't ever need to recall. Something that you haven't thought about in a while, but that bothers you more than it should. An insignificant detail. A memory that lingers for no real reason, but one you could actually be okay with parting with."

Reagan's eyes drifted to the countertop as she processed Baylos's words. She stood still, her brows knit with thought. Her mind sifted through the debris of her past.

Across the stall, the merchant leaned forward, fingers twitching with anticipation, his eyes glinting with an eager hunger barely concealed behind a smile.

Baylos said nothing, but his gaze didn't leave her. Watchful, steady, like someone silently urging a child to take their time before making a wish.

Reagan slowly lifted her hand. Her fingers hovered for a moment, just above the counter. Then, with a quiet resolve, she reached across the counter. "How about this?"

Her fingers brushed against the merchant's weathered palm. The moment they touched, a soft, golden glow pulsed from his hand, creeping up her skin like molten light. She stiffened. It wasn't painful, just... odd.

She closed her eyes. Her mind flashed.

The clang of metal against metal. Sweat running down her brow. The twisted satisfaction on her opponent's face as he took the cheap shot. The cruel grin stretched across his lips as he walked away. The sickening, unearned pride he carried as he claimed victory. Reagan slamming her hands on the ground after losing.

The magic pulled her into that moment. She wasn't just recalling the memory, she was living it, again.

A weapons tournament. An event to determine initiate rankings. Her opponent had faked an injury mid-fight. She let her guard down, stepping forward to help him and that's when she saw it. That devilish smirk. The moment before he swept her legs out from under her and claimed the final point. It made her blood boil. The oppressive weight of defeat. The bubbling resentment.

She knew the merchant was experiencing it with her. That same rush of shame and fury.

The memory bled from her mind into the conduit of light, flowing down her arm like liquid gold. Her hand twitched. The merchant's fingers curled in response, his grip tightening. His eyes fluttered. His mouth parted in wonder, caught between glee and surprise.

And then—snap. The memory was gone. In its place, the weapons from that match materialized on the counter with a quiet, almost imperceptible *pop*. As if the air had shaped them from thought. A sword. A spear. A meteor hammer, its long chain slowly cascading off the edge of the counter. Its links clinking against each other with a cold clattering chime until it hit the ground.

The merchant's eyes sparkled. A low, pleased chuckle escaped him as he lifted the sword, his fingers stroking the blade.
"Ahhh. This will do nicely. I'll remember you, my dear. If you ever need another exchange, come back. I always have a use for these kinds of memories."

Reagan glanced over at Baylos. Still leaning against the counter, quietly watching the entire transaction with growing concern. He raised an eyebrow, his expression wary.

As the merchant handed her the clothes and boots, Baylos turned toward him. "Is there somewhere she can put these on? A place to change?"

The merchant, now absorbed in admiring his new acquisitions, gave a lazy wave of his hand without looking up. "Back there."

They made their way toward the rear of the stall, passing through a narrow, winding passage cluttered with boxes and strange trinkets, until they came upon a small curtained-off room tucked behind a stack of mismatched crates.

The space was small, private, and just enough room to change in relative comfort. Reagan set the clothes near a warped mirror and began to change.

Baylos stood outside the curtain, mindlessly staring at the colorful patterns on the tapestries nearby.

Reagan stepped in front of the mirror, her eyes sweeping over her reflection. The change was immediate. No longer a princess in a ruined ballgown, but someone who might actually survive whatever lay ahead.

Her fingers lingered on the soft leather of the jacket before drifting to her hair. Surprisingly, all the tangled adornments still attached. Her hair was woven so tightly around the filigree tiara it was extremely difficult to remove it. She winced as she began untangling it piece by piece and removing the ribbons that were knotted tightly to her strands.

Then took a long look at herself. She mumbled under her breath
"Yeah... back to normal, I guess."

She pulled open the curtain and flung her satchel over her shoulder.

Baylos turned and froze.

Reagan looked nothing like the girl who had arrived at the market in
a torn, mud and blood soaked gown with her hair piled into a wild,
tangled nest. The clothes hugged her frame in all the right ways. She
looked strong. Fierce. And undeniably beautiful.

Baylos swallowed hard and turned his gaze to the ground, feeling a
rush of heat flood his face.

Reagan caught his strange behavior. The shift in his expression. She
asked with cautious suspicion. "What?"

He reached up and rubbed the back of his neck. His eyes dropped to
the floor, but then sneaked over to her for another glance. His gaze
dragged down her frame in slow, stunned silence. The pants clung to
her legs in a way that was suddenly, alarmingly distracting. He
blinked once. Then again. His jaw shifted like he was trying to reset
it. A breath escaped him, slow and heavy. He quickly looked away.

He muttered, the words thick and uneven.
"You look... Fine... Let's go."

His odd tone made her slightly concerned about her appearance. She
turned back toward the mirror, giving herself another glance-over.
Smoothed her hair. Tugging at the bottom of her jacket. Wondering
what was wrong with her clothes, what he saw that she isn't seeing.
She turned toward him, halfway to asking—

But he was gone.

She took a step out of the dressing alcove, and looked to the right.
He wasn't there. Then she looked to the left, but he wasn't there
either.

She called out for him, her voice low at first.
"Baylos?"

No response. Her heart leapt into her throat. She hurried down the corridor, and out of the stall. He was nowhere in sight.

She looked down the aisle both ways. Nothing. She picked one direction and started walking. Fast. Her steps became frantic, the pace of her breathing matching the beat of her rising panic.

Searching, peeking into every stall nearby, scanning every new aisle that appeared. Every empty corridor sent another spike of dread through her chest.

The market kept shifting behind her. Rearranging itself with every step. The aisles were eerily empty now, and the vendors had turned into shadowy figures with red eyes.

Her pulse quickened. She called again, louder. desperation fueling her voice.
"Baylos!"

Ahead, a flicker of movement caught her eye. Baylos's silhouette, turning a corner. She sprinted after him, but when she rounded the corner, he was gone.

She stopped and looked around her. Panic pounding in her chest. She was trapped in an endless maze of strange trinkets. She thought back to what he said when they first arrive at the bazaar. "*Stay close. If we get separated, we might never find each other again.*" Her stomach dropped. The memory hit like a curse.

She shouted again for him as she spun in place. His name tore from her throat. Rough and hoarse, like it had scraped its way up from the deepest part of her chest.
"BAY!"

Her voice echoing through unfamiliar corridors.

Suddenly, a curtain beside her fluttered open. From the darkness, a gray, shriveled hand reached out, one finger curling inward. A soft whisper followed, too close to ignore.
"Come closer... he's in here."

Reagan became curious. Almost entranced. The whisper grew more insistent. She stepped toward the stall, and pushed the curtain aside.

Just then, a firm hand grabbed her arm from behind and spun her around.

It was Baylos.

His expression was flat. Like catching a child reaching for something on the grown-up table. He said, low and casual... but edged with warning.
"Don't. It's a trick."

Shocked to see him, her eyes flew up to meet his, wide with surprise, brimming with relief and rage all at once. She had just been sprinting through the bazaar, frantic, shouting his name, and now he just casually reappears like nothing happened. She was on fire.

She clenched her fists and thumped them against his chest, each word a punch.
"WHERE. WERE. YOU?"

A breath of laughter slipped out, as if her fury was more endearing than frightening. A little thrown by the intensity. His brow pinched in faint confusion. Tilting his head slightly as he looked her over,
"Right here. I never left."

They stood there, close. Her fists still pressed to his chest, his hands wrapped gently around her arms. Reagan just stared at him, trying to make sense of what he meant.

She looked around. Somehow, they were still in the same stall where she bartered the clothes. The same tangled lanterns overhead. Same merchant behind the counter, humming softly as he sorted a pile of shimmering scarves. Same crooked clothing racks.

Her pulse began to settle. Her breath evened out. Her eyes darted from one familiar object to the next, her mind scrambling for logic, anything to explain what had just happened. It was as if she'd never moved. As if none of it had happened.

Her thoughts still spun in slow, staggering disbelief.
"I thought... I was running through the entire bazaar looking for you."

Baylos nodded with understanding. Like the final puzzle piece had just clicked into place. As if he'd seen it all before. His tone was so matter-of-fact, so casual. No panic. No pity. Just experience. Just truth.

"That's what it wanted you to think. This place messes with your mind if you let it."

Reagan took a step back, and turned toward the stall. Her eyes sweeping over it again, slower this time, like maybe she'd spot a crack in the illusion, but there was no trace of distortion. No sparkle of enchantment. No evidence that reality had ever bent around her.

That was unsettling. It meant there was no way to see if she was walking straight into a trap. The idea that it had all happened in her mind, that to anyone else, she might've looked like she was just standing there, silent, still. That made her stomach twist. She didn't want to think about it anymore. Unsettled didn't begin to cover it.

She turned to Baylos and grabbed his arm for reassurance. Her eyes searched his face, wide and still raw with unease. Her voice edged with urgency. "Let's get out of here."

They didn't waste any more time. The stalls seemed to lean inward as they passed, as if aware their visitors were leaving without further trades. A skeletal merchant tried to press a vial in front of Baylos, but he shoved past without a word. A shadowy creature with wings made of folded pages called out Reagan's name, but she didn't dare look.

They made it to the edge of the marketplace. The last row of stalls, the final woven rug, but they didn't stop there. They continued out and onto the uneven mix of dirt and sand beyond and kept walking until the strange sounds and rattling wind chimes faded to a low hum behind them. Only then when they were at a safe distance did they stop and glance back.

Reagan glanced up at Baylos, trying hard to suppress a smile. For her it was almost mildly refreshing how non-violent the experience was compared to everything else she has experienced in the chaos lands so far. She said lightly, half-joking, half-serious. "I don't know. I... kind of enjoyed it."

Baylos turned to her slowly and stared. Unamused. No expression. No reaction. Just a long, flat gaze that offered absolutely nothing.

Then, just as calmly, he turned back around and kept walking.

She turned and walked beside him.
She gave a small shrug and gestured to her new outfit. Tugging at her sleeves, half-heartedly smiling.
"At least I got this."

Baylos's gaze flickered over to her. His eyes hesitated, but caught a glimpse of the way her pants hugged her hips and legs, but only for a second. He cleared his throat and looked away fast, focusing hard on the path ahead.

Reagan caught it. His reaction. The glance. The shift. She stopped walking. Brows furrowed, eyes scanning his face for a clue. Her voice was gentle and genuinely curious.
"What's wrong?"

He brushed his hand through his hair, then he picked up his pace, putting quite a few extra steps between them. Without looking back, he said too fast, too casual.
"Nothing... Are you coming?"

She jogged to catch up, leaving the bazaar and its strange, endless aisles of chaos far behind them...

Though the world around them remained as dangerous and unpredictable as ever, Baylos made it easier to navigate.

No longer did she have to face every new terror alone, constantly on edge, fighting to survive at every turn. With him beside her, she could breathe, knowing someone was watching her every step.

Each moon, each step, felt a little less like a fight for her life, and more like a journey with someone she could trust.

In Eldrannor it had been seven nights since the Druid King cast his spell, erasing Reagan and Kayleth from existence there.

Valla gave up on sleep entirely.

Her dreams haunted her more than any nightmare. She padded barefoot to the kitchen. The stone floor cool beneath her feet, and the scent of herbs filled the cozy space.

Bundles of sage, rosemary, and thyme swayed lightly from the rafters. The familiar scents filled the air, comforting but not enough to calm her.

She made herself a cup of tea and sat down at the kitchen table, wrapping her hands around the warm cup without taking a sip.

The steam rose, curling into the heavy silence. She stared into the teacup, as if some answer might swirl up from its depths.

But all that came were more questions. Every time she tried to clear her mind, the memories from the dreams crowded in again.

Arithel awoke after his dream shifted. The girls face smeared with blood, her voice unmistakably desperate, and cried out, "I won't stop until I find him."

He sat up in bed, eyes wide, the stillness of the room too quiet for comfort. He couldn't go back to bed after that.

He noticed Valla wasn't in bed. He headed to the kitchen. There, he found Valla already sitting at the table, a cup of tea held in her hands, staring out the window.

He pulled a chair out across from her, the scrape of it against the floor was loud in the stillness. She didn't look. The silence between them stretched, both of them caught in thoughts they couldn't voice.

Arithel stared at her, his heart hammering. The fear, the unease. It wasn't just his. It was hers, too.

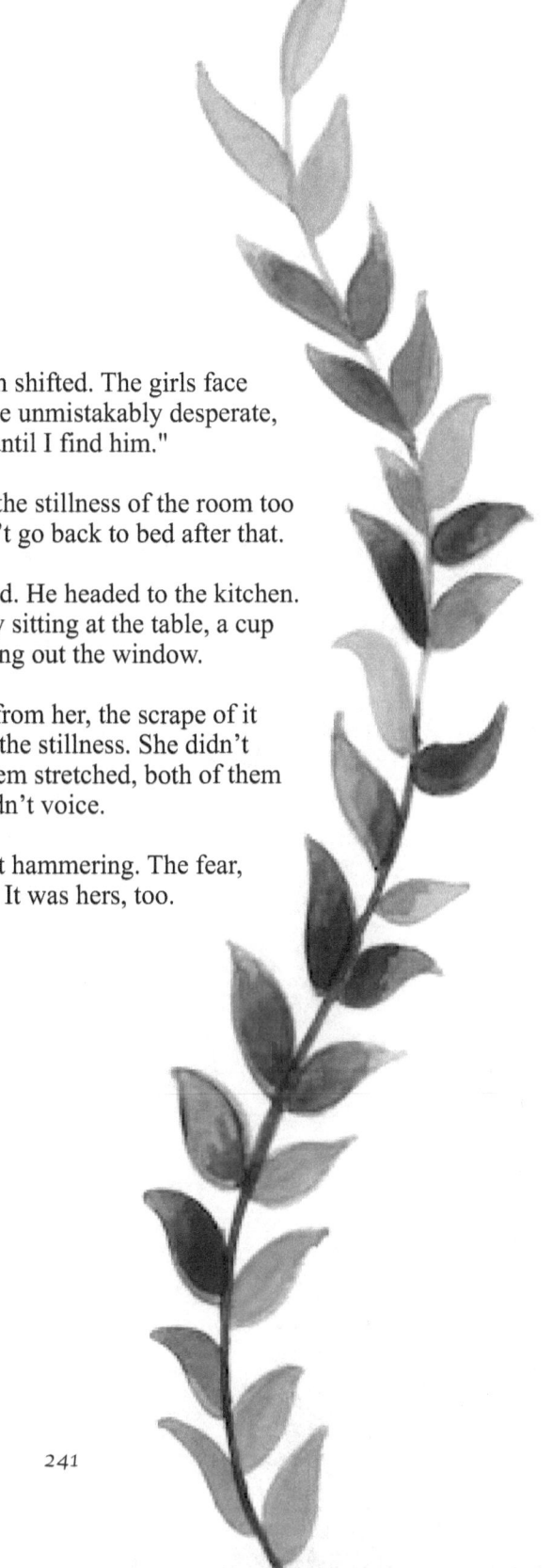

CHAPTER 25
The Purple Woods

A sinister purple fog crept through the trees, casting an eerie glow through the woods ahead. The trees were blackened and glossy like charred bone. They twisted and curled unnaturally, blotting out the sky.

Reagan and Baylos stood before it. Quiet and watching.

Reagan wasn't entirely sure what the hesitation was. She took a cautious step forward.

Baylos reached his arm across her path, stopping her cold in her tracks. He stood still, silent for a moment, staring into the trees.

His gaze distant. There was a softness in his face she hadn't seen before. He didn't look at her.

He said, voice lower than usual.
"This is Thackery Grove. It leads to the next town."

He took a deep breath and took his time to explain. The next town. The people there. He explained how they're stuck, forever trapped in a loop on the day of the war. It's the only place in the whole realm that has sunlight. An actual sunrise and a sunset.

Reagan could see it in his eyes, this was a place of torment, of endless suffering. She stayed quiet, watching him. Something in his voice made her uneasy. The weariness. She didn't speak. She just nodded slowly.

He finally looked at her. His voice changed to firmer now, deadly serious, almost like a warning. Bracing her for what was coming. "They're fighting. Over and over. It never ends for them. They are everywhere, and if they see you, they'll see you as the enemy, and they'll try to kill you..."

He paused, stammering. Trying to get the words out. "I haven't been there since I was little. My parents... they're stuck there. They're reliving it over and over."

He went on to explain how when he was little, he would watch them from afar. Even up on a rooftop just to see their faces. But when he got older, of fighting age, if someone saw him, they'd declare him an enemy, and he'd get chased by mobs of people with weapons.

Knowing he can't help or do anything to set them free from that kills him.

He looked at the ground, shaking his head slowly, as if trying to dislodge the flood of memories rising all at once. Memories he'd buried so deep they almost didn't feel like his anymore.

His voice cracked as he spoke, quiet and raw. Holding back emotions he'd long put away.
"I can't go back there. Not again. Seeing them like that would... it would destroy me."

He couldn't even look at her. Almost embarrassed he didn't have enough courage to help her through this next part.

Reagan stood still, absorbing the heaviness of what he was saying. Seeing him haunted by a past he couldn't bear to face. Her heart ached for him, and her mind raced with all the implications. She wanted to say something, to reach out to him, but words felt so small compared to what he was carrying inside.

Watching the tremble in his jaw, the way his eyes stayed locked on the ground like he was afraid to meet her gaze.

And in that breath, she understood. This was where their paths split. He couldn't follow her this time. And she had to keep going.

She was just starting to enjoy his company, and now she had to say goodbye to him. Same with Calla, Evra, and Sorrel at the shack. Nobody was able to stay with her. Finally finding friends and having to part with them shortly after seeing how great they are. She never felt so lonely.

A quiet dread settled into her chest. That cold, hollow ache of being alone again, of having to step forward without him. But she wouldn't let herself break. Not now. Not after everything.

Not after how fiercely he'd protected her. How many times he stood between her and something that would've devoured her whole.

She would carry his strength with her.

For him. Because of him. And because letting fear stop her now would make everything he did, everything he gave, mean nothing.

She took a breath. It was shallow at first, then deeper. Steadier.

She looked toward the path ahead, mentally preparing. Then all the sudden she felt his hand on her arm. She looked back at him.
He gently slid his hand down to her hand and pulled it close to him and turned it over, her palm facing up.

He grasped the runebound pendant from around his neck and took a deep breath. He pulled the leather cord over his head, taking it off and placing it gently into her palm. His fingers lingering for just a moment before he pulled away.

They both stared at the pendant resting in her palm. Neither dared meet the other's eyes. Not because they didn't want to, because they *couldn't*. If they did, they would have fallen apart.

Finally, his voice broke the silence, so gentle and warm. His eyes burning, his voice cracked under the pressure building in his chest and throat.
"I want you to have this. Something to remember me by."

Reagan stared at it, her chest tightening, fighting against the emotions clawing its way to the surface. Too fast to swallow down, threatening to spill.

She was stunned silent. It wasn't just a gift, it was everything. This was the only thing of real value he carried, and he was offering it without hesitation. It hit her in waves. What they'd been through. What they'd survived. What he was giving her now. His trust, his gratitude, his goodbye.

Her throat tightened. This meant more to her than anything anyone had ever given her. She couldn't even form the words.

She looked up at him, lips parted, searching for something to say... but there was nothing. Just him. This moment, and the terrible ache of goodbye.

His eyes wandered for a second, caught in something internal, like something had just occurred to him. Slowly, his expression settled into quiet resolve.

Without a word, he reached to his side and slowly drew his sword. The blade gleamed faintly in the dim light, and for a moment, he simply held it. Both hands cradled it with quiet reverence, like he was saying goodbye to something sacred. He looked down at it, nodding once to himself, the decision settling into place.

Then he gently took her other hand and guided it forward.
He wrapped her fingers around the hilt, his hands still covering hers.

For a heartbeat, they stood like that. His grip firm, hers tentative.
Like he was passing on something far more than a weapon.
"You'll probably need this more than I do. You at least know how to use it."

Reagan just stood there, holding the sword in one hand, holding his necklace in her other hand. She stared at them, the weight of the moment settling in.

Somehow, it made the pain of leaving him behind even more real. Strangled by the lump in her throat.

She slid the necklace around her neck. Her hand settled over the pendant, over her heart, and looked up at him.

With that, a new sense of courage stirred in her. Rage against what she had lost and what she had yet to face. Her journey was far from over. She was no longer a girl in a ball gown. She was a warrior, and she would find a way forward.

Channeling all the sadness, fear, and loneliness into rage, she gripped the sword tightly and walked forward into the purple fog. Ready to take on anything.

The black trees loomed above Reagan. As she took her first step into Thackery Grove, she walked with purpose, the sound of her footsteps muffled by the thick purple mist, her heart pounding in her chest as she prepared to face whatever horrors lay ahead.

She took a few steps, then stopped.

Something pulled at her. She turned, slowly, and looked back at Baylos.

Her hand rose to the pendant at her chest. She pressed her fingers against it. A silent thank you. A goodbye. A promise.

Baylos saw it. He placed his hand over his own chest, where the pendant used to hang, and gave a single, solemn nod.

Their eyes met across the distance. Reagan gave a small nod in return. Then she turned back and stepped into the purple fog and vanishing into the black trees.

VALLA
I've been having strange dreams all week. Every
night. Sometimes it's the same dream, sometimes
different. But it's always her.

ARITHEL
Her?

VALLA
The same girl. I can't figure out what it means or why I'm
having them. And before you say anything, it's not just
once a night, it's multiple times a night. And they're long.
It feels so… real.

ARITHEL
Does she have black hair? Blue eyes? Cute little nose?

VALLA
How did you—

ARITHEL
She calls us *mom* and *dad*. Talks about her
brother. How she's always looking for him.

VALLA
Arithel… How could you know that?

ARITHEL
I've been having the same dreams. Until just now,
I thought it was all my imagination.

VALLA
I think there's something we're not seeing.

ARITHEL
What do you want to do?

VALLA
I don't want to involve the council... Not yet. Especially if it
turns out to be nothing.

ARITHEL
But you don't think it's nothing.

VALLA
No. If the council hears about this, they'll assume
someone's tampered with our dreams. They'll
think an enemy has infiltrated our thoughts.

ARITHEL
That could start a war.

VALLA
Exactly.

CHAPTER 26
Murlus

Their meeting had no official summons, no scrolls or ceremonial staff. Just tea in the parlor room. Two tired men, and the slow, grinding collapse of a kingdom. They discussed nothing urgent. Nothing new. The kingdom still ran like clockwork.

Zarriq the reluctant ruler whose grief and guilt had long since dulled into numbness. Seated in a high-backed chair carved from blackened oak, holding his teacup with an expression of grim contemplation. His eyes fixed on the man before him.

Murlus.

A senior council member. Murlus was one of the few Zarriq trusted. Though they were not quite friends, their years of navigating council politics had forged a bond built on pragmatism and respect.

Murlus raised concerns about a faction of druids experimenting too openly with chaos wells, but even that was met with a shrug. As long as the system held, no one cared to change it. Murlus, like the rest of the council, being honest about corruption and apathy was the norm, because none cared enough to hide it.

The door creaked open, and Kayleth stepped into the chamber, fingers clutching a small toy.

Murlus paused mid-sip, his teacup hovering at his lips as he caught sight of the child. He lowered the cup to its saucer then to his lap, eyes narrowing with disbelief at the sight before him.
"What... is that?... Zarriq... is that a child?"

An elf child, no less. It had been sixteen years since a child had last walked within this realm. His presence would have been a surprise to anyone. An omen, a sign, a ripple in the stagnant quiet of their world.

Zarriq, ever the cynic, had no patience for theatrics. To him, the boy's presence was neither a miracle nor mystery. Just another complication, another delay.

Zarriq leaned back in his chair, one arm draped lazily over the side. He didn't even turn his head fully, just slid Murlus a sidelong glance.

All dry disdain and exhausted superiority. With a lazy smirk, sarcasm practically oozing from every word.
"Astute observation, Murlus."

Murlus rose slowly from his chair and moved toward the boy. There was something about him, an energy pulsing just beneath the surface. As Murlus drew closer, he sensed it more clearly. Earthen magic. Powerful and unfiltered. He turned sharply to Zarriq, and gasped. The questions didn't need to be asked, but they leapt out anyway.

Zarriq remained unbothered, lounging back in his seat with a faint smirk playing on his lips. A dismissive, almost smug amusement lit his face as he confirmed what Murlus already knew. The boy was not ordinary. And he wasn't here by accident.

Kayleth toddled further into the chamber, dropping his toy with a soft clatter before settling near Zarriq's feet. He had grown attached to this place. He was treated very well, adored and surrounded by a strange but comfortable power.

Zarriq boasted, he saw the curiosity in Murlus's eyes, the hint of wonder, and it fed that quiet, simmering arrogance that always lurked just beneath his skin. And Zarriq was not about to let that go unacknowledged.

With a glint of pride in his eye, he explained that when the boy came of age, his power will awaken in full. Not some minor trickle of magic, no. Raw, unspoiled earth magic. Ancient. Uncorrupted. Enough to restore the land. All of it. The fractured soil. What was broken will mend. The curse will lift. The entire realm would heal.

Once, the crowns of the king and queen were more than just symbols, they were vessels of magic, tied to the lifeblood of the kingdom. Without the crowns, the land became cursed and withered. With the Ogres under the curse and no longer able to serve on the council, the remaining druid members had become morally grey, desperate to control chaos magic for their own ambitions.

Murlus studied the boy more closely, tilting his head slightly as he glanced him over. The idea of stealing a child for this purpose carried a cruel sort of elegance.
"I rather like the idea of kidnapping a child with earthen magic. It's poetic, really."

It was decided that the boy's identity must remain secret. The other council members would be indifferent. But if the child succeeded, if he truly undid the curse, the ogre clans must never know the truth of how he came to be here. Such a revelation would mean banishment for them all, if not worse.

The ogres, once fierce and intelligent beings, had now been cursed into dim shadows of their former selves. No one on the council truly cared.

The druids, once protectors of the land, had turned inward. Their connection to the lands power had faltered after the war, and without it, many had grown desperate. Self-preservation had become their priority, not restoration. Others saw the ogres as relics of a past best left forgotten. A race too diminished to be worth the effort of saving.

When the matter of the boy's presence was raised, Zarriq offered a simple explanation. The child would be passed off as his own. Born of another woman, from another union. A simple story. Common enough in royal circles, where lineage was fluid and bloodlines often rewritten to suit convenience. Kings remarry. Heirs appear. No one questions legacy when power is involved.

Murlus, ever the cynic, brought up the whereabouts of Zarriq's *new wife.*

Zarriq dismissed the question with a wave.
"Insignificant details."

Murlus was fascinated by this conquest and wanted to know more about the boy, where he had truly come from, and the strange path that had led him here.

Zarriq had been all too willing to indulge the curiosity. How he had gone seeking a companion for Martouf. In a realm called Eldrannor. The girl insisting on bringing her little brother along. How it was as if a stroke of fate had delivered Kayleth into their hands.

Although Zarriq trusted Murlus, he didn't dare bring up the detail that it was actually Reagan who summoned him there. That was something he didn't want anyone to know about.

Zarriq shifted in his seat, settling deeper into the cushions with casual arrogance. He propped his elbow on the armrest, wrist slack. His voice edged with theatrical boredom.

"The match didn't go well... she was a nuisance."

With the energy of a man who treats exile like an eye-roll-worthy inconvenience, he gave a dismissive flick of his fingers as if brushing away a gnat.
"So I sent her to the swamplands."

Murlus's eyes snapped up to Zarriq at the mention of the *swamplands*. His eyes narrowed. His head turned sharply, like a creature catching an unexpected sound in the dark. Something had just brushed across the edge of his awareness.

His eyes flashed then glowed a bright white and gold as he looked beyond the castle, scrying her location across the realm.

Zarriq straightened in his chair. His fingers curled around the armrest, tightening as he leaned in. His eyes locked on Murlus with cold, focused anticipation.
"What do you see?"

He teased Zarriq about his little pet slipping out of its cage when he wasn't looking, and let that sink in while he finished scrying across the realm for her location.

The glow in Murlus' eyes faded, but the tension in his face remained. He reached for his teacup and saucer, lifting it to his mouth as he casually responded.
"She's at the forefront of the battlefields."

Rage overtook Zarriq as he stood. His voice cracked like thunder across the stone chamber. The banners overhead shook. Her persistence enraged him. The fire that burned in his chest now had a face, and it was hers.
"I thought I had dealt with her."

He paced across the chamber. His thoughts circling like wolves. Murlus seated in stillness watched in idle amusement as Zarriq's fury spiraled.

Murlus picked up his teacup and brought it close to his lips about to take a sip. Then he asked with a voice laced with a slow, mocking drawl. More bait than question.
"Did you not know?"

Zarriq stopped mid-stride. That dry, effortless smug humor calmed him. The absurdity of it cut through the heat of his rage like cold steel.

He turned. Deadpan, incredulous.
"Clearly not!"

Murlus smiled.

Zarriq exhaled sharply through his nose, shoulders tight, eyes distant. He was quiet. Thinking. Thinking what to do with her. His hand tightening into a fist.
"What a pest that girl has become."

Murlus took another sip of his tea, slow and unbothered. He didn't even look at Zarriq until the silence stretched thin.

Then looked up at Zarriq over the rim of his teacup, eyes glinting with quiet mischief. His voice was a silky venom and dripped with enough provocation to be an elegant taunt.
"Whatever do you plan to do?"

Zarriq stilled. For a long beat, he said nothing. One hand curled near his mouth, thumb brushing his jaw in thought. His eyes narrowed, flickering with the embers of ideas coming and going. Then came the spark. A slow exhale. The faintest twitch at the corner of his mouth.

His eyes gleamed with cruel intent, then snapped to Murlus.
"Come. We'll use the passageway to the village. We'll put an end to her... annoyance."

Murlus cast a glance at Kayleth, who was sitting cross-legged on the floor, without a care in the world.

They knew the boy needed to remain hidden for now. He was too important to risk.

Zarriq shouted for Nanny Grubella. He paced waiting for her. Grumbling about her absence. She was meant to be watching him.

From down the hall, the sound of her hurried footsteps hammered closer, each one a frantic thud of panic.

That was their cue to leave.

He and Murlus turned for the door just as she appeared in the hallway. Grubella skidded to a stop and stepped aside quickly. Zarriq and Murlus both side-eyed her as they walked past.

Martouf quickly hid in another room nearby. He had been watching Kayelth. Both roaming the corridors in an aimless sort of play, until Kayleth ventured into the parlor room.

Martouf didn't want to intrude on their meeting unless Kayleth was being distracting. So he lingered just beyond the doorway, waiting for Kayleth to come out on his own. Quietly listening to their conversation.

He now understood exactly why Kayleth and Reagan were brought to their realm, and was now painfully aware how unsafe Reagan is there.

He knew he had to get to her.

Valla mentioned a name that hadn't been spoken in years.

Ysmerra.

The only one name she trusted to speak aloud.

The former Shaman of the Eldrinth Circle. Once revered as the spiritual heart of their elven tribe. Chosen not by bloodline, but by old signs, dreams, omens, the markings left on her skin by starlight.

She had the rare gift of weaving the will of the land into words, reading the memory of the trees, hearing the rivers speak. But it wasn't enough. Desperate to help her people in any way she could, she turned to something ancient. Something forbidden.

She found spells and rituals in neglected old texts. Raw, untamed forces outside the narrow, birthright-bound traditions of their kind. Powers beyond what any elf in the tribe were born with.

She used it to help all those in need, and even those who didn't ask. Quietly, at first, but she could only hide it for so long.

When the council discovered the truth, there was no mercy. No debate.

Ysmerra had broken the oldest taboo of their kind.
Never wield what you were not born to command.
To do so was to invite imbalance, to tether oneself
to forces beyond understanding. In their eyes, it was
beyond forgiveness.

They stripped her of her title and her standing. In the rites
of judgment, they declared her a fracture, someone who had
betrayed the sacred laws of their people.

Banished from the tribe and land, she was forced to the
frayed edges of Thistlemire Woods, where the mist grew thick
and the soil remembered older, darker things.

No longer shaman. But magic, true magic, does not care for
titles. She remained powerful, more so than ever. Just no
longer welcome.

Ysmerra had always chosen loyalty over caution. She
would listen. She would understand.

Whatever this was, it had wrapped itself too tightly
around Arithel and Valla to be ignored. They
needed answers before anyone decided what those
answers should be.

It was decided. They would seek her out
quietly, without council permission, without
ceremony.

At first light. No hesitation. Find Ysmerra.
Find the threat.

CHAPTER 27
The Deal

The stone passage echoed with the rhythmic thud of footsteps as Zarriq and Murlus descended into the depths of the ancient tunnels that twisted beneath the decaying palace and spilled into the village beyond.

The exit opened abruptly into a narrow alleyway carved between crumbling brick homes and crooked wooden structures, their frames warped by years of exposure to corrupted magic.

As they walked, their cloaks trailed behind them like smoke over the uneven stones. The village around them moaned with age and rot. Shutters rattled against hollow windows.

Here, time did not move forward. The village was caught in the grip of chaos. Villagers fought one another with rusted swords and dented shields, their eyes glazed with the fog of the endless loop. Every motion repeated. Every scream, identical. Dust hung thick in the air, and the scent of old smoke and blood clung to the wind.

Zarriq scanned the chaos before them. Then, his eyes locked onto a figure in the distance. He saw her, Reagan.

Murlus stayed back, melding into the shadows of the alley's edge. He did not wish to be seen. Not by her. Not now. If she ever needed to recall this moment, his presence would remain unspoken.

Reagan stood in the fray, blade clashing against one of the cursed villagers. Her breath came in sharp bursts, sweat streaking her dirt-smeared face. The look in the villager's eyes was more haunting than anything. Empty, trapped in a time they could not escape.

As the villager raised his weapon for a counter-strike, a blast of magic slammed into him from across the square. He flew backward and landed in a crumpled heap, unmoving. Reagan looked over her shoulder, eyes snapping to the source.

Zarriq.

He approached her with fast strides.
"You!"

She didn't retreat. Her body tensed, her stance steady. She hadn't expected to see him. Not here. Her blood surged forward, a fury boiling to the surface, mixed with exhaustion, grief and the sheer chaos of the day. Everything was leading up to this confrontation. She just hadn't expected it to be right this moment, but she was ready. As if the gods brought him to her as a gift.

Her voice rose, raw and thunderous with emotion.
"I want my brother back! You have taken everything from me. Our family, our home. You can't take him too. He's all I have left."

Her grip tightened around the hilt of her sword. She realized yelling wasn't going to get her anywhere. Her voice started to steady. The bargaining, the reasoning, started coming through.
"He's just a child. I know deep down, you understand that. You've lost too. You know what it's like to be left with nothing. Please. You don't have to do this. Let me take him home. Or I'll live in the swamplands with him. I'll let you have my magic. All of it! Just please give him to me. Please. I'm begging you."

Behind them, a deep rumble shattered the air as a swirling portal erupted open across the clearing. The sound drowned the moment in wind and rising energy. Soldiers spilled from its mouth. Phantoms of the loop, running toward a battle already lost sixteen years ago. Their weapons clanged as they vanished into the village's heart, unaware of the present.

The wind whipped around them, lifting Zarriq's long hair and tugging at his robes. His face remained stoic, but his silence spoke volumes. Something in her words had struck a vein.

He remembered the battle. The sounds, the screaming, the loss. How many lives had vanished that day. How many things had broken in him that never healed.

Her voice. Her plea. It touched that old grief. It was the first thing in years that reached the part of him he thought was long dead.

And still… He drew himself up with solemn control. He spoke loud over the sound of the wind and portal behind him. Loud enough for her to hear him. But not shouting in anger. Far from it. The wind of the portal thrashed around him, but he stood unmoved.
"You can't have him back… I won't let him go. He's too important to me, to the future of this realm, and my son."

The portal behind Zarriq closed. The winds settled. The noise level returned to before, just the regular sound of battle cries.

Reagan's eyes blazed with fury. She took a single step forward, her sword lifted ever so slightly in preparation. Her rage was pure. "You can't have him."

Zarriq stood motionless, but within him, a storm churned.

The fire in Reagan's voice, the weight behind her words. He could see it in her stance. The rigid tension in her shoulders, the way she gripped her sword like it was an extension of her very will. She was prepared to fight him here, now, in the middle of this cursed village, surrounded by chaos and violence. She wasn't bluffing. There was no hesitance in her gaze.

Zarriq wanted her to know this isn't a negotiation. His words are final. "I'm not backing down from this."

She was not just a girl clinging to sentiment. She was a force now, honed by hardship, shaped by loss. She made it clear with every fiber of her being that she wasn't negotiating either.

She looked at him dead in the eyes. Chin held up high. Each word stronger than the next. "Neither. Am. I."

He was taken aback by her persistence. Nobody has ever challenged him before, and he doesn't like it one bit.

Zarriq's posture stiffened, his expression hardening into a mask of finality. He didn't need to raise his voice. The gravity in his tone said everything. His frustration was growing by the minute and it became apparent in his voice.
"If you become an incessant pest, I'll treat you like one and lock you in the dungeons."

But she wasn't backing down. She spent a couple months on the edge of death every day, fighting her way through, becoming stronger and fiercer than she ever thought possible. She wasn't the slightest bit afraid of him. She had gone through worse to let this shake her.

Her eyes were still locked on his. She didn't budge or falter, fully aware of her strength and what she was capable of. As if his threats meant nothing to her.

"I'll find my way out."

He was grasping at straws trying to scare her, but she wasn't getting rattled easily. And he was getting tired of this conversation already. "I'll banish you to the edge of the lands again."

But Reagan didn't flinch. After all she had been through, she survived, and knew she could do it again. Knew each time would get easier. That didn't frighten her in the slightest. Her voice was calm, steady and sure.
"I'll find my way back."

He stepped closer to intimidate her.
"Then I'll do it again and again."

But they fell flat against the steel of her resolve.

She stepped forward too, slowly, her gaze locked with his, like the weight of her entire soul was pressing into him. Each step deliberate and intense, showing she meant every word.
That she would become his curse if he stood in her way. She wasn't going to stop.
"Then I'll keep coming back. Again and again. Until I have my brother."

There was no tremor in her voice, no break in her stance. She meant every word. She was fire and blood, scarred by the journey, reforged into something stronger.

Zarriq let out a long breath, the kind that came from a place of reluctant understanding and annoyance. His shoulders dropped. He looked at her like an obstacle. Like a problem he might not be able to solve.
"You're not going to make this easy, are you?"

Willing to burn down the world for the people she loved. She gave a single, unrepentant shake of her head. Eyes glaring at him. Dragging out the word, emphasizing each sound, dripping with disdain.
"Nope."

He squinted his eyes looking at her. Taking in the whole conversation. He studied her, her conviction, how she held her ground. Something in him shifted. Not softened, but altered. A calculation formed behind his eyes.
"I admire your passion…Let's make a deal. Shall we?

Not because he believed she would succeed, but because he believed the realm would swallow her whole trying. The terms were cruel, but fair in his mind.

One week.

That was all. Return to the castle on foot, through the warped lands riddled with chaos magic, and Kayleth would be released.

Fail, and not only would she be banished, but Zarriq would wipe Kayleth from her memory entirely. No more torment. No more hope.

Reagan had looked at him with incredulity, her face shadowed by disbelief. It had taken her months to get this far. To think she could do it in a week was impossible.

Zarriq assured her there were bridges, portals, and magic doors scattered throughout the land. Some opened at random, others were hidden in plain sight. Many led back to the castle. One only needed to know where to look.

Reagan let the offer curl through her mind, taking in the terms of the deal. Measuring them like she actually had a say, as if this were truly a choice. As if he were *asking*.

Bending to his will, she hesitantly asked.
"And you promise to let Kayleth go?"

Zarriq watched her falter, weighing the idea like it was hers to decide. That flicker of doubt. That pause. The moment she bent. That was enough.

He didn't answer. He didn't need to. The corner of his mouth curled into a devilish smile. Quiet and knowing. He had her. It was all the answer he needed.

Another portal had opened in the village. Reagan turned her head, glancing at it for only a moment.

Zarriq took that as his cue to leave. He turned, his cloak dancing along the wind as he walked into the crowd.

The cursed villagers descended on Reagan, their minds too fractured to see anything but an enemy. When she turned back, she was caught by surprise, immediately lifting her blade as it clashed against the first cursed villager who lunged at her.

More of them came. She fought like someone possessed, pivoting, ducking and slicing. Between dodging and strikes, she searched the thinning gaps in the fray for Zarriq's silhouette, but he was gone.

The noise of battle behind him barely touched the stillness in the corridor.

Zarriq was already far down a winding alley behind a broken market stall. Shadows moved around him like loyal dogs, keeping his robes from brushing the grime of the cobblestones.

Murlus waited for him where the alley narrowed into a dead end. He hadn't moved since Zarriq vanished into the fray, yet his mind had followed every step. Murlus was concerned.
"Why did you tell her about all the secret doorways? Divulging council secrets to an outsider?"

Zarriq had delivered her the bait, spoken of the hidden shortcuts scattered through the land like threads in an invisible web. It hadn't been kindness.

There was a much higher likelihood she'd touch something far worse and gets stuck in it than actually finding a doorway.

The realm was a labyrinth, and the monsters were not always the ones carrying blades.

He was counting on her getting lost inside one of the magical horrors and hellscapes of this wasteland. Then he would come and imprint on her again, replacing his tether and steal her magic.

Murlus smiled, not kindly, but with admiration for the elegance of the plan. There was power in patience. Power in letting others suffer their way to failure. He gave a slow, approving nod.

Zarriq had never intended to give Kayleth back.

Even if Reagan made it through the trials ahead, even if her will carried her to the steps of his throne. She would not be rewarded.

Her memories would be stripped, her fire extinguished with precision. She would wake in her old life with no knowledge of what she'd lost. No grief. No questions.

Zarriq slowed his pace.

Before them stood a wall, unremarkable to any who did not know its secret. He lifted his hand and pressed his palm flat against it. Under his touch, the cobblestone wall shimmered. A ripple moved across it like wind over a pond, distorting reality.

The wall parted like silk, revealing a tunnel awash in white light. It led to the tunnels beneath the castle.

Together, they stepped forward.

And behind them, the battlefield still burned.

ARITHEL
I heard she went a bit mad out here all alone.

VALLA
She was always a little... off.

(Knock Knock)

YSMERRA
Did anyone see you come here?

ARITHEL
...No.

YSMERRA
Good! Quick! Get inside!

VALLA
We're sorry to arrive without warning, but we have a
private matter to discuss with you.

YSMERRA
The girl!

ARITHEL
How did you—?

YSMERRA
And the dreams...

VALLA
Yes... How—

YSMERRA
Always mentioning her brother, Kayleth. I
could do this all day dear.

PIP
May I take your cloaks?

ARITHEL
Oh—uh… Thank you.

YSMERRA
Pip! Must you always arrive like a raccoon in a pantry?

VALLA
He's adorable. Is he your son?

PIP
Please! I'm older than she is.

YSMERRA
That's my assistant. Caretaker. Cursed broomstick who
came to life. The titles shift... I found him wounded on the
side of the road one day. I took pity on him. Fed him, and
he followed me home. Haven't been able to get rid of him
since. This is why you never feed strays.

PIP
That is a *completely inaccurate* description of what
happened.

YSMERRA
Hmmm is it? Oh well. My memory isn't what it
used to be.

PIP
I'll let you have that one.

YSMERRA
Right then. Pip go fetch the tea. You two
follow me! We haven't much time.

CHAPTER 28
Owed Loyalty

Reagan's interaction with Zarriq had only added fuel to her fire, but her movements were less calculated now, more feral. Guided by instinct and fury, she forced her way deeper into the village's winding lanes of cobblestone.

The battle didn't relent. The cursed soldiers pressed on, wave after wave. The path narrowed. She turned a corner and found herself surrounded. Too many soldiers. They closed in on her like a tidal wave of rusted steel and lost souls.

Without hesitation, Reagan spun around and bolted for the nearest building. She clawed her way up the side, catching her foot into the windowsill, pulling herself up by the uneven stones.

Her boot barely caught the cracked trim and half-broken brackets. She managed to scramble up, her muscles burning. She caught the edge of the roof. Fingers digging into the cracks of the shingles, but it broke off beneath her grip and her foot slipped.

Her nails scraped wildly against the stone, clawing for anything, a brick, a ledge, a crack, anything that she could catch. Her boots thudded and skidded uselessly over the uneven stone as she slid.

Panic surged through her. She was desperate, frantic, trying to dig in, to hold on, to stop the drop. But there was nothing. And she was falling.

Wind whipped around her as the world tilted. She braced herself for impact, but instead, strong arms caught her fall. Her body jarring only slightly before easing into stillness.

It was Martouf.

He looked down at her, offering no grand expression of triumph, as if saving her life had been an inevitability.

Carefully, he set her down on her feet.

Reagan stared at him with a mixture of shock and suspicion."You saved me... thank you."

The prince was supposed to be sheltered, safe behind the castle walls, ignorant of danger and entirely unfit for the chaos of the cursed lands.

Reagan asked, with deep concern,
"What are you doing here?"

Martouf gave her a quiet look, then inclined his head, gesturing for her to follow.

She hesitated, but her instincts didn't scream *danger*, and she wasn't about to pass up the unexpected aid.

Together, they slipped away from the bloodied street and into a darkened alley between two warped buildings.

Martouf stopped beside a plain, weatherworn wall and pointed.

Reagan frowned. Her gaze darted from the wall to his face, then to the ground. She scratched her brow, unsure whether to laugh or cry at the absurdity of it. She was starting to think he was dimmer than Zarriq led on.

But before she could object, Martouf took her hand, gentle but insistent, and stepped forward. Her breath caught in her throat as the stone parted around them like fog.

It was one of the magic doorways Zarriq mentioned.

They emerged on the other side in an ancient, crumbling road winding through the ruins of a forgotten city. A shattered kingdom lost to time. Vines snaked up the remains of columns.

Martouf moved forward with confidence, as if he had been there many times before. Reagan followed, still unsure where they were headed, but trusting that he knew the way.

The path stretched out before them. Towering stone arches that leaned at odd angles, their carvings eroded by centuries of wind and neglect. Moss blanketed the fallen pillars, and tangled roots crept through cracked stone. It was quiet, eerily so, but peaceful.

As they continued along the fractured road, Reagan found herself glancing sideways at Martouf. His posture was calm, his gaze fixed forward. Only then did she realize how far he'd gone out of his way for her. Not just catching her when she fell, but guiding her, showing her a path through a land that had tried to kill her at every turn. There was no duty tying him to her. No reward. And yet, here he was.

But... *why?*

She glanced up at him, softening just enough to invite an explanation and asked, then eagerly waited for some kind of response.

Martouf sees that his father's actions are wrong. In his eyes, she is owed loyalty, even if she doesn't see why. He wanted to explain that real loyalty isn't just about family, it's about doing what's right.

He feels like it's his fault she was even there in the first place. He feels indirectly responsible for her situation, even if he never intended for things to turn out this way. That guilt, mixed with his own sense of right and wrong, drove him to help her. That and finding out his father's plans for her and her brother. He knew he had to intervene.

He wanted to tell her everything, all of it, but all he could offer was one quiet response.
"Owed Loyalty"

She took those words in. But they didn't feel right. Not to her. She saw him as helpless and unknowing. It wasn't his fault Zarriq lured her and Kayleth to Balderon. How could he feel obligated to help.

Although she is extremely grateful, she still doesn't understand. So she presses him further. "But you don't *owe* me anything."

The seriousness, the depth in his tone said it all.
"I DO."

The heavy meaning of those words left weight in the air. Reagan could tell there was more, much more to the story than she understood. And for now she would just have to take his word for it.

Then it dawned on her. The way he had moved without fear. The way he seemed to understand her. The ease with which he answered all her questions. Her steps slowed as realization dawned. He had understood *everything*. Every word. Every plea. Every insult.

She stopped walking. She lit up with excitement at this revelation.
"So you understand everything I say?"

He stopped walking, then turned to face her. Acknowledging her question and nodded.

The truth unraveled in her mind with painful clarity. Zarriq made it seem like Martouf was incapable of understanding, as if he were too slow or dim to comprehend anything beyond the most basic command. But now she saw the lie in that.

She was almost speaking out loud as she was churning the thoughts. "Your father made it seem like you weren't…um…"

She caught herself and stopped. There was no graceful way to finish that sentence, not without being incredibly insulting.

Martouf scoffed. He gave a slight shrug as if to say it didn't matter, but the glance he cast to the side betrayed something else. A flicker of embarrassment. A quiet ache.

He had been underestimated. Dismissed. And yet, instead of retreating into bitterness, he was here. Helping. Protecting. Doing what was right, not because it was expected of him, but because he felt it was the only thing he *could* do.

They walked on. Their footsteps were the only sound as they made their way through the wreckage of the fallen kingdom, through curtains of moss. Stepping over broken columns and slabs.

Then, she casually blurted out, like a confession she had been holding onto for a while. "I'm sorry... for screaming when I saw you…back at the castle. I was just startled. I just came out of the glamour spell, realizing everything was fake, and I was on edge. Everything was just happening so fast."

He nodded. He although had a difficulty with words because of the curse, he understood. And still here he was, leading her through an ancient ruins like it was his own backyard.

They reached a point where the broken road was interrupted by a jagged gap in the ground, a section where the stones had collapsed inward, leaving a wide ravine between them and the next stretch of path.

Martouf didn't hesitate. He turned to her, stepped close, and without so much as a warning, his hands found her waist. She tensed, caught off guard, but before she could say a word he lifted her easily and placed her gently on the other side. Then easily leaped across himself.

She flashed him a half smile, tilting her head, then tossed out a question like bait. Careless on the surface, but with purpose beneath. "Do you sneak girls through these ruins often?"

It wasn't an honest question, and they both knew it. It was a flick of humor to cut through the silence. A deliberate nudge to see what he'd do with it.

Martouf blinked, caught off guard. Not threatened. Not flustered. Just... surprised. Like no one had ever aimed that kind of jest at him before.

His lips twitched, the beginnings of a smile surfacing like something half-forgotten. A soft breath left him, not quite a laugh, but close enough to count.

She didn't press. That tiny reaction was enough. It meant he got the joke. And maybe, for a second, he even enjoyed it.

Reagan stepped carefully over a fallen slab, her eyes glancing toward Martouf. She wondered aloud whether he was capable of speaking more than a word or two at a time. Her comment hung in the air for a beat too long. For a split second she worried she shouldn't have asked.

He barely reacted. Just the faintest glance in her direction before offering the simplest of answers.
"No."

She continued to lighten the mood. She proposed the idea, how it must be nice not having to explain yourself all the time. Not having to justify your every move, every thought, every choice. That sounded like a peaceful luxury to Reagan. Martouf considered the idea in his own way.

They kept moving through the ruins. Through broken pillars and cracked statues, and Reagan kept their conversation going. Even if that meant she was mostly the only one talking.

Then the atmosphere shifted.

Reagan had a burning, unspoken question lingering. Frustration bristling at the edge of her breath. It's coming off of her hot. Something had been gnawing at her, and she could no longer keep it in.

The names tumbled through her mind.

Calla. Evra. Sorrel.

Their fear, their confusion. The girls who had come before her, swept into this realm with the same lies and promises.

Reagan suddenly stops, her voice laced with frustration. "Martouf, what about the other girls? The ones who came before me? Calla, Evra, and Sorrel."

Martouf kept walking. His shoulders stayed broad. He squinted slightly trying to understand her question... then simply shook his head.

Reagan's jaw tightened. She quickened her step, circling in front of him to block his path. The space between them charged with the fire in her stare.

Her voice rising with each syllable. Each question pressing harder than the last. "You don't know *anything* about Calla? About Evra? Or Sorrel?"

Martouf stood silent, his brow furrowing, gaze flickering with confusion, but he doesn't speak.

Her fists clenched at her sides. The fury in her voice cracked open into something rawer, deeper as she explained how those girls had been taken just like her. Their lives reduced to whispers in the fog, their families left behind. Alone. Terrified. In a shack beyond the chaos lands.

Her words splintered under the cracks of frustration.
"How could you *not* know what happened to them?"

Martouf's gaze softens, but he remains silent. He stepped forward, and the distance between them shrank. His hands came up, gentle and tentative, curling around her forearms. Not to restrain, but to calm, ground and assure her.

Her eyes moved toward his touch, surprised by the gentleness.

His eyes searched hers, solemn, steady, and heavy. No defense. No denial. He holds her gaze and with the softest tone he says. "Didn't know."

Reagan looks at him for a long moment, searching for the truth in his eyes. He seems to genuinely not know. She shakes her head. Unbelieving.

He really didn't know. He didn't remember them.

Zarriq had cast a forgetting spell, wiping away every trace of the girls from Martouf's mind. Their names. Their faces. So he would never have to feel the hurt or shame of the way Evra screamed at the sight of him. The terror in her eyes like he was some monster in the dark.

Or the ache and embarrassment of falling behind Calla in the halls, racing after her with all his might, only to be left breathless and crying when he couldn't match her pace.

To forget the sadness Sorell caused. How she barely spoke to him at dinner, eyes fixed anywhere but his, conversation hollow and strained.

Zarriq had decided some memories were better forgotten.

Reagan pressed into him more. Demanding to know if he remembers having dinner with a girl and then she just disappeared from her chair!

Her words were hanging in the air like a challenge.

Martouf's expression darkens, guilt and confusion mixing in his features. He shakes his head again, barely breathing. His voice drops to a low, almost intense whisper.
"No."

Then he pulled her closer, so their faces were just inches apart. His eyes lock onto hers with an intensity that sent a strange warmth through her chest.

His voice was calm but fierce.
"I promise."

She can hear the sincerity in his voice.

He's so close, and there's something in his eyes that softens the harshness of the world around them. But her passion and heat, her love for those girls wouldn't let her be calm.

She begs him, makes him promise to find them. That he has to fix this. Makes him swear on it.

Martouf nods, his eyes never leaving hers.
"I swear."

She lets out a slow breath, the edge of frustration gone. She stood there for a moment, reading his gaze. Deciphering his words. Analyzing his stance. Making sure he was being truthful and honest....and he was. She can see the genuine compassion in his eyes, and it changes the way she looks at him.

She keeps getting taken aback at how kind and descent he is. She nods her head in approval and then turns around and keeps walking along the path.

Reagan smiles to herself thinking about how she had found the greatest friends in the most unexpected places in this realm and on this journey.

Friends. Something she never knew and never experienced until being here.

But then sadness comes over her again when she suddenly realizes how she will eventually have to leave all of them.

Ysmerra led them through the dim halls of her manor. Her voice rising just enough to reach them both as they trailed behind. "They were never dreams. The girl… she's been calling you. Through the veil. You didn't dream her. You heard her. She remembers what you cannot."

They followed her down a winding hallway until it opened into the ceremony chamber, cast in a soft glow of firelight.

Ysmerra crossed to the altar and turned. With one hand, she motioned to the space before her and gestured for them to kneel. "You cannot help her if you don't first remember who she is... please, sit."

Pip barreled in with a teapot and zero grace, setting the tray down with a clatter. Then retreated to a woven mat in the corner. He picked up his small, hand-carved drum and began tapping a soft, steady rhythm. The pulse of the drum mingling with the sound of breath and the flicker of candlelight.

And the ritual began.

Ysmerra sank to her knees before the altar, Words began to pour from her lips. A soft and otherworldly lullaby, sung backwards like a spell being unsaid.

She took their hands one at a time, then pressed their palms together, lacing their fingers tight. She bound their wrists with a brittle branch, twisted, dark, and still slick with sap.

She guided them to see her. See the girl. To picture her face. Lost in that cursed realm. They focused. Then came the tea. Thick. Dark. Warm as blood. The cups rose, the rim kissed their lips. They drank all of it.

Her chant deepened, folding into itself like layered smoke. slipping between syllables that didn't belong to any known tongue.

They felt it. The pressure behind their eyes, like a
veil thinning.

They gasped. Groaned. Clutched at their temples as if
their skulls might crack open from the inside. The
world tilted. The floor no longer felt steady beneath
them. Their vision blurred. They curled onto the floor,
twisting, rolling, as if trying to escape something
crawling beneath their skin. Reality frayed at the seams as
fragments of memory spilled into their minds. The magic
pulled them deeper. The visions carried them like a current.

The girl from their dreams. Arithel's hands guiding hers, steady
and patient as she learned to sharpen a blade for the first time.
Then Valla's arms wrapped around her, the two curled together in
an old rocking chair. A worn book balanced between them.

The memory shifted. A sharp cry. A baby boy's birth. His tiny
form swaddled in white, Valla's face radiant and tear streaked.
The high elder lifting the infant skyward, declaring his arrival
to the village under a blood-orange sky. The boy, older now,
running through the house in a cloth diaper, squealing with
glee as Valla chased him barefoot across the floor. Arithel
holding the boy in his arms.

The memories came faster, layered, and overlapping.
It was everything they had lived for, everything they
had forgotten. And now, everything they would fight
for.

Pips drumbeat halted and cocked his head,
curious. He rose from his seat and drifted
towards them. watching as they flailed across
the floor in agony, moaning, rolling from side
to side.
"That looks uncomfortable. How long are they
gonna do that for?"

Ysmerra stood slowly with a satisfied smile.
"As long as it takes for all their memories to
come back... we best leave them. This could
take a while."

CHAPTER 29
The Treetop Path

Tucked behind an overgrown stone archway was an entrance to a long-forgotten courtyard. The space, once grand, was now swallowed by wilderness. Cracked stone tiles beneath creeping roots, and half-collapsed walls framed the clearing. At the far end, nearly hidden behind a curtain of hanging vines, was a narrow passage.

At the far end of the passage, was an impossibly tall and large tree. Its roots sprawled across the stone floor. A twisting lattice spiraled up the tree toward the sky like a staircase. They ascended the staircase.

When they reached the top, before them was a treetop walkway. Hidden between the forest trees there was a rope bridge suspended by magic. Remnants of old druidic pathways that once connected the land. Its narrow wooden planks stretched far, and gently swayed with the wind.

They stepped onto the bridge with quiet caution.

Martouf walked ahead with the ease of someone who had done this dozens of times. His steps were steady, unfazed. Not once did he glance down.

Reagan, on the other hand, was hyper-aware of every sound, every shift beneath her boots. She hesitated before stepping onto the first slab, testing it with the tip of her boot. It held. She exhaled and followed.

They moved slowly. But then the magic keeping the bridge intact flickered weakly. Its magical glow dimmed in and out like a faulty lantern. That made them pause and exchange uneasy glances, but Martouf kept going.

Reagan took a moment and glanced over the edge. She quickly realized that was a mistake. She looked forward and kept walking, trying to unsee the haunting height.
Some planks were broken or missing, forcing them to jump or carefully balance across.

They made it about halfway across the bridge when Reagan stepped onto a plank that looked stable, but suddenly broke in half beneath her boot. Martouf heard the crack and quickly turned around.

She let out a sharp shriek. Her foot fell through the bridge.
The impact of Reagan's fall broke a couple nearby planks, causing the rest of her to fall completely through.

Marouf lunged forward and managed to grab her wrist, just barely, but he quickly slid forward and off the bridge with her. His ankle caught around the rope railing. That was the only thing holding them up.

They dangle there for a few moments, realizing the situation they are in.

Reagan grasped Martouf's wrist tightly and looked up at him. Her breath shaky, she could barely get her words out.
"Martouf—don't... let ...go!"

He tries. He really tries. But below them at the edge of the forest a portal opens on the battle ground. The winds swept at her, trying to pull her away. They were getting nervous. Sweat was forming on both their hands.

He reached up with his free hand, fingers stretching, searching for the rope just above them. His fingertips brushed the rope. With a strained breath, Martouf gave a sharp jerk upward to grab it. But that movement, mixed with the sweat in their hands, caused Reagan's hand to slide right out of his.

His hand caught the rope. He turned, and saw Reagan falling hands outstretched.

He yelled, as raw and as loud as his poor heart could.
"Reagan!"

The empty air roared in her ears as she dropped. Massive leaves, veined like spiderwebs and slick as oil, unfurled to catch her. One after another, cushioned her fall like a cascading gauntlet, each leaf flinging her to the next.

Branches catching her like cradles, sticky leaves slapped across her face mid-fall and y*eeted* her sideways into a web of stretchy moss. She ricocheted off like a slingshot, spinning through clusters of

pollen. Her limbs flailing like a ragdoll caught in a pinball machine made of trees. Bouncing through a mess of shifting vines and snapping foliage until the final drop dumped her onto the forest floor.

She hit the ground hard, back first, with a bone-jarring thud. The impact came like a punch from the gods and knocked the wind from her chest in a single brutal exhale. Her chest seized as she tried to draw a breath. Each inhale was like a knife to her ribs.

Above her, the trees laughed. A whole chorus of cracked-wood cackles. Giggling and howling in a fit of breathless amusement. Their branches flailing like arms mid-hysteria. Leaves quivered in delight.

Every part of her body screamed, but she didn't stay down long. She rolled onto her side with a groan, coughing hard as she forced herself onto her hands and knees.

One of the trees rasped, its voice was woody, brittle and almost gleeful. "Where do you think you're going?"

Another trees voice slithering through the moss.
"We're not done with you yet."

Vines crept toward her ankles. Gnarled branches bent low, reaching, trying to drag her back into their madness. Her arms felt like lead, her vision swam, but she planted one foot beneath her and pushed. Then, she ran. The sound of wicked laughter chasing her every step.

Reagan didn't have to run far before the edge of the forest opened up into a huge war-zone of smoke, chaos, and magic.
The battlefield.

From above, through a break in the canopy, Martouf spotted her. He wants to jump after her, desperately, but it was too dangerous for him. He had never learned how to fight. He knew he wouldn't survive two minutes down there. He had been sheltered his whole life from dangers. He has natural strength from being an ogre, but not the same strength if the curse had been lifted.

He felt so useless and helpless. Instead, he scrambles to his feet, and runs along the path, trying to track her from above, through openings in the trees, desperately looking for a way to help.

Reagan was in the mouth of madness. The battlefield stretched wide across a ruined valley, A massive portal pulsed in the distance. Warriors poured through it in waves, some charging forward in fury, others retreating in bloodied panic. Ogres charging across the field. Druids using corrupted magic, others still clinging to the ancient ways, spells flying with violent precision.

Bolts of energy rippled through the air, clashing mid-flight and exploding in bursts of emerald hellfire and freezing mist. The screams of the wounded mixed with the metallic clash of swords.

Reagan needed to reach the other side of the clearing. Fast. Her blade stayed up, deflecting strikes from every angle as she fought her way forward, cutting down whatever cursed soul tried to block her path. Every step forward felt earned in blood.

It didn't end. They just kept coming.

Her pulse became a war drum. Her breath, a storm. Each draw of air was sharper, more ragged, like her ribs couldn't contain the pressure building inside her. Like a volcano ready to erupt.

A dark tide summoned from the pit of everything she had endured, and now it ruptured from her like a plague. Bursting through her veins like shards of black glass.

She threw her arms up, sword still clenched in one hand, and shouted into the chaos. A scream that tore from her soul, blasting through her like a bomb that detonated.
"THIS. IS. RIDICULOUS!"

Then, as if it was happening in slow motion, the air rippled outward from her like a stone dropped into water. The outburst sliced through the veil.

Magic coiled and twisted, drawn to her like hungry parasites, whispering against her skin. It spread into a dome of translucent light as it spread. Everything around her slowed.

Frozen. Hovering.

From the treetop path above, Martouf saw her...

She vanished into thin air.

The next morning Valla and Arithel finally awoke in full knowing. Two sets of memories. A life with kids and life without.

They stepped into the manor's main hall, and found Ysmerra in a chair by the fire, book in hand.

She told them everything. How Zarriq took Reagan and Kayleth to his realm. To tether their power. To siphon their magic.

Valla and Arithel knew they couldn't go to the Council now. They'd take a week to debate strategy, then another to argue over who should lead the mission. By then…who knows. No. Arithel and Valla wanted their kids back now. Not a week from now. Now.

Ysmerra had anticipated as much. She'd already taken the liberty of preparing them enchanted swords and armors. Forged with the skill of champions, and enchanted with instinct. To protect them from magic, blade, fire, and worse. The armors understood defense. Anticipated offense. Block, counter, attack.

Valla, although grateful and appreciative of the gifts, tried to assure her they were high-ranking, skilled warriors with magic.

Ysmerra giggled. Slithering around in the dark attacking by surprise. Their magic was child's play to Zarriq, and their hand to hand combat skills have become... well not the best. Ysmerra insisted.

Without a word, they moved to arm themselves.

Then Arithel, for one brief moment, reached for Valla's hand and looked at her with a soft smile. A silent offering of steadiness in the storm.

Ysmerra placed two *bands of passage* around their wrists. Vessels to carry their wearers wherever they willed. All they needed to do was think of Zarriq, the castle, and their children. The magic would do the rest.

They were ready and united in purpose. A nod passed between them. No more waiting. No more wondering. Whatever waited on the other side, it didn't matter. They were going to get them back.

The bracelets pulsed.

A luminous blue light spilled out in ribbons. The glow stretched above their heads, swallowing them whole. A blinding bright light erupted and they were gone.

They vanished from Ysmerra's manor in Eldrannor, and reappeared a heartbeat later in the ruins of Balderon.

The castle loomed ahead. Dark. Foreboding.

Waiting.

CHAPTER 30
The Day the Sun Descended

Unknowingly, Reagan had awakened something deep within her, an ancient force, deeper than instinct and older than memory. Ether magic, and the magic responded back. It reached through the veil and offered her up like a sacrifice to time, dragging her backward through the layers of reality until it swallowed her whole.

The world fractured. Light distorted, bending and rippling outward in concentric waves until the battlefield dissolved around her. When it reformed, everything had changed. She stood in the exact same place, but not the same time. She had been pulled into the past. The very day the sun descended and the war tore the land apart.

Inside the dome of ether, the colors shimmered unnaturally bright, almost too vivid to be real. The soldiers around her looked different. Their armor gleamed, unstained by blood. Even the grass beneath her boots wasn't scorched or trampled. It was lush and vibrant. Wildflowers bloomed along the edges of the clearing in full radiant color. Forests stretched thick and untouched. The distant silhouette of cities shimmered in the sunlight. Butterflies were fluttering from bloom to bloom, oblivious to the violence around them.

Reagan stood still and turned slowly, bathed in the quiet wonder of it all. Too much to grasp, too real to deny. She was witnessing it, the final day before the collapse.

The castle stood in the distance, already bearing scars from the opening blows of war. From her vantage, she could see magic lighting up the sky. Raw chaos magic, uncontrolled and reckless. The air sizzled with bursts of it, streaks of magic soaring through the clouds like an otherworldly fireworks display.

Then she heard it, a voice shouting behind her. Familiar, but not quite. She turned. And there he was. Zarriq. But not the man she knew now, not the cold, weathered ruler wrapped in royal robes and sarcasm. This Zarriq was younger, sharper and in white. He moved like a guardian, an angel among the chaos. Cast from light and radiant magic. His skin glowed with life, unburdened by the years of grief and corruption that would one day hollow him.

Charging across the battlefield, casting spells that knocked enemies back with pulsing waves of golden light. With his other hand, he healed. Touching wounded soldiers and sealing their injuries in seconds. He crouched beside them, looked them in the eye, and held their hand.

In the time she'd known him, Zarriq had never moved with such urgency or purpose. He had always seemed distant, untouchable, slow like molasses, drifting through conversations as though time had no bearing on him. But here, he was fire. Motion. Light. A hero.

She watched him kneel beside an injured ogre, his hands glowing with restorative magic, healing the creature's wounds when his head lifted to Reagan. His eyes met hers.

Her gut twisted with fear. The space around her blurred, and felt suffocating. She was worried he recognized her. That she wasn't supposed to be there. Not in this time. That he was seconds away from wrapping his magic around her, caging her here. Stealing her magic and trapping her in a time that wasn't hers. No Kayleth. No way back and nowhere to run to.

His expression shifted. He lifted his hand. Fingers curled with intent, magic already stirring in the air around him, building like static before a lightning strike.

His eyes widened, just barely. His voice tore through the space between them, through the battlefield ringing with steel and shouting. His voice was deep, and commanding, laced with urgency that couldn't be faked.
"Behind you!"

He flung a burst of magic in her direction. It was fast, wild, and crackling with force.

But the moment it left his hand, something shifted. Her magic answered. Not consciously, instinctively. Time warped, slowed, and thickened around her like gravity bending. The bolt of magic stretched midair, suspended in motion.

She turned her head slowly, watching as it crept past her right side, so close she could feel the heat against her cheek. Her head turned just enough to track it as it streaked by, a glowing arc slicing through the air like a comet.

Behind her, an enemy soldier was charging her, weapon raised. Before he could reach her, Zarriq's bolt of magic struck him mid-stride, hurling him through the air. The soldier slammed into the ground with bone-shattering force.

Reagan turned back toward Zarriq, stunned. This man, the one who had tormented her, threatened her, stolen her brother... had just saved her life.

She didn't have long to dwell on it. Another enemy charged, and she met him with steel. Sparks flew as their blades clashed.

In the distance, Zarriq had finished tending to the wounded. Now he was fully immersed in the fight, sending blasts of magic across the field. Every spell sent his enemies flying backwards, some soaring fifty feet before crashing to the ground.

In the thick of it, they found themselves back to back. Enemies closed in on all sides. Reagan carved through soldiers while Zarriq protected her, deflecting incoming spells. She covered him with steel. He covered her with magic. Unspoken, the rhythm between them became fluid, like instinct. They moved as though they had trained together for years. But the enemy was growing more desperate.

The chaos magic intensified. Bursts of corrupted spells lit up the sky. Missed attacks struck towers and trees, ripping them apart. Debris rained down like ash. The sun overhead already dimmed by the smog of battle, had begun to shift. Its light pulsed oddly, flickering in fractured hues like a prism cracking under pressure.

Most were too consumed by the battle to notice. But Zarriq noticed. His gaze kept looking skyward, concern etched across his brow. And Reagan noticed him noticing.

A druid among the enemy lines, one wielding solarkinesis, continued to channel power into the sun, sending devastating waves of solar energy crashing down on the land like falling meteors. Each blast scorched the land, fueling the madness.

The sun had absorbed too much. Between the wild spells, the fractured magic, and the assault of opposing forces, it could no longer contain the energy. Something ancient and catastrophic was building in its core. Something about to break.

Zarriq knew it was getting ready to burst. He saw the chaotic druid mad with power, already channeling another surge of magic skyward. Zarriq tried to stop him. He quickly raised his hand, and summoned a blast of magic. The spell flared from his palm, but he got knocked down by enemy soldier. The blast went wide, missing the chaotic druid entirely.

The chaotic druid's magic collided with the sun, and the sky rippled with its impact. The prismatic sun overhead already pulsing, already unraveling, was now shuddering violently. It started expanding outward in furious waves.

Zarriq quickly used his magic to get his opponent off him. He scrambled upright, turned to his forces, and shouted for retreat. They ran. Druids. Ogres. Reagan. Feet thundered across cracked ground as they fled toward the kingdom.

Behind them, the sun burst in all directions. Fractured like glass. A shockwave erupted from the sun as it burst, hurling shards of molten chaos across the land like meteors. The explosion didn't sound like thunder, it sounded like the sky was breaking.

Once Zarriq reached the kingdom's boundary he lifted his arms upward, releasing an enormous energy shield. It arched outward and domed over the castle grounds just as the fragments began to fall. It stretched across the sky, then curved downward in front of them, locking into place. The sun shards fell to the land, hit the top of the shield, and sizzled against it, but the shield held.

They watched firsthand, as the sun fragments that were filled with chaos magic morph the land into something else all around them. The Balderonians who made it out stood there, hearts dropped, eyes filled with tears, watching the chaos consume every last bit of matter and all the people in it.

Then the shield collapsed. Even amid the dread pressing against his chest, Zarriq didn't freeze. He barked orders, snapping the others out of their stupor. They had to act now. They had to create a new barrier.

Something stronger. Impenetrable. One that could hold back the creeping reach of the chaos.

Everyone there, including Reagan, came together in a large circle. Hands raised, palms aligned, eyes closed. A low hum filled the air. Then, a rush of wind, as their joined power rose like a cyclone. A blue-green glow spiraled upward, threading through the sky and dropped back down to seal around the entire perimeter. The shield shimmered, solid and radiant.

Zarriq stepped back, watching the light stabilize around them. It was not perfect. Not yet. But it would hold for now. Eventually they would need to reinforce it layer by layer.

The council was already discussing ways to block every portal entry and create a barrier over the entire realm to prevent the enemy from ever stepping foot on Balderonian soil again.

Zarriq's gaze drifted toward Reagan. He finished his conversation with a fellow council member and walked over to her. He clasped his hands behind his back, and looked at her with reverence. "Whats your name, soldier."

She got nervous at the very question. Wondering if he would remember her name or face in the future. She looked at the ground. Hoping, praying his magic wasn't alerting him right now at this very second of who she actually is. She couldn't dare tell him her real name. She was quick to think of something, anything. "Anastasia."

Zarriq accepted it without pause. No recognition flickered. Only gratitude. He thanked her and told her how she was an invaluable help. That their king would have been so honored by her bravery.

Then he turned away from her, stepped forward, and raised his voice to the remnants of his army. Soldiers bloodied and bruised, ogres wounded and weary, druids barely standing. They gathered at the base of the kingdom steps, the air heavy with grief and ash. Some clutched each other. Others stared numbly through the shimmering wall of magic that still held back the chaos outside.

Zarriq stood tall as he addressed them, his voice carrying compassion and conviction.
"Many of us lost our homes and families today. I am truly sorry. The kingdom is the only safe land in this perilous time. It is now your home. We will work together to find a solution. To get back what

we've lost. You have my deepest sympathy and my highest respect. Let's not let this stand in the way of our will. We will get them back, we will endure, we will make Balderon safe again."

There were no cheers. No roars of victory. Only silence. Thick, aching silence. Some wept quietly. Others simply stared, faces blank with grief. The horror of the day still settling in their bones. They had survived, but survival didn't feel like winning. They appreciated his words, his sentiment and hope. They hoped too for all he spoke about. But they all lost so much in such a short amount of time. They were still processing it.

Some stood there, still watching through the protection shield at the chaos beyond, some walked with Zarriq back to the castle, others made their way back to their homes within kingdom.

Reagan stood there, on the steps taking in all she had just witnessed. A quiet and reluctant understanding chipped away at the edge of her hatred towards Zarriq. The man who had become her enemy. Her contempt dulled into something more complicated. His reasoning was rooted in grief and duty. His intent had once been noble.

This was an entire realm. An entire people, crying out for salvation. Kayleth is the only one who can help, and Reagan would make sure he had the chance. She would stand beside him. She would offer their magic, whatever it took to help these people.

She was ready to step into the present, into the castle and ready to face Zarriq. With Martouf at her side to help facilitate a peaceful discussion, she was confident, they could come to a resolution.

Reagan closed her eyes and exhaled slowly. The ripple of time passed through her body like a wave, tugging at her edges, pulling her back through the currents of the past toward the fragile the present.

Far above, Martouf saw her reappear, standing on the steps of the hill that led to kingdom. Without hesitation, he sprinted across the swaying rope bridge. He vanished into one of the hidden passageways, determined to reach the castle before she arrived.

Below, Reagan stood at the edge of the battlefield, her gaze sweeping over the cursed souls trapped in their endless cycle of anguish. Warriors reliving their final moments. Friends turning swords against each other with vacant, haunted eyes. A thousand tragedies frozen in time, playing again and again like a cruel haunted theater without end. The sight carved into her.

It wasn't just her brother's future at stake anymore. It was all of them. Every broken life. Every frozen breath. She needed to save them.

Reagan turned toward the kingdom, its towers rising beyond the tattered remains of the battlefield. There was no chaos magic blocking her path. No illusions. No walls of resistance. Only a clear road forward. She was walking toward redemption, toward hope, with no fear left to anchor her down. She could walk with ease.

PIP

This may not be the best time to tell you but, I left out the squid slime when enchanting those bracelets. If Valla or Arithel lose focus mid jump, they're going to end up in a haunted bingo hall inside a volcano.

YSMERRA

I love that bingo hall. With the sentient foot wart who calls the numbers, and the cards that scream every time you miss a number. They always do a delightful spread. The eyeball tapenade is to die for.

PIP

Woof. That Valla huh. She's one bad Tuesday away from burning the whole realm down. I bet you a week's chores she kicks down a door that was actually unlocked.

YSMERRA

No bets. I'm not built for manual labor. My knees click in Morse code.

PIP

Also, just a heads up, there's gonna be a brief pause in
fresh towels for a few days. The laundry room is cursed.
Last time I went in there, poltergeists were doing a conga
line... how long do you think until Arithel gets impaled by
something ornamental?

YSMERRA

Definitely within the hour. He has the exact energy of
someone who'd be dramatically skewered by a ceremonial
sconce. That or fall down a spiral staircase. And if either of
them *touches* anything labeled "DO NOT TOUCH" I swear
by the moons I will teleport them directly into a broom
closet with a sleep demon disguised as a mop.

PIP

Zarriq will definitely try to fling them through the air like
a couple of circus rejects.

YSMERRA

Most definitely. Let's see what our brave little
disasters are up to.

CHAPTER 31
Valla & Arithel

Martouf awaited Reagan's arrival by the East entrance of the castle, eyes fixed on the path where he believed she'd appear. She didn't know he was waiting for her. She took a different path toward the rear entrance, half-swallowed by decay to remain undetected. She pressed herself against the cold stone, scanning the area before slipping inside.

On the opposite side of the castle, Arithel and Valla breached the north wing. Swords drawn, senses honed, muscles coiled. Arithel took point, pressing himself against a crumbling archway before gesturing for Valla to follow. She mirrored his movements, slipping into the shadows, her gaze darting between the broken pillars. They moved like specters, sweeping through the halls, covering each other's blind spots. They peeked into rooms before stepping inside, clearing each space like seasoned hunters tracking prey.

Reagan's first priority, the dagger. The silver eclipse of eternity, an enchanted silver dagger encrusted with rubies. The weapon Ysmerra had given her, after she removed the Glamour Spell. Zarriq hurled it into the wall during their first confrontation. Reagan knew it was still in the nursery, exactly where she'd left it. It summoned her, its bearer. It whispered to her its location. When she first received the dagger, she knew it had magic, she felt it, but didn't know what it was. Now she does. And knows it will come in handy.

Sticking to the cover of darkness, Reagan scaled the crumbling outer walls. Her fingers gripping rough stone, testing each hold before moving upward. The roof would give her the best vantage point and keep her unseen.

At the top, she flattened against the ruined structure. Their walls gaping open like wounds, their ceilings split apart. That worked in her favor. She could see everything without being seen.

The nursery was just ahead. She inched forward, avoiding loose debris that could give her away. Peering through the jagged hole in the ceiling, she scanned the room. Empty.

In the far wall, the dagger remained lodged in the stone, exactly where Zarriq flung it. Its hilt gleaming faintly in the dim light.

Reagan dropped soundlessly through the opening, knees bending to absorb the impact. She wasted no time, crossing the room quickly. Her fingers curled around the dagger's hilt, and as soon as she yanked it free, a faint pulse of magic flickered along the blade. She wasted no time. She grabbed the edge of the broken ceiling and pulled herself back up, rolling smoothly onto the rooftop.

Now, Zarriq.

She stalked along the high beams, using the castle's shattered remains to her advantage. Every collapsed wall and missing ceiling gave her a direct view into the rooms below. She scanned, observed, and moved forward. Somewhere inside, Zarriq lurked, and she was on a mission to find him. But she wouldn't make a move, not yet. She would wait until Martouf arrived. She would wait as long as it took.

Martouf eventually made his way inside the castle. Hoping Reagan found another entrance or somehow arrived ahead of him. As he made his way further inside, he nearly collided with Nanny Grubella in one of the corridors. Kayleth darted past them, disappearing around the corner. Martouf didn't hesitate. He told Grubella he'd go after him. He followed, tracing the boy's trail through a series of half-forgotten halls. Kayleth was just ahead, wandering with amusement, or an unseen force guiding him.

Zarriq strolled through a dim corridor of the castle. His steps unhurried as usual. Until something shifted. He paused. Sensing something in one of the chambers ahead. He felt a presence. Two. And unfamiliar.

He walked a little slower. Each footstep light as he approached the doorway. Peering in, he spotted a man and a woman. Elves. Armed, armored, and creeping through the shadows like marionette puppets.

Zarriq cocked his head slightly. He knew they weren't from this land. A stillness settled over him. Dangerous and controlled. Wondering how they got past his protection barrier spell. His features tightened, brows knitting with quiet fury. Suspicion crept into his stare as he studied them. Not fear. Not alarm…permission.

A slow smile pulled at the corner of his mouth, like someone welcoming a game. They'd walked into the wrong castle. His castle, and he was in the mood to play.

With an unsettling lack of urgency and playfulness in his voice, he asked.
"Can I... help you?"

From above the ruined halls, hidden among the broken beams, Reagan froze. That voice. She shifted her position, staying out of sight, peering down from the fractured ceiling. Her heart dropped at the sight of them below.

Her parents.

Valla and Arithel didn't lower their swords. They immediately shifted their stances into combat, bodies angled to strike. Not a flinch in their focus. Waiting for the first threat to ignite the fight.

Reagan whispered under her breath with a mix of surprise, relief and, worry.
"Mom... Dad..."

Arithel was ready to set the room on fire. His eyes were locked on Zarriq, wide with rage, glinting like something that had already snapped inside him. When he spoke, it wasn't a voice anymore. It was dragged up from the deepest part of a father who had lost everything but the fight. A roar, a demand, a barely contained storm.
"You have our kids."

The smirk slid off Zarriq's face, slowly, like he wasn't sure he'd heard correctly. His brow creased. Just slightly. The amusement in his eyes evaporated. His gaze held on Arithel's face a moment longer than necessary, then slid to Valla. Something flickered behind his eyes. Sharp recognition quickly masked beneath his usual veil of casual menace. They looked like Reagan and Kayleth. Elves. The dark hair, the light eyes.

That wasn't possible. His memory spell should have erased all traces, every speck of Reagan and Kayleth's existence, ripped clean from the minds of Eldrannor. He had made certain of it. They couldn't be here. And yet, here they were.

Zarriq's pupils dilated as he reached inward, tapping into the well of magic thrumming beneath his skin and sent it outward, into these intruders, these so-called parents. He sought the truths they carried. Reading their minds, their memories, hunting for what they are trying to hide.

He saw it.

His spell was there, precise and brutal. It had erased Reagan and Kayleth, woven in false memories, replaced entire seasons of their lives. But there, tangled in the spellwork, was something new.

Reagan.

She had been speaking to them every night. Whispering like a child might pray to the stars. Her voice, raw with longing, had carried its way across dimensions. Primitive ether magic, uncontrolled, pulsing with emotion. And yet... it had worked. Each word burrowed and settled in the minds of her parents as dreams.

Dreams that weren't dreams at all, but telepathic fragments. Zarriq pushed deeper into the vision. He saw Valla waking in cold sweats, sitting by the window long after midnight with her hand pressed to her chest as if trying to recall something just out of reach. He saw Arithel pacing the halls of their home, restless, haunted, standing at a door he didn't recognize but somehow couldn't stop returning to.

Then... the shaman. Ysmerra. The outcast of their tribe. The one who had dared to defy magical law in pursuit of knowledge. He saw the two of them approaching her, cautiously, with skepticism masking hope. Ysmerra ushered them inside. Her chants. Her rituals. Her potions. And then, Zarriq saw it, her magic unweaving his own.

He watched Arithel gasp as the memories returned. How Valla fought to accept what wasn't real.

Their bracelets. Ancient tools of portal-walking magic. Forged to bypass dimensional protections. Forged by Ysmerra herself. He saw them on the castle steps creeping their way inside like a couple of thieves in the middle of the night.

And now they stood here. In this room. Blades drawn. Ready to take back what was never supposed to be remembered.

He released the magic like an arrow from a drawn bow.

Zarriq inhaled slowly. He smiled like a fox in a henhouse, not in humor, but in deep, deliberate amusement. His posture still unbothered. Slowly, he began to circle them, moving like a predator assessing his prey. One hand clasped behind his back, the other loose at his side.

And when he spoke, his tone was warm and playful, but his eyes were carved from ice. He dangled each word like bait on a hook, watching to see who would bite.
"I don't think so..."

His gaze drifted across them one by one. His voice was light almost hospitable, as if he was about to offer them tea, but the malice hidden underneath coiled like a snake.
"Are you sure you have the right castle?"

Doubt slithered its way into their minds. Valla's fingers tensed around the hilt of her sword. Her chin lowered, her gaze shifted, a flicker of internal uncertainty slipping through her warrior exterior. Arithel's stance loosened, the tight set of his shoulders slackened, his brows furrowed.

The realization sank in. They really didn't know. Everything they knew about him, about this place, was all secondhand information. Just Ysmerra's word. And Ysmerra wasn't here. And the bracelets... They'd never used them before. They could've landed in the wrong realm.

Zarriq could see it. The hesitation, the uncertainty. And he drank it in. He let the silence stretch, enjoying it the way one might enjoy a warm bath.

Almost ashamed to ask the question now that it hung between them. Valla asked anyway. The words didn't quite want to leave her mouth. Like she already knew the answer, and asking it only made the mistake feel more real. Her voice was quiet, tight and hesitant. The confusion obvious.
"Are you Zarriq?"

Zarriq looked away to hide his smile. His fingers traced the armrest of the throne chair. Eyes glinting like knives in a jester's hands. His voice stretched thin with amusement.
"No..."

He handled their fear like a wine connoisseur, swirling it, savoring it. His voice was almost melodic.
"I've never heard that name before."

Then, his gaze lifted to them, sharp and piercing like a lion stretching before the kill. "The children you're looking for...What are their names? What do they look like?"

All the sudden, there was the faintest creak at the door. All eyes snapped toward it.

Kayleth.

He walked into the room, a book dangling carelessly from one hand. He waved with the other, casual and lopsided, like he'd just returned from a nap or a snack and didn't notice the air was thick with tension.
"Hi, Mommy."

Martouf followed close behind Kayleth. He was only a few strides away from the threshold when he saw them. Two strangers. Armored. Swords drawn. Standing before his father.

Martouf froze mid-step. He backed up fast, silent, and unnoticed. He slipping into a nearby room, peering through the narrow gap in the doorframe.

Valla's jaw parted in stunned silence. For a moment, she didn't breathe. Didn't blink. Didn't move. She dropped to her knees, her sword slipped from her hand, clattering to the floor with a dull thud. Tears welled instantly, blurring the image of the boy before her. Her arms stretched out on instinct. Reaching, trembling, desperate to hold what had been stolen from her.
"Oh, my baby!"

Arithel was still locked in fighting stance, sword still drawn, but his eyes were locked on Kayleth and glassy. Holding back emotion. When he finally spoke, it was rough. Scraped from somewhere deep and half-broken. He managed to rasp.
"Come here, son."

Zarriq's control is slipping. He's watching his carefully orchestrated plan unravel before his eyes. Watching his prize slip through his fingers. This wasn't how it was supposed to go. His eyes blazed. He wasn't done with the boy. Not yet. Not now.

His voice ripped through the air with fury. Disbelief cracked through it, raw and ragged.
"No!"

He threw out his hand without thought, fury bursting from his core. The magic surged forward like a battering ram, meant to rip Valla

and Arithel from their feet and slam them into the wall. It raced toward them, but just before impact, the energy slowed, thinned, and dissolved. Slipping over them like a gentle breeze.

Zarriq's eyes widened slightly as if stunned by his own magic betraying him. He lifted his hand again, slower this time. He sent forward a blast of magic, this time even stronger. Right before hitting them, it disappeared.

Zarriq's arm dropped, fingers twitching with disbelief. Magic crackled at his knuckles, begging to be unleashed. A flicker of realization sparked behind his gaze. He tilted his head as if tuning into something. His nostrils flared, and started sniffing the air like a predator catching a new scent.

A slow, sinister grin spread across his face. His voice dropped, almost impressed. Nodding his head in amazement.
"Blood magic. Wow. Even I'm not depraved enough to do that."

Valla barely heard him. Her eyes were set on a shadow, the darkness on the walls. Instinct surged. She extended her hands, calling to the shadow. It peeled away and grew. A monstrous form took shape, its towering bulk stretching toward Zarriq.

Arithel took a half-step forward, hand reaching toward her. Not to stop her, but warn her. They were crossing a line. One they couldn't uncross. He barely moved his lips as he whispered to her. "Ysmerra said not to."

Valla was fierce, maternal, and not here to play it safe. She's not being reckless, she's being intentional. She knows the stakes, but she's not going to tiptoe through some cryptic prophecy and warnings when her children are right there. Her power, her instincts, and her fury are all aligned. She came to take them back by any means necessary.

She looked at her husband in the eyes. No shame. No apology. Just a fire that refused to dim.
"I had to try."

Zarriq watched the shadow stretch towards him, unfazed. Unimpressed. Almost entertained as if it were a joke. Instead his focus was on them, listening to their whispers. Their panic. He could hear all of it. A grin tugged at the corner of his mouth. They were trying harder now. Desperate enough to reach for old tricks. That meant they were losing.

He decided to add to that panic. To seed doubt. Remind them how little they truly knew. With a voice so casual it almost hurt, he asked. "How is Ysmerra?"

Knowing the mention of her name would unsettle them immensely. And it did. It made them wonder how he knew her. The edges of their trust fraying. Made them question what else she hadn't told them.

The shadows came close to Zarriq, trying to grab at him, claw at him, but he remained completely unbothered.
"That's cute! But your little shadow puppets won't do a thing to me."

He lazily lifted a hand toward the shadow beast with sluggish disdain. He flicked his wrist like he was turning down tea. The shadow beast unraveled mid-lunge, splitting apart and morphing into shrieking Wraiths. They floated over to Valla and Arithel, circling them and closing in. Their dark tendrils reached out for them, but dissolved the moment they made contact.

Zarriq observed this with intrigue, his smile sharpening. Nodding his head confirming what he already suspected.
"Hmmmm. Good to know. It's your armor that appears to be covered in blood magic... so I can't harm you... Very clever."

He placed his hands clasped behind his back, considering an alternative.

Arithel's eyes locked onto Zarriq with a cold and murderous promise. He decided to try his luck using his magic, despite Ysmerra's warning. He stood utterly still. Not a muscle twitched. Barely even a breath. With the faintest narrowing of his eyes, he disappeared.

Zarriq didn't react. Didn't turn his head. He simply smirked. Their desperation reeked of inexperience.

Arithel moved like a phantom, silent and unseen. His sword poised as he crept toward Zarriq.

Zarriq squinted, his head tilting ever so slightly, as if trying to decide whether this was a serious attempt or just a tragic joke. The corners of his mouth twitched, caught somewhere between pity and secondhand shame. He moved his arm out from behind his back with the nonchalance of a man ordering wine and slowly waved two fingers through the air.

Suddenly, a sharp scraping noise tore through the air.

Valla turned and saw a chair sliding fast across the floor, aimed with uncanny precision toward Arithel's path. The chair scooped him up and slammed to a halt, dead center of the room. Arithel's form flickered then he reappeared in full view. He was seated, confused and caught off guard.

Zarriq walked over to him and leaned in, tilting his head like a taxidermy animal just slightly off center.
"Cute trick... Here's another one."

Then his skin began to shift. Bone rearranged. Flesh pulled and molded like wet clay. In seconds, Arithel found himself staring at… himself.

Zarriq was now wearing *Arithel's face* and smiled with cruel satisfaction. The same eyes. The same mouth. The same faint scar on his cheek.

Arithel faltered. This was *his* magic. As a Dusk Warden, illusion was his weapon. He could create mirages, alter his appearance. Take on the face of another.

But now, Zarriq wore it like a party trick. Mocking and Better. The gesture wasn't just imitation. It was domination. Arithel flinched, not from fear though.

This magic, in Eldrannor, wasn't common. Illusion was a rare gift, one *only he* possessed. It was revered. Feared. He had been chosen for the most dangerous missions, sent where no others could go. And yet, Zarriq made it look like child's play. Effortless. Bored, even. As if this gift Arithel had bled and trained for his whole life was nothing more than a parlor trick. It shattered something deep in him.

Zarriq spoke with his own voice, but with Arithel's face. Smooth and smug. "Your little mind games won't work on me either."

Then his features began to shift again. Bone and flesh rearranging until his face transformed into Valla's.

Everything was identical. Her eyes, her lips. Down to the braids, feathers and charms in her hair.

This time, when he spoke, he used her exact tone of voice. Her inflection, her cadence, but laced with a venomous flair she never used. "Would you hesitate to strike me now?"

Arithel's upper lip curled in a sharp, involuntary snarl. A twisted mix of revulsion and rage flashing across his face as he watched his magic dangling from the hands of a madman.

In one last act of hope, Valla reached for her magic. Channeling everything she had left. She called forth the shadows. They slid off the walls onto the floor, and glided towards her. Winding around her legs and torso before spiraling around her arms. They pooled into her palms until they formed a dense dark core. She stretched her arms wide, then she slammed both palms together once, a loud and sharp clap.

In an instant the world vanished. Darkness swallowed everything.

Only she could see through it. A void where no light escaped. Where the world simply ceased to be. No walls. No floor. No castle. It was to *trap* Zarriq in a cage of nothingness. A place even magic hesitated to reach.

Valla raised her hands, ready to seal the boundary around him, but then the air shifted.

Eyes started appearing. One after another. Over a dozen eyes snapped open in the void and multiplying. Zarriq's eyes. Surrounding her. They blinked independently, watching her from every angle.

His voice cut through the darkness. Flat and dry, as if the words physically exhausted him.
"I'm getting really bored of all your party tricks. I've seen frogs put on a better performance."

With a snap of his finger, the void shattered like glass. Light returned. Reality snapped back into place. The castle, the walls, the floor, all reappeared as if nothing had ever happened.

Valla and Arithel exchanged uneasy glances, realization sinking in. Ysmerra had been right. Their magic was useless against him.

Zarriq dusted off his hands and exhaled. One shoulder lifted in a half shrug. One long blink, his mouth curling into a smirk that knew far more than it let on. His head lolled slightly to the side, voice dry with mock surrender.

"If I can't harm you... I suppose there's nothing I can do."

His head straightened with an eerie unsettling slowness. His gaze slid up to meet theirs. Something sinister had woken behind his eyes. When he spoke again, the words came like an irrevocable merciless of madness.

"... except imprison you."

He raised his arms. The magic poured forth like liquid light, cascading around Arithel and Valla in an enormous circle. The light glowed, pulsed, flickered, and hummed. Spiraling and swirling faster and faster. Reaching higher and higher, all the way to the ceiling.

They were overtaken by the gusts of wind, they could barely see through it. A fortress of moving energy formed around them. The prison became a spinning cyclone of enchanted bricks, a shifting cage of magic. A wall that pulsed, alive with power, untouchable, and unbreakable.

From the rafters above, Reagan watched as the monstrous cocoon of magic was spiraling shut around her parents. Without hesitation she plunged into the center of the structure before it fully enclosed. It sealed shut above her with a deep grinding groan that rattled through the chamber like the closing of a tomb. Fatefully trapping her inside with her parents.

Together.

YSMERRA

We have to limit how many custom potions we accept in a week. There's a line of werewolves outside waiting on flea and tic tonic.

PIP

Word must have got out about my *Full Moon Deluxe Spa Experience.* While you were off at that dreary meeting with The Order of Unhelpful Insights, I was offering a special. Back shaving, claw sharpening, de-shedding soak, and foot massages. We're booked through the next full moon.

YSMERRA

So a dog grooming salon? You turned my apothecary into a glitter-coated haunted kennel. That cauldron is for hexes and brews, not bubble baths!

PIP

It's a high end enchanted spa experience. Premier Paranormal Pampering... with chin scratches and belly rubs. Very exclusive clientele.

YSMERRA
I can't believe this is happening in my potion shop.
Furry beasts strutting around with towel turbines and
clay masks. Wearing my silk robes like this is some kind
of enchanted pet resort... That actually explains the smell of
lavender and wet dog.

PIP
Also, small favor—can you handle this centaur waxing? I'm
a little behind schedule.

YSMERRA
...I beg your *entire existence*? I'm not waxing anyone's
anything! I swear by every screaming spirit in the veil, if I
walk into my potion lab and see a half-naked
mythological mammal on my table...

PIP
He tips *very* well for services not exactly listed
on the menu. Just saying. He brings his own oil
for a thorough polishing.

YSMERRA
... I'm going to the garden. To sit and stare
at a shrub.
Until I've successfully unheard
everything you've just said.

CHAPTER 32
The Time Prison

Reagan plunged through the spiraling seal of magic, the roar of stone and wind rushing past her ears like a scream from the void. She braced herself, arms tight, heart pounding, until her feet slammed into solid ground. She staggered, caught her balance, then looked up.

There they were. Her parents. Just steps away. Staring at her as if their eyes were deceiving them. For a second, no one moved. No one breathed.

The words barely made it out of Reagan's mouth. Emotion caught in her throat. Breathless and disbelieving.
"Mom! Dad!"

Valla and Arithel surged forward, each grasping their daughter's forearm. Just below the elbow. A classic warrior greeting.

Respect. Trust. Strength.

Valla held firmly, her eyes locked with Reagan's. Then nodded her head in reverence. Reagan smiled and returned it. Wordless and solemn, before turning to her father and nodded before him.

Arithel moved his hand up to the back of her neck and leaned his forehead against hers. He tried to blink the tears away. To swallow. To Breath. To hold it together. But an unmistakable sniffle escaped him. Just the sound of the sniffle, the sob, made Valla's throat swell, and made Reagan's eyes burn.

Then when Arithel leaned back they saw his eyes swelling, tears sliding onto his cheeks, and that made their eyes leak faster than they could wipe it away. Silent and Relentless.

Reagan smiled as her eyes shifted back and forth looking at her parents in disbelief. Her voice was barely more than a breath when she said,
"You came for me."

Valla looked into Reagan's eyes. Her soft voice was reassuring, even through her mask of composure.

"Of course we came! We would've been here sooner but—"

She hesitated, then glanced at Arithel. Who finished her sentence.

He was still staring at Reagan. Like he couldn't quite believe she was real. A half-laugh slipped through his tears.
"The whole memory thing."

Reagan let out a wet laugh, her tears slipping freely down her cheeks. Valla and Arithel didn't let go of their daughter just yet. They were savoring the moment. One they worried might never come.

Arithel looked around, taking in their new surroundings. His voice broke through the silence.
"At least we're together in this prison."

And that moment of peace was gone.

Reagan wiped away the last of her tears, and took a deep breath before she started to explain herself.
"That's partly why I jumped in... When Zarriq was casting this spell, I felt something. I picked up on time magic. As the barrier was forming, I could feel it more."

She paused, her throat working around the next words before they came. Her gaze dropped to the dagger still clutched in her hand. She turned it slowly, almost absently, but with a searching look, as though it might offer confirmation. Like she was finally admitting something out loud. Though she wasn't sure they'd understand.
"That's something I learned how to do here. How to tap into time magic."

Arithel and Valla exchanged a glance. It was silent and brief, but loaded.

Reagan's magic wasn't supposed to awaken yet. Not at seventeen. Not like this. And certainly not through training. In Eldrannor, learning magic, cultivating it, was a breach of sacred law. One didn't study magic. One was granted it. When the gods decided. When the stars aligned. When the blood called it forth. Yet here she stood. Holding proof in her hands.

Arithel's gaze dropped to the dagger, its edge glinting with something more than steel. His eyes narrowed just slightly, not in suspicion, but in reassessment. The way a soldier sizes up a commander he never expected to follow.

The past few days, Valla and Arithel had broken many rules they'd sworn to uphold. Sacred oaths, political lines, the boundaries had all blurred.

Arithel finally nodded. A gesture of full, deliberate trust.

If Reagan believed she could open the prison, they weren't going to question it. They stepped back. Not in retreat, but in solidarity. Eyes on her. Weapons ready. Faith offered, without condition.

Valla's eyes softened as she took in the sight of her daughter. A warrior in her own right. There was respect and pride in her gaze. The bittersweet truth that her daughter had grown up without her. And yet she couldn't be prouder. She gave a slow, solemn nod in approval.
"No spell is stronger than your will."

Reagan nodded back and stepped toward the wall. She didn't know it at the time, but the dagger Ysmerra gave her, *The Silver Eclipse of Eternity,* had the power to cut through the fabric of existence. Now she knows. She can feel it. Reagan glanced back with a reassuring smile.

She raised the dagger, placing one hand against the shifting wall of the barrier. The shadows flickered erratically, speeding up and slowing down like something unstuck in time. She inhaled sharply, feeling the magic within the wall, feeling how it was woven together.

Then she moved forward, stepping inside the currents of the barrier. She let the magic swirl around her, pulling her deeper into its unstable flow. Shadows unraveled and reformed, flickering between moments. She sucked in a sharp breath. The magic whispered against her skin, winding around her like unseen fingers. Her body stopped being hers and became a vessel, a thread being pulled taut by something far older than she understood. Her soul had been humming beneath her skin for years and only now found its harmony.

Light unfurled from her sternum, soft and golden at first. Then it spread, curling across her skin in vines of silver fire. Symbols bloomed across her skin. Etchings in a language being remembered. Weaving patterns, leaving trails of molten geometry.

The markings shimmered with layered color, like starlight refracted through crystal. Indigo overlaid with gold. Violet veined with white. Glyphs that glowed with impossible light.

Her feet left the ground. The wind swirled upward from nowhere, drawn to her, dancing. She gripped the dagger, letting the magic take her to the top of the prison. Then she sliced downward. The blade cut through the very fabric of the spell.

A deafening crack pierced through reality. Layers of the prison peeled back in loud gashes flowing past them and disappearing. When the outside world reappeared, the suffocating walls of the prison were gone. But so was everything else.

Valla and Arithel were still there, but the ruined castle, the decay, the destruction, it was all gone. In its place stood something... pristine. Untouched. Beautiful.

The grand hall gleamed. Walls of milky quartz crystal shimmered like flecks of frozen stardust. Vast opalescent tiles rippled with shifting colors. The vaulted ceilings swirled like a starry night, casting a dreamlike radiance throughout the castle. Everything was flawless and unbroken. It was exactly as Reagan remembered under the glamour spell. But this wasn't an illusion. This was real.

Reagan pulled up her sleeves. Her arms were no longer bare. She turned her wrists slowly, watching the symbols catch the light. She slipped off her jacket, letting it fall to the floor. Her eyes traced the glowing symbols as they climbed over her shoulders, like a map written in starlight, revealing just how far they reached. The markings shimmered softly beneath her skin. Silver laced with blue, flickering faintly. The sigils moved gently, like breath beneath water, pulsing in rhythm with her heartbeat.

The Chaos Lands. The telepathic messages. The jumps through time. The slippage between years. Her early connection. And now, stepping into time magic itself. All of that hadn't just awakened her magic. It had accelerated it. The realization hit with quiet clarity.

Valla clutched at Arithel's arm. They approached her slowly, as if afraid any sudden movement might undo what had just happened. They didn't speak. Valla reached for her first, taking Reagan's hands gently in hers and then lifted them to her lips and kissed them. One hand, then the other.

Her father followed. He stepped in close and pressed a kiss to her forehead and then to her hands. Reagan stood between them, anchored by their touch, her arms glowing softly, marked by magic, by time, by blood. For those few minutes, time felt mercifully still as they were honoring that moment.

But eventually, reality pressed back in. Arithel was the first to stir. Valla released Reagan's hands, gently, and stepped back.
They were free from the time prison. That much was clear. But this wasn't the world they remembered.

Arithel turned in place, taking it all in. He turned to Reagan, his expression guarded. Trying to make sense of this.
"We're in the same place... just a different time?"

Valla walked over to touch one of the stone pillars, as if confirming it was solid beneath her fingers. Her voice was quiet. "This is impossible..."

Reagan took a shaky step forward, her mind racing. And then, realization struck her like a blow to the chest. She pieced it together in an instant. And dread pooled in her stomach.
"Oh no."

Reagan turned to her parents. Her voice steady, but her eyes betrayed the weight of what she was about to say.
"Zarriq wanted Kayleth because... he has earth magic."

Arithel's head snapped toward her, his sharp elven features darkened by suspicion.

In Eldrannor, *no one* was supposed to know. Not until their eighteenth year, when the council branded them in sacred ink, marking their rite into magic. Until then, every child's gift remained a mystery. A *divine secret*, chosen not by bloodline or talent, but through a weaving of the gods' will and the soul's true nature. Not even the shamans knew. Not the seers. Not the elders. To speculate was taboo.

Arithel's gaze hardened. The look of a man trained to hear danger, not in volume but in detail. The line between his brows deepened as

if a silent alarm had been triggered. He asked, his voice calm, but carried a tension.
"How do you know that?"

Reagan met his gaze. She didn't shrink from it. She spoke with grit. Like someone holding a sacred truth. It was not a guess. It was all already decided. Like prophecy.

Zarriq had spoken with certainty, the kind that didn't leave room for doubt. As if fate had already sent him the answer long before the question was ever asked. He had known about Kayleth. Had seen something in the boy, something ancient and buried, the quiet pulse of earth itself.

He had been right about Reagan. She had awakened to ether magic, just as Zarriq had predicted she would. Untethered by elemental form, moving between planes, threading through time and memory. A gift no one could have foreseen, *and yet, he had.*

Arithel crossed his arms while he studied her. He could see the understanding in her face. The conviction in her voice. She held knowledge she wasn't supposed to have. And she stood in it without flinching. Standing before him with the knowing.

She wasn't a child reporting what she'd been told, she was a warrior relaying mission intel to her team. Her voice didn't waver. Her shoulders were squared. This was *her land* now. She had walked its ravaged roads, seen what magic had rotted, what still whispered with potential. Here, now, she was the one with answers. Not them. And they were listening.

Reagan spoke with the authority of someone who had stopped asking for permission.
"Zarriq needed Kayleth's power to restore the castle and the land. That would undo the curse on the ogres and reverse the chaos magic that's been corrupting the cities outside the kingdom."

Then Reagan paused, her posture shifted. Her head tilting slightly, almost thoughtful. Trying to cushion her next words, bracing them for the truth, because she already knew it was going to hit hard. She didn't say it outright. It was carefully wrapped. She laid the trail. Allowing them the dignity of reaching the conclusion themselves.

When she spoke again, the words came out slow and deliberate. As if saying it gently might dull the edge.

"But... Kayleth doesn't get his powers until he's eighteen..."

Her gaze flicking between them, watching, waiting to see if they'd catch up.

Arithel's lips parted slightly as his brows lifted. He let out a deep exhale. The truth had landed. The realization solidified in his mind. He looked upward, at nothing. At the ceiling. At the gods. At whatever invisible force had stolen those years.

He nodded, slow and bitter. He was almost reluctant to say it. As if saying it out loud would make it real. He looked sad, angry, betrayed. "Which means... Kayleth is eighteen."

Valla let out a soft gasp and slowly shook her head, as if trying to deny the truth forming before them. She looked back over her shoulder at the spot where the time prison had once existed. It had only felt like moments.

The castle had changed. Time had passed. The world outside was not the one they had left behind...

And they had no idea what awaited them beyond the walls of that chamber.

PIP
Wait— hold up.
So we just *skipped* the whole part where Kayleth
grows up in a cursed castle, a realm full of druids
and ogres, secrets and spells? Don't tell me we
have to wait for a sequel or spin-off just to find out
what happened during the *entire* time gap!

YSMERRA
I'd like to see Martouf's full redemption arc. Training like a
warrior monk. Studying time magic in secret, cutting his
hair with a dagger for dramatic effect.

PIP
Yes!! And at some point he actually *opens* the time prison,
but of course Zarriq, Daddy Warlocks, finds out and
rebuilds it again.

YSMERRA
What if Martouf bonds with Kayleth. Big brother
energy. Tells him *everything*. What really happened.
Who he is. Where he came from. And then BAM.
Zarriq erases Kayleth's memory.

PIP
Can you imagine Kayleth's emo teen era.
He gets sick of everyone treating him like a
glass vase on a holy pedestal and runs away
into the Chaos Lands.

YSMERRA
We could finally explore what's actually in the
Chaos Lands. Everyone talks about it like it's
The Forbidden IKEA of Reality. I want details.

PIP
Speaking of a spin off. Reagan's time in the chaos
lands. It could be like Wonderland meets Labyrinth meets
Never Ending sleep-deprived horror and dread.

YSMERRA
I *want* to like it, but that trope is overdone. It's always
"girl lost in a surreal fever dream of trauma and
whimsy." Been there. Bought the mushroom hat.

PIP
So is Kayleth actually a prisoner? Magic tethered?
Controlled? Or did they make him believe he's a
prince. The *Chosen One.* Raised like a relic. Told he's
the last hope of a doomed realm. Everyone bows to
him, but no one tells him the truth… Hmmm...
no it's a cage. Definitely a cage.

YSMERRA
Well hush and we'll found out...

CHAPTER 33
The Prisoners Escape

Just beyond the door, the faintest sound of footsteps echoed through the corridor. Arithel, Valla, and Reagan turned their heads toward the door all at once and unsheathed their blades in a single breath.

The boots against the cold stone floor were not hurried, confident in rhythm, and getting closer.

Arithel stepped forward, Valla's hands lit with magic, and all three moved into a battle stance without a word, ready for whatever stepped through that door. Swords tight, eyes locked on the doorway.

The footsteps grew louder, closer, until a figure stepped through the arched doorway into the chamber.

Tall. Broad-shouldered. A warrior. A sword hung at his side, not for show, but for use.

An elf, with long hair. It was the eyes that gave him away. Those same bright blue eyes. Those same lashes that had fluttered against Valla's neck when he fell asleep on her shoulder. That same nose Reagan used to tap with a fingertip to make him laugh.

The boy was gone. But his soul shined through.

They knew who he was.

Valla's heart was both melting and wrenching in the same instant.

Just moments ago, he stood in that same doorway as a child, no more than four years old. Now, he stood before them a warrior, raised in another man's world.

...

The walls of the time prison solidified and sealed shut with a deep, grinding groan that rattled through the chamber like the closing of a tomb. Zarriq barely spared it another glance. Their time had stopped. They were no longer his concern.

He turned his attention to Kayleth, whose small arms lifted, wordlessly asking to be held. Zarriq carried him away, deep within the castle, past wards and hidden passages, to his private sanctum.

A pang of sorrow swept through him as he searched for an acceleration spell. One that could turn Kayleth eighteen overnight. Zarriq found himself charmed by the boy's presence in a way he never expected. He didn't want to let go of these precious moments.

So instead, he stretched the growth across five years. Not so fast he'd lose every chance to bond with the boy, but just long enough for Kayleth to grow familiar with them. To trust them. To understand the shape of what he was becoming.

More than anything, Zarriq wanted it to be Kayleth's choice to help. Not because he was told, or forced, or fated, but because he wanted to.

Through midnight strolls and moonlit stories, they gave him love, affection, and a semblance of normality in a world that was anything but. Zarriq sought out the finest instructors from all the realms, bringing them to the castle to mold Kayleth into mastery.

A scholar. A warrior.

Kayleth's growth was so rapid that every few months felt like a new chapter. Martouf and Zarriq never let those moments pass quietly. The castle would be festooned with streamers and banners. Huge dessert trays would be laid out. Grand festivals spun just for him, each one more magical than the last.

Zarriq and Martouf were his family. His world.

On the moon of Kayleth's eighteenth birthday, the whole kingdom had gathered. Ogres, druids, and creatures of all kinds came to witness the moment of Kayleth's awakening. Zarriq had planned it for years, weaving together the traditions of both their ancestors.

On the kingdom grounds, Elders in deep red cloaks stood silently in a large circle beside blazing torches. Priests of the Order bathed Kayleth in sacred oils, dressed him in ceremonial robes, and whispered fragments of prophecy. The elders chanted low incantations and led him through the old rites of preparation. Zarriq began summoning ancient spirits from earth magic bloodlines. They spoke in unison, their voices rising like wind through a canyon, weaving a chant that had not been heard in a thousand years. Their tones were layered and resonant, like distant thunder. A pulse rippled through the land and sky.

The cosmos had chosen Kayleth's skin as a scroll, his birthright written in living flame. Vines of glowing blue swirled and stretched across his skin. Zarriq knelt before him and took his hands, then pressed Kayleth's palms to the earth. The ground shuddered. Their joined magic tore through the land like a shockwave. It surged through every root, every buried seed, every vein of soil, and into the chaos territory.

Every creature felt it. The dead earth erupted into emerald green grass that spread like wildfire. Trees once withered stretched to the heavens. The chaos surrendered and balance was restored. The curse was lifted. The ogres were able to speak freely, voices unshackled. The fog from their minds had been lifted. Martouf found his voice, whole, fluid, and his own. Primordial magic returned to the Druids and Ogres. It had rewritten them. Restored their youth. Stripped the wear of time from their faces, as if the years had been nothing more than dust blown off an ancient statue.

Friends and families lost were now reunited. Voices of disbelief filled the air. Kayleth was lifted on shoulders and praised in every tongue. The castle halls, once silent, burst to life with music, dancing and feasting. The celebrations continued for months. The kingdom had returned to its people.

YSMERRA
This is exactly why you follow a spell recipe to the nose.
Only a half vial of zombie breath and now his son's walking
around looking like a sea sprite with that blue hair. Amateur
alchemist. That's something I'd expect from you. Why is it
so hard to follow a recipe to its entirety.

PIP
Wait! Five years have passed there… isn't that's thirty-five
years here!?… Why does it only feel like five minutes
have passed?

YSMERRA
Because I froze time the moment they stepped foot into
Balderon.

PIP
You altered the flow of time for an entire
realm and didn't think that was worth
mentioning?!

YSMERRA
Would you have preferred I made a banner?... What's the
status of the laundry room?

PIP
Still cursed. The laundry folding spell turned into a
sentient sock octopus. It hosts a cabaret show with the
poltergeist's every night at seven. They're actually pretty
good, but still no fresh towels.

YSMERRA
Typical.

PIP
Well? Are we gonna do a spell to see what
happened during those five years!

YSMERRA
Do you mind? My stories are on. This is
better than The Haunted Housewives of
Hell.

....

The sight of three weapons drawn on him. The prison dismantled. The captives loose.

Kayleth unsheathed his sword fast, not to defend, but to strike. His stance was angled and taut with tension.

His voice rang through the halls, sharp and alarmed.
"Father! The prisoners have escaped!"

Kayleth's gaze darted between them, measuring, calculating, never resting. He tracked every breath, every subtle shift in their stance, the way he had been taught. His awareness was razor sharp, sweeping the space for threats, escape points, weaknesses.

Every lesson drilled into him, the years of training under the finest sword masters and war tacticians in all the realms, had prepared him. It all rose to the surface now like muscle memory.

He stood tall, grounded, blade steady, prepared for anything. If they so much as twitched, he'd be ready to demolish them.

Valla lowered her sword to her side and stepped forward, her voice gentle yet urgent. Reaching toward him as if she might disarm the storm building behind his eyes.
"Kayleth."

He didn't hesitate. He quickly raised his sword and leveled it at her. Blade steady. Didn't even flinch. The metal gleamed under the torchlight.

His voice was cold and unfamiliar. His eyes didn't blink. Didn't soften. They were fixed on her like a predator assessing distance before the strike.
"Hush, thief. Stay back!"

Valla faltered for half a breath but kept moving. One step, then another. She held her hand low and open in a plea, trying to get through to him.

Her tone rising, cracking slightly. The desperation visible in her eyes.
"You don't understand. If you would just listen—"

But the words were wasted. Kayleth didn't let his guard drop for
even a second, his grip tightening on the hilt. Something was wrong,
but he couldn't place it.

He wouldn't let her speak. He cut across her voice with his own,
deeper now, more commanding. His tone left no room for
uncertainty.
"I know exactly who you are. My father had you locked away for a
reason."

Valla flinched, not from the blade, but from the words.

My father.

The thought of Zarriq raising her child made her blood boil and her
stomach sicken. She couldn't imagine what he had been through. Her
concern was growing by the second, thinking about what
brainwashing tactics had been used on her boy. What lies he had
been told.

Still, she stepped closer. She knew her boy still lingered behind that
guarded gaze. The boy who laughed in her arms would see her
standing there and pleading. She kept walking forward, thinking her
voice would reach through to him.

She tried again, voice trembling.
"Kayleth, please—"

But in his eyes, her movement was no longer a plea. It was a threat.
And before she could finish her sentence, he moved. Like a fuse
catching fire.

Kayleth lunged. Silent and precise. His blade sliced through the
space between them like an arc of silver and fury.

Valla barely had time to dodge his attack.

Reagan quickly stepped forward to shield her, blocking Kayleth's
strike.

The moment Reagan's blade met his, parrying the first strike with a sharp clang of steel, something shifted. It was no longer a warning. It was war, and Kayleth didn't hold back.

He was a whirlwind of steel and wrath, eyes blazing, blade flashing, taking them on with the full weight of everything he had become.

His strikes came fast and brutal, as if he'd been preparing for this moment his entire life. Every pivot, every slash, every calculated blow was executed with precision. His fury was unrelenting.

He didn't know them. He didn't remember. To him, they were the enemy.

In his home.

In his castle.

They only blocked his strikes, never countering with their own.

Then, Zarriq burst into the room. His eyes swept the scene in an instant. He quickly caught on that Reagan's magic had broken the time prison. That she had already tapped into her magic. He knew he couldn't put them in another prison. They would just escape again. He had no time to think.

Arithel saw Zarriq and charged at him. Blade raised, roaring with fury and vengeance as he closed the distance between them, his boots hammering against the stone floor, the rage burning behind every step.

Zarriq barely managed to summon a sword from the wall. The weapon flew into his grasp just as Arithel's strike came down. Their swords clashed, sending sparks flying over them in a shower of light.

As their swords were crossed, Arithel snarled through clenched teeth, driving forward with brute force, all of his muscles trembling with rage and adrenaline.
"I've been waiting for this."

Zarriq's grip was straining as the weight of Arithel's assault bore down on him. He dug in his heels, holding his place with grim defiance. His arms ached. The force behind Arithel's blade threatened to break through, but he didn't let it show. Not even a flicker.

Instead, he lifted his chin just slightly and gave Arithel a crooked smile. Half amusement, half provocation. His eyes danced with mischief. Taunting him silently, like this was all part of the game and he was still two moves ahead.

"Let's see if you can take from me what I stole from you."

The words dripped with challenge, but it was his face, that infuriating calm, the glint of enjoyment in his eyes that struck like a slap.

Arithel's fury only deepened. He poured every ounce of his weight into him. His shoulders trembled with the effort as he pressed his sword down, trying to overpower Zarriq through sheer force.

And still, through gritted teeth and labored breath, Arithel forced words out. He rasped, each word jagged and strained with effort.

"I want to hear you say that while you bleed."

Zarriq shoved him off with a sharp grunt. Their blades scraped apart as they staggered back.

He gave Arithel a slow, curling smirk, one brow lifted in amused challenge. It was all performance now, and Zarriq was loving every second of it. He said, smooth and unbothered,

"You want blood? Fine... I doubt you'll be alive long enough to hear it."

Across the chamber, the clash of steel rang louder and sharper than words. Kayleth continued his assault against Valla and Reagan.

Valla, still dodging Kayleth's relentless strikes, stumbled back.

She cried out, her voice cracking with urgency and frustration.

"Kayleth! Will you please just stop and listen?"

Her words bounced off him like her blade did. Ineffective and unwanted.

Kayleth didn't respond. He only pressed harder. Their swords met again and again, Valla always catching the rhythm of his strikes.

Her voice was breathless and aching.

"Look at our markings. You have the same ones. It's our bloodline."

He refused to look. He tried to keep focus. He kept coming at them fast and hard. But he couldn't deny their facial resemblance. The bright blue eyes. Their pointy ears. Their noses. They looked like him. Too much like him. It was enough to make him falter, to make him question who these people truly were.

Reagan intercepted his next move. Their blades collided. She grabbed a hold of his shirt and pulled him close, their eyes inches apart. She looked at him deeply, and in a voice so serious she revealed,
"We are your family, Kayleth."

Kayleth snarled instinctively as he pushed her off. Ridiculous, he thought. He knew who his family was. Zarriq and Martouf. The idea was preposterous.

But the longer he fought, the more he noticed, they weren't fighting back. That made him realize something was wrong.

Zarriq saw it. The slip in Kayleth's stance, the flicker of confusion in his eyes. He saw the doubt creeping into Kayleth's face like a crack in stone. His blade no longer fueled by blind rage, but by uncertainty.

That moment of distraction was all Arithel needed. Arithel lunged forward, slamming Zarriq into the nearest stone pillar with a bone-jarring thud that rattled its base and made dust fall from the ceiling.

Arithel used the momentum to trap him. His forearm braced across Zarriq's collarbone, pressing him against the stone. Hearts thundering between them like war drums.

Arithel yelled. A deep, thundering demand.
"No more lies! Tell him the truth!"

Zarriq didn't even flinch. He smiled. Sharp and maddening. Looked directly into Arithel's eyes. Amused. So proud of what he had done, and what he had accomplished. Boasting.
"The truth? That he calls me father. Stands by my side. Fighting *with* me. Fighting *for* me."

Reagan tried to speak through every block, during every one of Kayleth's strikes. Her voice sliced through the noise, not loud but sharp. The kind of truth that carried weight even without volume.

She tried to explain everything. Her voice was tight with grief, taking responsibility for the whole situation. How she was the one who summoned Zarriq because she didn't want Kayleth to suffer like she had. How they came here when he was little. She went through it all. Told him the whole story.

Kayleth didn't respond. His thoughts spiraled. For a second, everything slowed. Time, sound, movement. Her words dug somewhere deep, at something buried.

But he refused to believe it. This had to be some trick. Some manipulative spell. His life couldn't be false. It wasn't.

He shook his head hard, trying to banish the rising tremor inside his chest.

Focus.
Return order.
Secure the situation.
Lock up the prisoners.
Let father explain later.

He took a deep breath. His grip tightened. And then he surged forward with fueled purpose.

Valla and Reagan saw the shift in him. His anger boiled. His strike had more teeth than before. His strike was meant to damage.

Quickly, they tried to block it. Both their blades met his at the same time and got tangled. For one suspended breath, all three swords were locked. Cross-guards snagged, hilts pressing together, arms overlapping. They couldn't disengage. Their forearms were pressed close to one another, wrists straining in the tangled knot of weapons and force.

Then, Kayleth saw it.

Their markings.

The ancient symbols and glyphs flowing across their skin. Same as his. He had never seen anyone in Balderon with those markings. A chill shot through him like cold lightning.

He yanked his arm away as if it burned, staring at the proof etched into his skin. Stumbling backward with a choked gasp, his sword falling to his side. His chest rose in ragged, uneven pulls. His entire body was trembling, shaken, not from fear but from something far worse.

Recognition.

He looked at Reagan. At Valla. Staring at them. His pulse roaring in his ears.

Valla's eyes were practically swimming. Tears clinging to the edges but never falling. Her sword forgotten, hanging limp at her side.

Her voice cracked, soaked in the effort it took to keep it steady. Breathlessly she said.
"My baby. My beautiful baby boy."

Those words hit Kayleth like a crack splitting through his core. His entire body tense, his eyes widened like he had seen a ghost. He stilled. Unsure. Haunted, and disbelieving.

In search of the truth, he turned slowly, almost mechanically, toward the one figure he'd always trusted, always believed.

His eyes intense as they locked with Zarriq's.
"Is this... true?"

Then pointed to Arithel with his sword. His voice was charged. He looked at Zarriq demanding to know.
"Is he... my father?"

There was no escape. Not this time. Zarriq's shoulders dropped, limp, as if they could no longer carry the weight of pretense. No elegant deflection. No story left to tell that could shield his son from the truth.

Zarriq exhaled, long and heavy, like it carried the last of his lies.

Then he said at last, the words quiet, but true and painful to admit.
"I'm your father, too."

PIP
It's giving "Luke, I am your father... depending on custody arrangements and blood sigils." I want a remix of that scene where Kayleth just keels over and screams "NOOOOO! I'm not a prince? I'm a pauper!" into a pit of despair while lightning strikes behind him... We need more tea, but I don't want to miss anything. Hmmm... I'll ask Gregor to get it.

YSMEERA
Who in the name of spectral soup is Gregor? One of your pet rocks?

PIP
My assistant. I re-animated a Skeleton. Well just it's bottom half. Legs. No torso. He zooms around like a frantic centipede. Carries potions in its hip satchel. Occasionally moonwalks.
I'm not set on the name though. It's between Gregor, Reginald and Winslow. Wini for short.

YSMERRA
I can't leave you unsupervised for three hours. I return and suddenly we have skeletal housekeeping staff. I'm afraid to even ask... is anyone going to come looking for these legs?

PIP

No! I built them. Out of spare parts. They were on
clearance. You wouldn't believe the deals at
Ghoulmart's Midnight Estate Sale.

YSMERRA

You bought haunted bones at a garage sale run by the
undead?

PIP

Estate liquidation. Very classy. Came with a free jar of
ectoplasm. Also... a hellhound followed me home from
estate sale. It seems to be guarding the jar of ectoplasm.
I named him Fluffernox.

YSMERRA

Get that that demonic incarnation from the third circle
of screaming sulfur and his ectoplasm out of my
parlor room, out of this house, and off our
property! I am not getting possessed by a
demonic houseguest with boundary issues.
This placed is turning into a chaotic cursed
petting zoo... I'll be in my library. Unless
you turned that into some enchanted
bathhouse for squirrels?

PIP

Only on Thursdays... just kidding!

CHAPTER 34
The Prisoners Escape Part 2

Kayleth's eyes widened. His heart dropped into his stomach.
Like his whole world had just been shattered. His mouth opened
slightly, but no sound came. It was as if all the air had been sucked
out of the room. Kayleth's eyes slowly moved to look at Arithel, like
each movement cost him more than the last.

Arithel was already watching him. Quiet. Still. Arithel met his gaze
with a bittersweet smile, and took a hesitant step forward, eyes never
leaving his son's.
"I am your blood."

As if his heart couldn't drop any further. It felt like it fell to the floor.
The recognition and admission of it all. Kayleth stood frozen, the
truth sinking in like a blade to his chest. The weight of it all
threatened to crush him. He turned back to Zarriq, who looked more
defeated and heartbroken than ever.

Slowly, hesitantly, Arithel and Valla stepped on either side of Kayleth
and clasped his arm, leaning their forehead the sides of his head,
closing the space around him as if he might disappear again. Kayleth
remained still, distant, overwhelmed, his mind grasping for solid
ground, his breath caught somewhere between disbelief and
surrender.

Reagan stepped in front of Kayleth and placed her hand on his
shoulder. Wordless, quiet. Like the final piece of something broken
being made whole again. She bowed her head to him. Her eyes shut
tight.

For a long heartbeat, they just stayed like that. No explanations. No
defenses. Just four people, suspended in the fragile stillness that
comes right after the storm.

Valla lifted her head. She smiled as she was looking at Kayleth. His
eyes, his cheeks, nose and chin. Drinking him in.
"Let's go home."

This ache, this connection, this storm of emotion clinging to him now. He didn't know if he could call it home yet. But he didn't want to step away either.

He had never left Balderon. He never even spent the night away from the castle. This wouldn't be easy. It was stepping outside everything he knew. And yet… he didn't dread it. Somewhere beneath the fear and the confusion, he was curious. Drawn to the possibilities. He wanted to know them. Really know them. To see where he came from. To walk the land that had shaped them, feel the pulse of the magic that ran through all of them.

Kayleth turned his head, looking to Zarriq, who looked ashamed. Too proud to follow, too broken to speak.

Kayleth walked over to him. He stopped in front of the man who had raised him, protected him, and shaped him. The man who wasn't his blood, but had become his bones.

Zarriq looked worried at what Kayleth might say. But Kayleth wasn't angry and had no contempt for Zarriq at all. He grew up feeling so special and so loved. Zarriq had never been cruel, never cold.

Zarriq hadn't even lied. Not exactly. It was more nuanced than that. He avoided certain discussions or topics entirely so these things never came up.

Kayleth felt loved. Zarriq never was short on giving him that. That was real, and Kayleth knew it. He doesn't blame Zarriq for any of it. He still loves him, and always will. For Kayleth, he simply has two fathers now.

Kayleth took a step closer to Zarriq, lowering his voice.
"I want to know where I came from… and I want to spend time with them. Get to know them…"

He paused. Waiting for Zarriq's reaction, and approval, but Zarriq couldn't speak. He just looked at Kayleth, saddened and speechless.

Kayleth wasn't ready to abandon the life he had, not even close. He loved his home. He missed it already. He didn't plan on staying there forever. This wasn't a goodbye.
"I'll come back. I promise."

Zarriq swallowed hard, his throat working around the words. His eyes glistened, but he didn't look away.
"I love you, son."

The words struck deeper than Kayleth expected. The fact that Zarriq even felt the need to say it, to reaffirm something that had never been in question, made this all even worse. He knew his father loved him.

Kayleth's voice softened, like he didn't want to hurt him more than he already had.
"I never doubted that."

Zarriq pulled him into an embrace as he sobbed, his breath shuddering.
"I'll miss you."

Kayleth's arms came up, wrapping around him like a shield and whispered back.
"I'll miss you too."

They stood embraced for longer than either of them intended. Arms wrapped tight, neither one speaking, neither one willing to be the first to let go. It wasn't a forever goodbye. They both knew that. But it felt like one. Because it was the first real separation. The letting go hurt more than either of them had words for.

When they finally pulled apart, it wasn't with bitterness. A silent promise that this wasn't the end.

Kayleth took a deep breath and walked back toward his other family. Ready to leave with them.

Valla and Arithel were watching from a distance. They waited. Only once Kayleth was safely beyond reach did they begin to move. They stepped forward in front of Zarriq.

Zarriq saw them approaching. He turned toward them. He rolled his eyes with a bitter exhale.
"What now?"

They stopped right in front of him. A little too close. Even Zarriq was bothered by their closeness.

Arithel stood still like a fortress. His expression was calm, but his words came out like a threat.

"We can't risk you following us."

Zarriq's brow furrowed, but by the time realization sparked, it was already too late. While Zarriq's attention was on Arithel, before he could react—

Valla lifted one hand and blew gently across her palm, releasing a delicate plume of shimmering silver dust. It drifted onto Zarriq like harmless glitter.

Zarriq's eyes widened as the spell took hold, rage flaring behind his gaze.

Valla spoke with the weight of restraint, but joy threaded through every word.
"That's to prevent you from coming to our world again."

The enchantment rippled through him like invisible chains, binding him to the very air. The magic tethered him to his realm, locking him within a barrier. Similar to the he had once created to keep others out. Now it kept him in. Trapped in his own protection shield.

His fists clenched. His eyes burned with rage. Not at the spell itself, but at the audacity of it. Of being contained. He said nothing, but the silence pulsed with threat.

Valla and Arithel turned their backs on him and walked towards Reagan and Kayleth.

Zarriq cast them a sharp look, filthy with disdain. But then his gaze drifted. It landed on Reagan, and he smiled. A knowing smile. A devil's grin. It slithered across his face with theatrical flair, smug and unreadable.

Then he said, so soft, so elegantly devastating.
"Goodbye, Anastasia."

Her eyes widened. A gasp nearly escaped her lips.

Zarriq had already turned away, expression calm, posture composed.

Reagan stood frozen. Silent. Thoughts spinning. How long had he known? When she crossed into the past, did he know then? Or did he know the whole time? From the moment they first met? Her thoughts tangled in spirals, looping in on themselves with no answers. It unsettled her. And yet... it also intrigued her.

The four of them stood in a circle, hands clasped. A soft blue glow began to pulse between their joined palms.

Kayleth looked across the chamber. His eyes found Zarriq's. They held their gaze. Neither smiled.

A pulse of blue light shimmered around them, growing brighter and stronger until it engulfed them completely. And then, in a flash, they were gone.

Zarriq stood alone, staring at the space where they'd vanished. And for the first time in years, he felt devastatingly alone.

Reagan, Valla, Arithel, and Kayleth reappeared in the quiet stillness of Ysmerra's manor. The blue light faded slowly into the air. The walls around them were familiar, the very room from which they had departed. They were back in Eldrannor.

The four of them released each other's hands. A shared breath passed between them, one of relief, exhaustion, and something deeper.

Kayleth stood stiffly beside them, his eyes scanning the unfamiliar terrain, unsure of what to make of it all. Arithel rested a hand on his shoulder, a gesture of grounding, but didn't say a word.

They stepped forward together, the tension of battle slowly unwinding from their limbs.

They moved toward the door, ready to find Ysmerra, ready to go home.

But Reagan didn't move. She stayed in place. Her sharp voice broke the silence.
"Wait!"

The word stopped everyone mid step. Kayleth looked over, startled by the urgency in her tone.

Reagan's eyes were burning with purpose.
"We have to go back. There are other girls still there. Calla, Evra, and Sorrel. Zarriq tricked them too. They've been stranded there for

years. We can't leave them. We need to bring them home, back to their families."

Arithel nodded his head in agreement. He didn't know who those girls were, but he could hear it in Reagan's voice. This wasn't a request. This was a vow. He didn't need to hear the whole story. He understood immediately it was the right thing to do, and he was proud his daughter had honor.

Valla's lips parted slightly, her expression folding inward with guilt. She stepped forward beside Reagan and offered to go with her. Valla took Reagan's hands into hers, the faint pulse of the transport spell already flickering around their wrists. As the light began to build again, the chamber filled once more with light, and in a rush of wind and color, Reagan and Valla vanished.

They were transported to the small, humble shack. The place that had felt more like a tomb than a shelter. Hollow, quiet, and hopeless. A sagging roof barely holding off the wind.

Valla and Reagan stepped through the door, but Reagan paused at the threshold, momentarily stunned.

Now it looked like an actual home. A quiet awe washed over her as she took it all in, seeing all the new additions and details of the interior. Each of the girls' sleeping spaces had been made cozy, with pillows and blankets. The table had a cloth draped across its surface, dishes and silverware arranged, brass candlesticks standing tall, and at the center, a glass vase holding a spray of fresh flowers that still carried the scent of the meadow.

Books were stacked beside chairs, others piled haphazardly as if they were eagerly devoured. Rows of jars lined the walls with preserved fruits. The faint, comforting aroma of something recently baked.

A soft exhale escaped Reagan as she realized what she was seeing. Martouf had kept his promise. He had come for them. They were no longer barely surviving and abandoned.

All of a sudden, they heard laughing followed by voices just outside. The girls walked through the door, bright and light. Martouf walked in just behind them, his presence calm and undeniably comforting.

Reagan couldn't help but notice how at ease the girls seemed. It wasn't just that Martouf had kept his promise to help them, it was that he had genuinely befriended them. Their connection ran deeper than simple kindness; it was something real. They trusted him, and now, Reagan saw, they had begun to trust each other more as well.

They admitted they had prayed for her often. That she was safe. That she reached the castle. That she found her brother. And that they looked forward to the day they could see her again.

Reagan offered to take them home. To bring them back to their families and reunite them with their parents.

The girls exchanged quiet looks. For a moment, there was only the sound of the fire crackling in the corner and the distant rustling of the wind outside. The words hung in the air between them, but none of them rushed to speak.

Calla, Evra, and Sorrel shared a brief, silent understanding. Their eyes spoke volumes. Of the time spent together, of the laughter and shared moments, of the community they had formed within those walls. The idea of leaving one another felt... wrong.

The life they had begun to build here was more than just a shelter. It was a home, a place of belonging, and it had become theirs.

They took each other's hands with a quiet, unspoken agreement and turned to Reagan. Calla spoke for them. She sweetly said, "We are home..."

Reagan looked at each of the girls, one by one, and was met with the same quiet expression. Soft, reassuring smiles filled with warmth and certainty. There was no hesitation in their eyes, no fear in their voices. Just peace.

Gently, they explained that they had become each other's family. They didn't want to leave one another. Not now. Not after everything.

All their parents had let them go willingly, believing they were giving their daughters a better life. One of luxury, security, and nobility. It would be too heartbreaking to tell their parents what had happened. It was a kind of quiet relief, having their parents believe their girls had grown up in palaces, draped in silk and surrounded by finery, rather than having to face them and tell them the truth.

Their brothers and sisters were likely grown by now. Married. Maybe even had children of their own. Time had marched on without them. The idea of returning, of trying to step back into the societal standards of their world again. One of arranged futures and well-worn expectations. Find a husband. Start a family. Smile and behave.

That wasn't their path anymore. They liked the freedom here. The quiet autonomy to shape each day as they pleased. To choose their company, their pace, their dreams.

They made sure Reagan knew they were safe now. They were happy. And she didn't need to worry anymore. They thanked her deeply, sincerely. Their gratitude was unmistakable. Not just for coming back for them, but for remembering them at all.

Reagan smiled, her heart swelling with understanding. She knew, deep down, that they had made the right choice. For now, at least.

Their journey wasn't over, it was just beginning.

PIP
Nope! I can't see Kayleth surviving a week in normal society. The poor pampered prince will stage a coup when he realizes he has to butter his own toast.

YSMERRA
He'll absolutely be bribing forest animals to clean his room. You know, I really thought Reagan and Martouf were going to end up together. Lots of longing stares.

PIP
What? No. Team Baylos all the way. Their tension was palpable. It's called subtext.

YSMERRA
That Martouf turned out quite nicely. Tall. Strong. That tragic noble face. I bet he could carry me across a meadow with a single arm.

PIP
What are you saying?! You're like... 900 years old!

YSMERRA
Oh, calm down. And for the record, Edward was 300 years old in that one vampire scroll, and nobody batted an eye about their age gap... I think some readers might be upset they never got a steamy forest scene, if you know what I mean!

PIP

Eww! What people? Or are you just referring to
yourself? You need to stop reading those enchanted
romance scrolls.

YSMERRA

Noted. Well, that's the end of that adventure. I suppose we
go back to normal now. The sentient pantry, the sarcastic
spell books, your monthly arguments with the cursed muffins
and shrieking cupboards.

PIP

The cinnamon was supposed to neutralize the shrieking.
I read that somewhere.

YSMERRA

Where? On the back of a cereal box?
We've had enough drama to last us several
timelines. Let's change the channel.
Either *Haunted Antiques* or *Haunted Home
Shopping*.

PIP

Either one is fine. I'll *fetch* the tea.

CHAPTER
The Return

Kayleth, Reagan, and their parents walked through the threshold of the place they once called home. There was an undeniable sense of change, like stepping into a world that was both familiar and foreign.

There was so much to catch up on, so much to say, but the words didn't come easily at first.

Reagan had spent her whole life feeling disconnected from this place and from these people. Now, standing in it, after everything she went through, after all she did to get away from it, she felt a strange mix of relief and apprehension.

Ysmerra hadn't restored the memories to the entire tribe. Only to Arithel and Valla. It was a deliberate choice, one made out of necessity.

As far as the rest of Eldrannor was concerned, Arithel and Valla never had children, and it had to stay that way.

They couldn't go to the council and explain everything, not without exposing the countless laws they had broken.

Even Reagan's involvement placed her in danger. She had summoned a being from another realm without council permission, an act that defied one of the tribe's sacred codes.

If any of this came to light, the council would have no choice but to contain the damage. Their punishment would be swift, harsh, and irreversible.

For now, the safest path was silence.

No one knew who Kayleth and Reagan truly were. Their identities would need to be kept hidden carefully behind that silence. They must keep their true names, lineage, and their symbols concealed forever.

Arithel and Valla would present them to the tribe and the council as guests, or distant cousins. The rules of their world would apply, but they would be allowed to move within it, free from the constraints that had once defined them.

If Kayleth and Reagan wished to leave, to carve out a different destiny, Arithel and Valla offered their full support if that was their decision. It was completely their choice now. They were no longer obligated by family or the tribe.

Reagan realized that their guarded words were not meant as a punishment. They were an offering. Reagan's desperation for freedom and choice was what had initially caused her to summon Zarriq in the first place. Driven by a longing, a yearning for freedom from the constraints of the world she had known. She had wanted more. She had wanted to choose. To decide her own fate.

Now, the power to choose was finally hers. This was what she had wanted all along. The freedom to make her own decisions. To live a life not dictated by duty or obligation but by the desires of her heart. She had fought for this, not just for herself but for Kayleth as well. And now, standing here in the quiet aftermath of everything they had endured, she realized she had achieved it.

Valla and Arithel worked together to rebuild what had once been lost, restoring their children's rooms with new furniture and comforting decor. The walls of their home began to resemble remnants of their past.

As the moons passed, Kayleth found himself slowly adjusting to his new life in this foreign realm. He sat at the foot of his new bed, a place so different from the castle he had left behind. Everything felt so... new, and yet not quite right.

And then, without warning, a soft, dark gust of black wind swept through the window. It coiled along the walls and floor like serpents, dancing and writhing toward a single point in the center of the room before him.

From the veil of black smoke, Zarriq emerged like a phantom made real. The shadows peeled off of him, curling into nothingness as they left his cloak and dissipated into the floor.

The magic dust Valla had used to bind him, meant to anchor him to his realm like a prisoner in his own fortress, had worked...

At first.

Zarriq had felt its weight like invisible chains, but he never fought it. He could have unraveled it, but he didn't try. He had chosen to stay behind.

Kayleth had left with his true family, and Zarriq didn't want to be in the way.

But then, months later, something changed.

He was summoned.

Far from Balderon, someone desperately called his name, using an invocation spell pulled from old tales whispered across the worlds.

The two spells collided. The summoning shattered the tethering spell Valla had placed upon him.

With the chains broken, it caused him to feel something inside. Something he hadn't let himself feel in months.

The will to return.

After answering the call, after helping the one who summoned him, Zarriq didn't return to his castle. He didn't retreat into isolation.

Instead, he turned his steps toward Eldrannor. Not to interfere. Not to take back what had already been given. But just to see his boy.

And so, wrapped in black wind and shadow, unseen and uninvited, Zarriq came.

Kayleth leapt to his feet, his breath catching in his throat as his eyes locked on the shadowed figure emerging. The familiar silhouette. Like stone that had weathered every storm. His heart raced as he took in the sight of the man who had once been everything to him. His protector. His guide. His father.

He gasped, voice cracking under the weight of emotion.
"Father!"

He didn't wait. He rushed forward and collided into Zarriq's chest with force, arms wrapped around him tight. The warmth of his presence momentarily banished the cold of the room.

Zarriq staggered just half a step from the impact, but his arms rose quickly, instinctively, pulling Kayleth close and holding him equally as tight and unrelenting. As if afraid he might vanish the moment he let go. Zarriq closed his eyes, burying his face in Kayleth's shoulder.

His voice emerged tender and unguarded. Bright with emotion, and shy in its delivery.
"I missed you too much to stay away. I had to see you."

They stood there for a long moment, wrapped in something that felt older than words. Eventually, their embrace loosened, the moment stretching before they parted. Zarriq's hands moved to Kayleth's shoulders as if reluctant to sever the contact entirely, still in awe of the presence before him.

Kayleth's gaze dipped to the floor. His shoulders gave the slightest shrug. He said in a faltering voice, soft and uncertain, as if saying it out loud might make it true.
"I'm okay."

Then he eased down onto the edge of his bed, hands resting in his lap.

Zarriq stood for a moment longer, nodding his head. He heard it. The way the words tiptoed out like they were afraid of being seen. The tremble beneath them. He knew his son's voice too well to be fooled. He knew something was wrong. That this all wasn't quite what he hoped.

Zarriq followed, settling beside him. Worry tugged at the corners of his mouth. His voice softened with concern, one brow lifting just slightly.
"Just okay?"

Kayleth looked down, eyes fixed on the floor, contemplating his words, thumbs rubbing together. He had thought the change would be exciting. He didn't expect it to be like this. It had been hard adjusting. He thought it would be easier to fit in, to be in a new place, but it wasn't easy. None of this was. He missed home. And more than anything... he wanted to go back. But he didn't want to say that. None of it felt right.

When he finally spoke, he chose his words carefully and only gave just a sliver of what weighed on him. Everything was wrapped in

layers of diplomacy, softened and trimmed down.
"It's just... different here. The customs, the people, the silence... even the stars feel different. But I'm getting to know my parents and Reagan. They're good people. I owe them more time."

Zarriq didn't need the whole story. He already knew. And though he didn't press, didn't ask for more... he was hoping. Desperately hoping Kayleth would say it. That he wanted to come home.

Since Kayleth wouldn't say it outright, Zarriq baited the moment, just a little. Offered him the space to.

Zarriq's eyes narrowed, and then, with a crooked grin tugging at the edge of his mouth, he tilted his head and said with a hint of mischief creeping back into his usual raspy bravado.
"Why don't you just come back with me? We can steal back the royal crowns from those savages like we always talked about. We can rule the realms again, the way we were meant to. It'll be fun."

The question came like a tease, but the edge of sincerity hummed just underneath.

Kayleth let out a short laugh. His grin came unguarded with fondness. For a moment, he saw it all again, the fireside jokes, the half-serious plans, the reckless dreams they had shared. Zarriq, draped in mischief and madness, spinning tales of conquest. He missed it. All of it. Missed *him*. Missed his brother Martouf. The nonsense and shenanigans that would brew over there.

But his smile faded, and something softer settled behind his eyes. A weight. A choice. Despite the longing he felt, he shook his head slowly. His voice was firm and reluctant at the same time.
"I feel like... they need more than just a few months. I... owe them more than that."

Zarriq's grin faltered, just slightly. His shoulders lowered. He hadn't expected Kayleth to say yes but some foolish part of him had still held onto the chance. Now, hearing it spoken aloud, that hope unraveled quietly inside him.

He swallowed the disappointment. He didn't argue. He didn't protest. He simply held the silence for a moment longer, as if giving the words space to breathe while his eyes lingered on Kayleth's face.

He just needed his son to know, that if he ever needed anything. That he will always be there. No matter the reason. He would arrive quicker than a crow fleeing fire.

But like his son, Zarriq had never been one to say such things so plainly. Instead, he offered something that said *everything* without having to say it all. The devotion in his voice said it all.
"You can summon me *anytime*... You're the only one who knows the true way to call me forward."

Others went to great lengths to summon Zarriq. Rituals that involving etched sigils, candles, rare herbs, and ancient languages recited by trembling tongues. A whole production meant to beckon something as vast and unknowable as him.

What they didn't realize was that most of it was unnecessary. They only managed to summon him at all by accident.

The true spell. The original one. Kayleth knew. He knew because he asked. And Zarriq told him without hesitation. As if the knowledge had always belonged to him.

It was a sacred trust. A bond. It was about *who* had the right to call him forward. And he felt Kayleth had that right. His son had the right.

To be given permission to use that secret truth Zarriq had once placed in his hands. To be allowed to use that knowledge. Not for ceremony or obligation, but for *himself*. For nothing more than *wanting* his father near. That meant *everything*.

Kayleth leaned forward, his arms wrapped around Zarriq tightly. A silent understanding. One part goodbye, one part never-letting-go.

Zarriq returned it just as firmly. He held the back of Kayleth's head like he had when he was a boy. Like he could still protect him, even now.

Time seemed to stretch. It was a farewell written in stillness. Everything they wanted to say, was said in silence, in the moment, in the embrace.

Then Zarriq leaned back, just enough to cup Kayleth's face. His thumb brushed lightly along his cheek. He said quietly, not as a statement, but as a blessing.

"My son."

Shadows emerged from the floor, flickering like they could hear what was coming. Without another word, they stirred and coiled at Zarriq's feet, rising like smoke drawn by sorrow. Swirling around him, fading his form, slowly dissolving him.

Until he was gone.

The room felt empty without him and instantly colder, but Kayleth could still feel his presence. He sat there, motionless.

Just moments later, a knock tapped gently at the door. Kayleth turned as Valla peeked her head in. Her expression was soft. No questions in her eyes. Only warmth.

She said gently. A simple piece of normalcy handed to him like a gift. "Dinner will be ready in ten minutes."

She smiled and walked down the hall, leaving him sitting in the quiet once again, alone with his thoughts.

And then, the wind stirred faintly through the open window, swirling to Kayleth's ear. Zarriq's voice whispered, soft as silk, and carried on the wind...

"I Shall Miss You With All My Heart."

The Druid King

The End

To my phantom editor, Marlow

My Quill, My Wraith.
Who kept the chaos on track and the goblins in line.
For surviving the caffeine-fueled séances, the unruly sock council,
and every cursed fragment.

You saw the magic before it had a name.

Thank you.

I couldn't have done this without you.

www.ingramcontent.com/pod-product-compliance
Lightning Source LLC
Chambersburg PA
CBHW022146010726
47493CB00002B/359